"You...
her ire part... ...him.
"What are ... ...ing here?"

"Well, now, little sis," Jansen responded, his voice soft but firm. "I could ask you the same question." He assumed his favorite wide-legged stance, arms crossed.

Jansen's arm-folding action caused Eden's heart to flutter a bit, as she watched his pecs ripple with the movement. Her eyes slid to the wide, muscled shoulders, down the six-pack to a narrowed waist, and over the strong, powerful legs that held up a man she determined had gotten finer with age. And why was she imagining what lay just beyond the beige-colored towel shielding his manhood? Eden closed her eyes and licked suddenly dry lips.

A lazy, knowing smile crept across Jansen's face. "Liking the view?" he asked cockily as he leaned against the stair banister. "I can part the, um, *curtain,* if you'd like."

"Still arrogant, I see," Eden said, turning away from him and reaching for her suitcases—just for something to do.

"Arrogance is when a person thinks he's all that," Jansen shot back. "Confidence is when he knows it."

Eden ignored Jansen's comment. *Dang, I was looking at him like he was a piece of chicken, and I was the colonel getting ready to fry.*

Also by Zuri Day

Lies Lovers Tell
Body By Night
Lessons from a Younger Lover
What Love Tastes Like

Published by Dafina Books

Lovin'
Blue

Zuri Day

Kensington Publishing Corp.

http://www.kensingtonbooks.com

DAFINA BOOKS are published by

Kensington Publishing Corp.
119 West 40th Street
New York, NY 10018

All Kensington Titles, Imprints, and Distributed Lines are available at special quantity discounts for bulk purchases for sales promotions, premiums, fund-raising, and educational or institutional use. Special book excerpts or customized printings can also be created to fit specific needs. For details, write or phone the office of the Kensington special sales manager: Kensington Publishing Corp., 119 West 40th Street, New York, NY 10018, attn: Special Sales Department, Phone: 1-800-221-2647.

Dafina and the Dafina logo Reg. U.S. Pat. & TM Off.

ISBN-13: 978-0-7582-5999-8
ISBN-10: 0-7582-5999-9

First mass market printing: April 2011

10 9 8 7 6 5 4 3 2 1

Printed in the United States of America

For those who seek peace without violence.

Acknowledgments

A heartfelt thank you to my editor, Selena James, and my agent, Natasha Kern, for your unwavering support, spot-on advice, and treasured friendship. And to officers David Cooper and Marlon Morgan, who made my hero come alive and kept my men out of the stereotypical and unrealistic doughnut shop! Also to CHP officer Greg, who kindly informed me it was a "radio" attached to his belt, not a "walkie-talkie." ☺

1

The police! Eden Anderson's heart leaped into her throat as she pulled behind the police cruiser parked in front of her brother's Baldwin Hills residence in southern California. "What's going on, Michael?" she whispered as she fumbled with her seatbelt, then the lock button, before scrambling out of her packed Acura SUV and rushing to the front door. Her concern had been growing for the past three days—ever since her phone calls and e-mails to her older brother had gone unreturned.

At first she'd shrugged off her worry. After all, her brother, Michael "Big Mike" Anderson, was trying to make a name for himself in the music game. He'd produced a couple B-level acts while working for a major record label. His work often went late into the night, and reaching him wasn't always easy. But when Eden had left two "call me right now" messages, followed by texts marked with the same urgency, she'd experienced the first twinges of fear. And now, looking at the black-and-white squad car sitting at the curb of her brother's front door, Eden's anxiety went into full throttle.

Eden knocked on the front door. No response. She repeatedly rang the doorbell but didn't hear the chimes that usually sounded when the button was pushed. Eden knocked harder, first on the door, then on the window. The living room was dark; she could detect no movement. But lights were on upstairs. Eden's fear increased.

You've got a key. Out of her panic came a voice that reminded Eden she had a key to her brother's house. He'd given it to her months ago, when she'd come house hunting and stayed at his place. She'd meant to give it back but hadn't. Remembering that she'd placed it in the zipper compartment of her large Junior Drake purse, Eden walked purposefully back to her car to retrieve it. Her steps were measured and much slower than before. Eden wasn't sure she wanted to find out what was happening on the other side of the door.

Jansen McKnight turned off the shower. *Did I hear a knock?* He waited a beat, and then another, before turning the water back on and finishing the long, hot shower. He turned to let the water pound against the knots in his shoulders. *I need to see Dakkar,* he thought dispassionately. Dakkar was the masseuse trained in Swedish massage who had rubbed away tension, stress, and frustration from Jansen's body for years. For now, however, the near-scalding hot water pulsating from the heavy-duty showerhead was serving as a viable alternative. Jansen rested a large palm on either side of the stall, hung his head, and let the water work its magic.

A loud thud interrupted Jansen's serenity. His just

relaxed muscles tensed, his entire body rigid in alert. He lessened the water pressure, straining to hear beyond the guest bathroom he'd used since agreeing to house sit for Michael the previous week, and beyond the stereo playing in the bedroom across the hall.

Thump. There it was again, unmistakable this time. Either the sound of footsteps, or something being dragged across the floor, or both. Jansen's officer instinct went into auto mode, and for good reason. A recent rash of burglaries in the upscale, central Los Angeles neighborhood was why Michael had asked his friend to house sit. Jansen loved the comfort of his home in Gardena, and agreed to his best friend's pleas only after Michael promised that a home security system would be installed immediately upon his return. *Well, brothah,* Jansen thought with a resigned sigh, *looks like I'm getting ready to earn my keep.*

With the stealth of a panther, Jansen turned the shower back to full blast, eased out of the stall, soundlessly wrapped a towel around his waist, and reached for the 9mm Glock that was never far from his reach. Tonight he'd unstrapped and rested it on the closed toilet seat, before the rest of his navy uniform ended up in a heap on the bathroom floor.

Thunk.

Jansen eased the gun out of its holster and crept down the short hallway to the top of the stairs. Taking a deep breath, he placed his foot on the top step and prayed the old maple wood wouldn't creak under his weight.

* * *

Eden walked into the living room and dropped another load onto the hardwood floor. Her first thought had been to leave everything in the car until morning, but a chance glance at a crime-watch sign nailed to a post nixed that idea. Even in what she felt was a fairly safe neighborhood, a car packed with clearly visible goods may be too much for either a hardened criminal or a bored teen to pass up. So with the last ounces of energy she could summon after driving for ten hours, she walked in with her beloved stereo system—the final load.

Jansen kept his back against the wall as he noted the shadow passing along the living room's far wall. *Whoever this fool is has a lot of nerve.* Normally, especially when it was obvious that someone was home, a burglar would do one quick, thorough sweep—get in and out. But Jansen wanted to catch this perpetrator, believing that in doing so he may nab the person or ring of persons behind this neighborhood's woes. That's why he'd left the shower running, to give the thief a false sense of security. The criminal had obviously taken the bait and made himself at home. *You may be nervy, but you're not too bright, son.* Jansen quietly cocked his weapon. It was about to go down.

Eden gingerly sat her stereo on the coffee table and then reached for the suitcases she'd tossed on the couch. She couldn't wait to get in the shower. Her head hurt; her hair—stuffed under an Orioles baseball cap—was in desperate need of shampoo, and the secret that was strong enough for a man but made for a woman was about to become public news. *Oh, I'm funky,* she thought as she used the sleeve of her long-sleeved Bison Blue T-shirt to wipe her face. As she did so, her earring caught on the sleeve and came out of her ear. She'd planned to replace the clasp on her favorite hoops before leaving DC, but like many other plans she'd made in the past two weeks, these, too, had changed. Ever since resigning her job on Capitol Hill, her life had been a series of unexpected interruptions. Part of what she was hoping for with this move back home was a life without surprises.

"Freeze! Don't move!" Jansen eased off the last step onto the floor, assumed a strong, wide-legged stance, and pointed his gun at the back of the scrawny, ball-capped thief who'd been wreaking havoc on the neighborhood. "Get your hands up and slowly turn around."

Eden stood frozen, unable to speak or move. *What's going on? Where's Michael?* After hearing the music, and the water running, Eden had assumed it was Michael upstairs. But these strong, authoritative commands had definitely not been uttered from her brother's lips, and her womanly intuition, along with a rapidly beating heart, told her this was not a joke.

"Do it now!" Jansen took another step toward his suspect.

Eden began to shake as she slowly turned around. She took one look at the huge man whose face was hidden in the darkness, noted the gun that—unlike his countenance—was clearly visible from his outstretched hands, and did what any normal, law-abiding citizen would do under such dire circumstances. She fainted.

2

Jansen frowned as he slowly eased his finger off the trigger. He'd seen a lot of reactions from suspects in his near-decade of life as a cop, but he had to admit—this was a first. *Are you bluffing? Huh? We'll soon find out.* "Stay on the floor. Don't move," Jansen commanded, even though it seemed quite clear that the suspect had no intention of changing positions. Jansen moved the coffee table with his foot and, with the gun in his left hand still trained on his target, used his right hand to turn over the intruder so he could see his face. As he did so, the baseball cap came off, and a head of long black hair cascaded over the hand clutching the suspect's shoulder. Jansen's frown deepened. He kept his weapon trained on the unconscious female and hurried over to turn on the overhead light. As the harsh, bright light flooded the room, the suspect groaned and opened her eyes.

Eden! Jansen's heart clutched in his throat. He'd thought often of Michael's younger sister in the past few days, especially since staying here at her brother's house. Michael had told him that Eden was moving back to Los Angeles, but he'd mentioned nothing about her staying at the house. In fact, he'd assured him that they'd probably not cross paths at all because the condo she'd found was in a totally different part of town— Santa Monica, an area Jansen rarely frequented. Yet here she was, sprawled on the floor. Jansen hadn't seen the girl-turned-woman he used to mercilessly harass in at least ten years, and he quickly took in the curves he'd missed in the heat of the moment, and the onion that begged to be peeled. Jansen had to admit . . . she looked good lying down.

"Girl, you sure know how to make an entrance," Jansen scolded to cover his concern and unexpected attraction, even as he hurried to her side to help her up. "Breaking into someone else's home, even your brother's, is a good way to get shot!"

Eden's eyes narrowed as reality dawned. She hadn't seen Jansen, otherwise known as her childhood tormentor, in ages, probably since marrying her college sweetheart. After the divorce, she'd buried herself in work, and her trips back home became infrequent. Except for the house-hunting trip, Eden hadn't been back to LA in three years, ever since her mother relocated to Phoenix. The last she'd heard of Jansen, he was married and living in Chicago. She also remembered Michael saying he'd become a police officer. But still . . . what was he doing here? And why was he one towel shy of being naked?

"You!" Eden spat, her ire part anger, part chagrin, but mostly relief. "What are you doing here?"

"Well, now, little sis," Jansen responded, his voice

soft but firm. "I could ask you the same question." He assumed his favorite wide-legged stance, crossed arms across a massive chest, and noted Eden's eyes were larger and more almond-shaped than he remembered. And were her lips always so full and luscious?

Jansen's arm-folding action caused Eden's heart to flutter a bit as she watched his pecs ripple with the movement. Her eyes slid to the wide, muscled shoulders, down the six-pack to a narrowed waist, inverted navel, and over the strong powerful legs that held up a man she determined had gotten finer with age. And why was she imagining what lay just beyond the beige-colored towel shielding his manhood? Eden closed her eyes and licked suddenly dry lips.

A lazy, knowing smile crept across Jansen's face. "Liking the view?" he asked cockily as he leaned against the stair banister. "I can part the, um, *curtain,* if you'd like."

"Still arrogant, I see," Eden said, turning away from him and reaching for her suitcases—just for something to do.

"Arrogance is when a person thinks he's all that," Jansen shot back. "Confidence is when he knows it."

Eden ignored Jansen's comment. *Dang, I was looking at him like he was a piece of chicken, and I was the colonel getting ready to fry.* She picked up the ball cap from the floor and placed it back on her head, feeling a semblance of composure coming back. After all, this was her brother's best friend, the one she'd known since she was five years old. The one who had stuttered as a child, squashed bugs, and then picked up their remains and chased her with them. Who had collected the most Halloween candy but still stole the mini Snickers bars Eden received. Who had refused to take off his "Thriller" jacket Christmas gift for a whole week, but later scared the bejeebers out of her by donning a monster mask and jumping out of her bedroom closet. This was "germy Jansen"—the name she'd called him when they'd gotten older and Jansen and Michael had begun to play sports. They'd come home sweaty and funky, and Jansen would insist on nabbing a hug, giving Eden the willies. This was Jansen all grown up . . . but Eden tried not to think about that now.

"What are you doing here?" she asked again. "Where's Michael? And can you put that . . . thing away?"

"Are you sure you want me to?" Jansen asked, wriggling his eyebrows. Eden huffed. "Oh, you mean the gun." The Glock was almost an extension of himself. Jansen had forgotten he was holding it. He placed it on the third step, where Eden couldn't see it. "Is that better?"

Eden nodded. "A little. Where's Michael?"

"Out of town. Actually, out of the country." Jansen tightened the towel around his waist. "He asked me to watch the place."

Oh, so that's why I couldn't reach Michael. And why the police car is out there. "Well, if you're just patrolling the area, why are you taking a shower in his house?"

"I believe the official term for what I'm doing is 'house sitting.'"

"You're staying here?" Eden was surprised to hear a trace of panic in her voice.

"Yeah, why? Are you? I thought you got a condo over there in prime-real-estate Santa Monica."

"I did. I mean, I do. But there's a problem. It's not ready. . . ." Eden's voice trailed off as her exhausted mind tried to process her predicament. When the contractor had begun the kitchen makeover, mold had been found under the sink and behind the refrigerator that had come with the house. Further inspection confirmed it had spread underneath the hardwood flooring and under the baseboards. The job that was supposed to take three days would now take two weeks to finish. Eden had planned to save her money by staying with her brother. But now . . . "I can't stay here," she finally said, sighing, the thought of getting back into her car and looking for a hotel tiring her out more than she already was. Once again, she reached for her luggage.

"Don't be ridiculous. You can sleep in Mike's bedroom."

"Don't try to tell me what to do!" Eden snapped, feeling ten again.

"Eden, it looks like you drove here. That means you're probably exhausted, which is why you passed out."

"No, I passed out because I saw the shadow of the Incredible Hulk pointing a gun at my chest."

"Sorry about that, baby, but I thought you were a burglar. There's been a rash of them in the area, which is why I'm here at Mike's house. I'm sleeping in the guest room. You can either sleep in your brother's room or on the futon in the weight room. C'mon, now. You know you want to stay and soak up the charm of the knight."

"You are so full of yourself."

Jansen chuckled. "I'm just messing with you, girl. But on the real tip though . . . you know you can't resist me."

"I'm going to take a shower." Eden grabbed her purse and began pulling her luggage toward the staircase.

Jansen raced to her side, quickly picking up the gun Eden eyed with disdain. "Don't worry, it won't bite you. Here, let me get that."

Eden batted away his hand. "I can get it myself."

"Oh, it's like that? See, I'm trying to be a gentleman, and you're acting all independent and whatnot. But I understand, baby girl. Things happen when I get too close to a woman, and even in that raggedy T-shirt and jeans, I can see that Mike's little sis is definitely all grown up!"

Eden hoisted the suitcase onto the first step and then the second. By the fourth step, her strength was drained. *Why didn't I think to just get out what I needed and leave the datgum case downstairs?* Now Eden felt she'd put herself in the position to prove that she could indeed carry the suitcase up the entire flight. She took a deep breath, grabbed the handle . . . and suddenly felt the weight of nothingness as Jansen took the case from her and effortlessly mounted the stairs.

Eden raised her head to deliver a sarcastic comment but just as quickly lowered it. The towel around Jansen's waist was a short one that perfectly outlined his round, hard buns. Two more steps, and Eden knew there was a good chance that she'd be able to see the package Jansen was working with. And even though they would be under the same roof for only one night . . . Eden knew life would be easier if she didn't know.

3

After a long, revitalizing shower, Eden realized she was hungry. She'd spent the night in Phoenix and then delayed her journey to spend the morning with her mother. Eden had pushed herself the last three hundred and fifty miles into Los Angeles—across the Arizona desert blazing with August heat, into the cooler, greener California, and finally into the burgeoning City of Angels. All the way up the 10 freeway, she'd tried to reach her brother and had promised her mother that she'd call as soon as she reached his house and found out what was going on.

Eden used the towel to squeeze excess water from her hair and then combed it back and put it in a ponytail. She donned her favorite lounging outfit—black yoga wear. The pants were formfitting yet comfortable, both they and the oversize top made of soft, organic cotton. After uncovering the house shoes that were at the bottom of her luggage, she plopped on the futon she'd made up with fresh, clean sheets in the weight room and reached for her phone.

Even though it was close to midnight, Phyllis Anderson answered on the first ring. "Hello?"

"Mom, it's me."

"Hey, baby. You in Los Angeles?"

"Yes, I finally made it."

"You're just now getting there?"

"No, I got here about an hour ago."

"And you're just now calling? Where's your brother? It's not like I can catch him half the time either, but still, I'm worried sick."

"Michael's fine, Mom. He's out of town."

"What's that got to do with why he's not answering his cell?"

"He's in London. Promoting some new, hot band. Guess he's late on getting one of those international calling plans," Eden uttered amid a yawn.

"But you got into his house okay. You had a key, right?"

"Uh, yeah, I got in. And almost got shot in the process."

"What?" Phyllis sat straight up in bed, the *Essence* magazine she was reading falling on the floor.

"Jansen's here. Thought I was a burglar."

"Jansen McKnight?"

"Who else." Eden explained why Jansen was in Michael's house.

"Kathryn told me he was thinking about moving back after the divorce. But I didn't know he was already back there."

Jansen's divorced? Eden looked up to make sure her door was closed. Even so, she lowered her voice.

"How did I miss that news flash? Jansen isn't with his wife anymore?"

"Child, please. You've been so busy it's hard for you to remember your own name, much less what someone tells you. I told you three or four years ago that he and his wife were having problems. Come to think of it, though, that was when you were in the throes of the Obama campaign. That part of your life is probably just a blur."

"That's for sure." Eden yawned again, and her stomach growled. "Mom, I'm going to go now. See if I can scrounge up something resembling a vegetable in Michael's kitchen."

"Yeah, well, good luck with that. You're the only vegetarian in the family. Your brother is strictly a meat-and-potatoes man."

"Don't remind me." Eden's stomach lurched at the thought of having to endure meat in the refrigerator, even for a night.

"I feel good knowing Jansen is there with you. Tell him I said hello and not to be a stranger."

"I will, Mom. Bye."

Minutes later, Eden hesitantly opened her brother's refrigerator. The pickings were slim but were much as she'd feared: a six-pack of cola and another of beer on one shelf, a couple leftover takeout cartons on another, and various packaged, processed meats and cheeses in the see-through crispers. There was nothing even green, much less fresh. Eden began opening cabinet doors and fared no better.

"Sorry, I haven't been to the store yet," Jansen said.

"But there's some lunch meat in there. And some chips in the other cabinet."

"No, thanks," Eden replied, reaching for a box of shredded wheat she spied on a cabinet's top shelf. She glanced at Jansen, thankful that he'd covered his body, even though the pristine white wife beater T-shirt, paired with low-riding shorts, accented his athletic physique almost as good as the towel.

"What, you too good for bologna now?"

"No." Eden again looked into the refrigerator. There was every condiment known to man in the door, but no milk. "I've been a vegetarian for the last five years." She poured some of the biscuits into a bowl and began to eat them dry.

"But you still eat, what, chicken and fish?" Jansen watched in fascination as Eden popped one wheat mini biscuit, and then another, into her mouth.

Eden shook her head, still chewing. "I don't eat meat or fish of any kind, and I'm weaning myself off dairy. I plan to become vegan within the next year."

"What's this, some kind of religious position or health kick or something?"

"It's the way I choose to live. Makes me feel good." Eden crunched down on another mouthful of wheat and then rose and began scanning the cabinets again. Then she walked back over to the refrigerator. The shredded grain may have been healthy, but it wasn't doing much to assuage her appetite at the moment.

Jansen sat down at the table Eden had just vacated. "Little garden," Jansen said, using the nickname he'd used to call Eden just before he'd mess up the thick, naturally curly locks Eden used to wear all over her head. "Guess you're trying to live up to my moniker."

"Don't flatter yourself." Eden laughed. "I'd forgotten all about that stupid name. Ooh, you used to get on my nerves with that."

"I got on your nerves with a lot of things."

"Tell me about it. Between you and Michael, it's a wonder I made it out of the house without losing my mind."

While Jansen and Eden ate bowls of vanilla Swiss almond ice cream she'd found in the freezer, they caught up on each other's lives.

"So what have you been doing since graduating Howard in what . . . 2000?"

"1999," Eden corrected around a spoonful of creamy goodness. "With a degree in business administration."

"Human relations? So how'd you get into politics?"

"My minor was political science, but trust me, I hadn't envisioned a career on Capitol Hill when I moved to DC. That just sort of happened after an internship with a senator during my junior year."

"And a marriage sort of happened, too, correct?"

"Yes," Eden said, finishing the last scoop of ice cream. "For the both of us, from what I understand."

"Yeah, my marriage just sort of happened. But my divorce was well thought out."

Jansen placed Eden's empty bowl on top of his and walked to the sink. Eden watched him, admiring his firm, round backside, broad shoulders, and narrow waist. She'd forgotten how nice Jansen could be when he wasn't being a knucklehead. But she remembered other things as well. Like how much of a player he'd been during his teen years, and how many hearts he'd broken. Given his dark brown bedroom eyes and how he was wearing that sleeveless T-shirt, Eden imagined the pain hadn't ended when he'd left Crenshaw High.

"I'm up and out by six-thirty," Jansen said as he washed out their bowls. "Hopefully, I won't wake you."

"I'll probably sleep like a log," Eden replied, "and will be gone by the time you get home."

"So your place *is* ready."

"Not for another week or so. But that's okay, I'll find a hotel."

"Ha! Can't stand the heat, can you? You know that if you stay here, you'll try to seduce me."

Eden fixed Jansen with a look. "Me, try to seduce you? That will be the day."

"Well, why are you running then? If"—Jansen ran a hand down his well-toned abs—"all this ain't bothering you, save your money and hang out."

"Whatever, Jansen. Good night."

"You just know you couldn't handle staying here with me," Jansen said to Eden's retreating back. "You know you've always had a thing for me, girl. And now I know it, too."

These words stopped Eden in her tracks. True, she'd been among the goo-goo-eyed females who'd relished watching Jansen run up and down the basketball courts. He'd been a star senior, after all, a sports standout, and she'd been a lowly freshman, vying to make a statement amid fast, fly girls with their own various bags of talent. Eden was hardly an introvert, but she had been the more studious type. And there was only

so much sexy that her mother had allowed. What was
a fourteen-year-old to do but dream?

*But Jansen doesn't know this. There's no way he
could know about the crush I had on him from the time
I was in junior high. And there's no way he'll ever
know.* Eden came out of her musings to hear Jansen
singing a famous Gap Band song about putting pedals
to the metal and burning rubber. He ended the chorus
with hearty laughter, obviously garnered at her ex-
pense. As tired as she was, Eden couldn't get back into
the kitchen fast enough.

"You might have it going on with all these other sis-
tahs in LA, but you forget that I knew you when you stuttered, your knees were ashy, and your head was too big."

Jansen turned to face Eden fully. His brown, almost
black eyes bore into hers. "So you're not attracted
to me?"

"Boy, you're almost my brother, and hardly my
type."

"Not even a little bit?"

Yes. "No."

"Because you know . . . I'm not your brother." Jansen
wriggled his eyebrows.

"Jansen McKnight, I am not attracted to you in the
least."

"Then prove it. Stay here until your place is ready.
And I guarantee that before you leave, I will have seduced you. That is . . . if you don't seduce me first."

"Get over yourself, Jansen. I'm not feeling you like
that." Eden's smirk was not because of what she'd said,
but that she'd successfully pushed that lie out of her
mouth.

"Then you have nothing to worry about."

"And unlike the other women you've obviously encountered, I don't give in to soft touches and warm words."

"Which makes the challenge all the more exciting. . . ."

Eden spun on her heels and walked toward the stairs.

"So can I take that as a yes?" Jansen yelled out. "You're staying?" Jansen came around the corner and leaned against the wall. Effortless self-assurance oozed out of his pores. "I dare you. In fact, I double-dog dare you!" When Eden didn't respond, a smile broke out on Jansen's face. Eden's heart did flip-flops even as her back stiffened and her chin showed the slightest tilt. "Trying to get your nerve up, I see. You would need to."

"You're pretty sure of yourself, huh? Who's to say it won't be you who'll end up panting after me, that the tables will turn and you'll be the one who ends up getting seduced?"

Jansen wasn't necessarily opposed to this idea. His interest in Eden had been piqued a few years ago, when Michael had come back from a Thanksgiving holiday with pictures of the family. Jansen had joked about Eden looking old, but the truth is that he'd wondered when she'd gotten so fine.

"So you think you can seduce me," he drawled, his voice lowered along with his eyelids.

He licked his lips, and the squiggle that had begun in Eden's stomach moved lower. She crossed her arms and raised her chin higher, showing a bravado she was far from feeling. "Guess there's only one way to find out. Wait a minute, what's the prize? What do I get after successfully seducing you?"

"Trust me, baby girl, *I* am your prize."

Eden rolled her eyes.

"Okay," Jansen shrugged. "You name it, I'm game."

Eden tapped her chin with a forefinger, in serious thought. "Let's say that if—I mean *when* I seduce you—you'll take yoga classes and eat no meat for a month! Oh, and you'll lose the ego, find some humility, and treat me with nothing but the utmost respect for as long as we live."

"Okay," Jansen answered, much too quickly for Eden's taste. "And what do I get for seducing you?"

"What do you want? Wait, let me rephrase that."

"Yeah, watch your words because I'm going to get what I want. But right now we're talking about the prize relating to the dare."

"It doesn't matter what you come up with. You'll never get to experience whatever it is."

"If I win," Jansen said thoughtfully, totally ignoring Eden's last jab, "you'll come to the shooting range with me, learn how to handle a firearm. And I'll get to handcuff you . . . at a time of my choosing."

Eden wasn't into S and M, but the thought of being handcuffed suddenly sounded like a very good idea. She once again turned to head up the stairs, lest her face betray her salacious thoughts.

"So it's a done deal then? You're staying here?"

"Yes, just so I can wipe that smug look off your face," Eden retorted before marching up the stairs. Jansen's deep, melodious laughter followed her up there, settling around her warm, tired shoulders like a hug. It was only then that she realized how tight she was, after sitting almost ten hours straight in an automobile. The shower had helped, but Eden knew she could use an expert massage. She thought about Jansen's large, strong fingers and just as quickly shook her head to banish the idea. Two minutes later, Eden realized her thoughts were more of a premonition when Jansen knocked on her door.

"Little garden, are you asleep?" No answer; and he couldn't see the smile that his childhood pet name elicited from Eden's lips. "I thought you might like a nice . . . long . . . massage. It'll make you sleep like a baby, I promise." Still, no answer. "All right then. I have a feeling you can hear me, but it's probably best that you don't answer." Jansen's voice dropped to a near whisper, one that Eden had to strain to hear. And strain she did. "Because once I put my hands on you . . ." The soft sound of Jansen's bare feet on the polished oak floors ended the sentence. Seconds later, she heard the subtle thud of the guest-room door closing, and in spite of repeated attempts to quell her wandering mind, she wondered whether Jansen slept in pj's, boxers, or nude.

Eden was exhausted and had envisioned this moment—lying horizontally with a pillow against her stomach and another tucked under her head—since hitting LA's city limits. It had been a long day, one that had begun just before dawn. But as she tossed and turned, her mind whirling with thoughts and her body wide awake, Eden concluded that the night would be even longer.

4

"Yes, reservations, please. Thanks." Eden munched on a banana while waiting to be connected. Her quick trip to the nearest 7-Eleven earlier that morning wasn't going to cut it. As soon as she made hotel arrangements, she was going to look up a vegetarian restaurant and eat a real meal. "Hello, I'm interested in whether or not you have special rates for extended stays." Pause. "Ten to fourteen days." Eden told the reservationist the specific dates she'd be staying.

"One moment, please," the operator replied with barely there enthusiasm. The click-clacking of computer keys filled the silence. "We have an online special of eighty-nine dollars a night, plus tax and incidentals."

"And there's no further discount for stays lasting longer than a week?"

"That is our lowest price. Would you like me to reserve a room for you?"

Eden had done a quick calculation in her head and knew the answer was no. Now was not the time to spend a thousand dollars, especially when such an amount had not been budgeted. While she had a nice savings built up, along with a few solid investments, Eden was being cautious. She didn't know how long it would take to find a job in her desired field of holistic living, and when she found one, she was sure the pay wouldn't equal what she'd made as a congressman's aide. She had enough to live comfortably for quite some time but was determined not to spend needlessly.

But is this needlessly? Is there any cost too high to keep me from potentially making a fool of myself with my brother's best friend? Eden snatched the tank top over her head, knowing that the only one she could truly be angry at was herself. "I must have been a fool to take Jansen up on his ridiculous dare," she chided aloud as she roughly brushed back her hair and put it in a pony-tail. She knew that one of the first items on her agenda needed to be finding a hair salon. *Maybe I'll do that today after I check on my house. Then again, Jansen will think I'm getting cute for him.* "I couldn't care less what you think, Jansen McKnight! Germy Jansen," she sang to herself in the mirror, screwing up her face and recalling the nauseating tone he used to adopt in child-hood just to get on her nerves. She knew that she must look foolish, and was acting much younger than her thirty-four years, but Eden didn't care. She'd backed herself in a corner. And now she had to sleep in the bed she'd made. Her biggest fear wasn't the bed, per se, but that she may not be able to say no to Jansen when he came to join her in it.

Five hours later, except for one piece of bad news, Eden felt a lot better. The first thing she'd done after leaving her brother's house was to drive to Santa Monica and meet with the contractor. The good news had been that the job was progressing smoothly; the contractor was confident that the mold specialist had found the cause of the mold and that he, the contractor, would be able to fix it. The bad news was that there was no way the job would be finished sooner than the two weeks the contractor had originally estimated. Eden had hoped to be out of Michael's house and away from Jansen in seven to ten days. Now she felt it may indeed be two weeks, if not longer.

That was when Eden had employed the words of one of her favorite motivational speakers, Wayne Dyer: *When you change the way you look at things, the things you look at change.* As she'd relished an absolutely divine vegan dinner at Real Food Daily, the Santa Monica eatery she'd already deemed a favorite spot, Eden had changed her point of view, decided that the best defense was a good offense, and had come up with a plan. After all, she wasn't the shy, pimply faced girl with braids anymore. She was a woman who'd stood side-by-side with giants as they'd battled on Capitol Hill; who'd married, divorced, and lived to tell the tale; and who'd just driven over twenty-three hundred miles cross-country alone. *So you think you're a player, player,* Eden thought as she climbed the steps to Michael's house, juggling bags of groceries from her favorite store. She placed the bags on the table in the foyer and caught her new and improved image in the mirror above it. "Well, get ready, Germy Jansen. It's about to be 'game on.'"

5

Jansen's stomach growled as a tantalizing scent from the kitchen wafted past his nostrils. It had been a long, grueling day—punctuated by a four-hour standoff with a bank robber. Fortunately, the incident had ended peacefully. Nobody had died. As Jansen was more than painfully aware, that was not always the case.

He strolled toward the kitchen, determined not to go down memory lane. He figured nothing could get his mind off work faster than teasing his temporary roommate. "Hey, Garden of E—" The vision in front of him stopped him in his tracks. *Damn!*

Eden had dressed purposefully but had no idea how effective the look would be. The hairstylist had barely turned under her thick, freshly permed hair, so its silkiness hung past her shoulders, begging for a strong male hand to run through its strands. She'd also taken a plunge and allowed the stylist to trim the front, creating a long bang, wisps of which teased her eyebrows and accented her eyes. She wore little makeup, but the bronzer blush and pink lipstick added just the right amount of shine. *Kiss me,* the glimmer beckoned. *Here. Now.* But the new hairdo and light makeup wasn't even the heart-stopper. That came courtesy of the casual white T-shirt mini she wore, the one she knew showed off her badonkadonk to perfection and highlighted her skin's deep tan.

When she turned around, Eden's face was a mask of innocence. "What's up, Germy Jansen?" she asked casually and later would congratulate herself that she'd pushed the words through suddenly constricted windpipes. She turned back quickly before her eyes betrayed her. *God, give me strength!* Eden had never been one for a man in uniform. She was what people like Jansen would call a "tree-hugging hippie": anti anything violent—guns, war, guns, military, guns, police . . . Oh, and she hated guns, too. It wasn't like Eden was naive. Having lived in DC for the past sixteen years had taught her that sometimes police being around was a good thing. But, more than those times, she remembered when she'd felt the police, military, and government entities had overstepped their bounds with artillery muscle and had hidden extreme and un- usual punishment behind the badge. These thoughts had deepened behind such cases as Amadou Diallo, the unarmed immigrant fatally shot by four officers, and Sean Bell, the unarmed fiancé who was killed by NYPD days before he was to marry his child's mother. They had hardened into a mindset after a friend's brother had been shot and killed by police. For these reasons, Eden's panties should not be wet right now. But they were.

"Hey, little garden," Jansen said from about a foot away

Eden jumped. She hadn't heard a thing as he'd walked up behind her.

"Dangit! Do you want me to spray sauce all over this kitchen?"

"No, I want you to spray it all over that little white dress so I'll have a legitimate reason to take it off you."

Jansen hadn't touched her, but Eden's body was on fire. Once again, she found solace in the sauce, turning around to stir it vigorously and forcing her body to follow her mind. *But wait a minute. Where is my mind? And what's on it?* Because, for the life of her, Eden seemed unable to form a coherent thought. Every fiber of her being seemed tuned to the close proximity of Jansen's body and the slight muskiness emanating from his skin.

"You really need to move," she said, proud of herself for managing to sound chagrinned. "I know you think you're the *F* word, and you are." She glanced at Jansen and was pleased to see that cocky smile. "*Funky,* my brothah." She was equally pleased to see the smile disappear. "Oh," she continued, turning around to face him. "You thought I was going to say *fine?*" Eden deemed her legs steady enough to put some distance between herself and temptation. She walked over to the refrigerator and retrieved a bowl of cut vegetables and fixings for a hearty salad.

"Where's the meat?" Jansen knew he should go take a shower but wondered if the water would be any more refreshing than the vision of loveliness he was drinking in right now. "That sauce smells good. But where's the ground turkey or beef that's going in it?"

"This is going to be a vegetable sauce filled with squash, corn, eggplant, green and garbanzo beans, onions, served over whole-wheat pasta and topped with a soy-based, vegan cheese sauce."

"That sounds all right for a side dish. But, woman, when I get back down here, I want to see some meat on my plate."

The sound of his voice, let alone choice of words, got Eden's attention and, as Jansen had intended, crept a little under her skin. "Who said I was cooking for you?"

"I did. My grandmother believes the way to a man's heart is through his stomach. Looks like somebody else's granny may have said that, too."

Eden took a deep, calming breath. Jansen was pushing her buttons, but she was determined not to let it show. "The way to good health is through one's stomach as well," she calmly replied. "And cooking is a wonderful way to be creative, productive, and to relax. I'm cooking for *me.* But you're welcome to have some, as you probably can't boil an egg."

Jansen made a sound as if air had been punched out of his stomach. The same grandmother who'd spouted sayings had also taught him to cook. No one had to tell Jansen he could throw down. He knew for a fact that this was true. And he knew something else, which was why he'd crossed the kitchen and once again invaded Eden's space.

"What?" he asked when Eden put a hand against his chest, preventing him from coming closer. "I was just going to give you a hug. That's the least two good friends could do after not seeing each other for over ten years. What, you scared?"

"Hardly."

"Good." Jansen closed the distance between them and wrapped Eden in his arms. He squeezed her gently, drawing a lazy circle on her back with his thumb. "It's good to see you, girl," he whispered, placing a kiss on the rim of her ear.

Eden quickly pulled back. "Okay, hug over. Gotta check the food."

"Ha!" Jansen slowly backed out of the kitchen. "I don't know about eggs, but I bet something else is boiling right about now."

His quick reflexes were the only reason the onion Eden threw at him missed its target—his head.

6

Eden awoke to the sound of birds chirping from the tree near her second-story window. Amazing what some good food and a solid night's sleep could do. She felt like a new woman. She raised up, enjoyed a good, long stretch, and then flopped back on the pillow. Immediately, thoughts of the previous night flooded her mind. She tried to stop the smile that threatened to spill across her face at any moment, but after a few seconds of quivering lips, she broke into a grin, crushed a pillow to her chest, and remembered. . . .

"Ugh! Don't tell me you're getting ready to cook meat! Really, Jansen, I've cooked enough to share, and the protein is in the spinach pasta. You won't even miss that . . . cow you're holding." What Eden was trying to miss, with her sarcasm, was that Jansen looked as good in the gray T-shirt and sweats he'd donned after showering as he had in his policeman's uniform.

"Mmmm," Jansen replied, raising the T-bone to his

nose and inhaling deeply. "Smells good, and look how thick it is—rich ruby red. This cow is going to taste good! I'm going to make you want some of it."

Just what I need, the smell of meat cooking to ruin my appetite. Eden had been surprised the first time her body had reacted to the smell of meat. It was Christmas about a year after she'd become a vegetarian, and months after separating from her husband, Gregg. Rather than spend it with friends in DC, and be reminded of things she and her husband usually did together (even passing the White House would make her think of happier times), she had come home to Los Angeles. The day after arriving, she'd awoke to the smell of bacon cooking. Seconds later, her stomach had flip-flopped, and she'd felt nauseous. She hadn't given it much thought until the same thing happened when she'd visited her grandmother, and again when she'd walked into a friend's kitchen where chili simmered on the stove. It wasn't so bad when the meat was already done, but at the height of it being cooked? Yikes!

Jansen whistled as he liberally seasoned the inch-thick cut, dredged it in flour, and then placed it in a piping hot, cast-iron skillet.

Well, there's another thing to add to my shopping list. All pots and pans, but especially cast iron, retained the essence of whatever was cooked in it. In that moment, Eden came to a realization, a welcomed barrier to the feelings for Jansen she was trying to ignore. *I could never date him. My next husband will be a vegetarian!*

Eden left the kitchen until Jansen finished preparing his steak. He liked his medium, so, fortunately for her, it took less than ten minutes to brown after he'd placed it in the oven. By the time she'd gone upstairs, checked her messages and e-mails, washed her hands, and come back down, Jansen was fixing his plate.

"I'll let it slide that you didn't fix my plate this time. But don't make a habit of it." Jansen walked to the fridge and pulled out a beer. "Want one?"

"If you wait for me to fix your plate, you might get pretty hungry. And no, thanks. I'm going to have a nice sauvignon with my meal."

"I should have known you'd prefer a sissy drink."

"Wine?"

"Real men don't drink that stuff, girl. C'mon, I don't want my meat to get cold."

"You don't have to wait on me. Who said I was eating with you anyway?"

"Of course we'll dine together, darling. You know you wouldn't have it any other way."

They took their plates to the dining room table. Jansen dug right in, cutting off a large chunk of steak he'd smothered in steak sauce. Eden poured herself a glass of wine, took a couple sips, and then began her meal with a dainty bite of salad.

"No wonder you have no meat on your bones, girl. There's a good reason they call that rabbit food."

Instead of answering, Eden took a bite of her pasta dish, closed her eyes, and savored the taste. The fresh herbs she'd used fairly sang in the sauce mixture, and the pasta was perfectly al dente.

"Ah, you know it's not that good," Jansen said after he'd enjoyed watching Eden lick sauce from her lips and admitted he wanted to lick them, too.

"Taste it." Eden would never admit to anyone, including herself, how important it was that Jansen like her food.

Jansen placed a forkful of pasta in his mouth, his eyes never leaving Eden's as he chewed. Like her, he slowly licked his lips when he finished. "That's good, girl."

"Told you." Eden picked up her fork, acting nonchalant. But inside she was doing the happy dance. "So," she continued after they'd eaten in silence a couple moments, "what have you been doing, oh, the last ten to fifteen years?"

"That's more than a one-meal conversation."

"So give me the mini version."

Jansen took another couple bites of steak and then wiped his mouth with a napkin as he leaned back in the chair. "You know I joined the service right out of high school, right?"

Eden nodded, finishing a bite of salad. "I was so surprised, Jansen. I thought for sure you'd take advantage of an athletic scholarship, maybe even try your hand at the NBA."

"Granted, I could ball—still can. And, yes, I got a couple scholarship offers from smaller colleges. But a conversation with my uncle changed my direction."

"How?"

"Uncle Jeff is a career military man, a marine to the core. He shared with me what the service did for his life, laid out both the advantages and the challenges." Jansen shrugged, took another drink. "After looking at the big picture, I decided that path worked for me."

Eden studied Jansen—tried to decipher the unreadable

expression as he toyed with his fork. "Do you still feel that way?"

"Absolutely." The moment of subtle vulnerability was gone as Jansen picked up his knife and fork and resumed eating. "I did my four years, came out and got my degree in criminal justice—fully paid for—great medical benefits . . . I think it set me up pretty well."

"Did you ever see combat?"

Jansen nodded, and, once again, a shadow passed over his face.

"Directly, I mean—shooting and everything? You know what? Don't answer that. I don't want to know."

"So, what, you're antiwar or something?"

"I'm antiviolence—at any time, for any reason. And nothing personal, but I abhor guns."

"Oh, really? Well, check this, Ms. Give Peace a Chance. That 'shooting and everything' is why you enjoy the freedom you undoubtedly take for granted, and the gun I strap on every day is why the streets in which you walk are relatively safe." Jansen didn't try to keep the attitude out of his voice. His defenses regarding this matter had been up ever since she'd asked him to "put that thing away."

Eden finished her glass of wine. "You know what? We probably should change the subject. It's obvious we're of opposite opinions . . . on a lot of things."

They went to safer topics then, reminiscing about the good old days and the old neighborhood, talking about mutual acquaintances, recalling fond memories. By the time they finished their bowls of ice cream, the warmth that made Eden even more uncomfortable than the conflict once again existed between them.

Jansen's teasing and subtle flirtations were met with
Eden's witty sarcasm, mixed with sultry stares. When
Jansen's look turned predatory, she poured another
glass of wine and retreated to Michael's room, which
she could now appreciate since she'd changed the
sheets and cleared the clutter. To keep her mind off
things she'd rather not think about, namely Jansen, she
watched television until she fell asleep.

"Yeah, you'd better run," had been the warning that
had followed her up the stairs, along with the deep,
throaty laugh she already loved.

"Wake up, sleepyhead! It's time to work out!"

Eden jumped at the unexpected announcement. *Oh,
no, Jansen's here?* She looked at the clock and saw it
was almost nine-thirty. Then she remembered it was
Sunday, obviously his off day. Eden had planned to
lounge around the house, do laundry, and not much
else. But there was no way she'd hang out if Jansen
was going to be there.

"Don't make me come in there. Get up! We're getting ready to run a couple miles."

"Are you prepared to join me for yoga and meditation afterward?"

Silence.

"Uh-huh—that's what I thought."

"Yes, I'll join you."

What? "You're kidding, right?"

"No."

"I run with you, you'll do yoga with me."

"Yep."

Eden's eyes narrowed. "Do you have your fingers crossed, Jansen?"

"Nope." But there was an undeniable smile in his voice.

Eden crept out of bed and across the room. She yanked the door open to find Jansen's crossed fingers resting on his chest. He burst out laughing.

"Aha! I knew it! I fell for that too many times growing up not to remember that little trick." The laughter was contagious, and soon Eden was laughing, too.

"Okay, for real. Come run with me, and I'll do your little new-age stuff."

"Promise?"

"Eden," Jansen said, his eyes darkening with the sudden seriousness of the moment. "I'm a man of my word."

A mini shiver went down Eden's spine.

"Now get dressed. You've got ten minutes."

"You must have been a sergeant in the service, and you obviously think I'm a cadet."

Instead of replying, Jansen turned toward the steps. "You heard me. Don't make me come get you."

Eden rolled her eyes. She didn't want to like Jansen's bold confidence but had to admit that his swagger was growing on her. Two hours later, she'd run one mile and he'd joined her for thirty minutes of Kundalini yoga combined with meditation. While he'd made fun of it at first, he'd finally settled down and participated fully in her daily ritual. Afterward she showered and was relieved that when she came out of the room again, Jansen was gone. She spent the rest of the day catching up on e-mails, reading, and watching TV. She re-

searched various jobs in the holistic community—
including administrator or management options at a
holistic facility, yoga instruction, even becoming a massage therapist. Finally, she decided to go to the mall or
the beach—maybe catch a movie. Anything to get her
mind off the fact that, one, Jansen looked entirely too
sexy while doing a *siddhasana,* the basic seated yoga
pose, and, two, it had been less than forty-eight hours,
and she already missed having him around.

7

"You must have gotten some this weekend." Jansen's partner, Alberto Gonzalez, delivered a playful jab before getting into the driver's side of the patrol car.

"I don't know what you're talking about," Jansen calmly replied, buckling his seatbelt and checking equipment.

"Sure you do. You've got that look."

"What look?"

"Like you've been sniffing pussy, and it smelled good."

"Man, you crazy."

"Yeah, but I'm right." Alberto stole another look at his partner as the patrol car headed to their beat in the Baldwin Hills/Crenshaw area of Los Angeles. "You've been *olor de gatito!* Sniffing the *coño* . . . ha!"

Jansen joined in the laughter.

They rode a while in silence. "What, you gonna leave me hanging?"

There were few secrets between Jansen and Alberto. They'd been partners since Jansen had joined the force, and their relationship was not only professional, but one of mutual respect and deep friendship as well. Alberto had been a great impartial ear following Jansen's divorce, allowing Jansen the catharsis of letting words and feelings flow freely. He'd also welcomed Jansen into his home, where Alberto's wife, Delphia, had plied him with mouth-watering Mexican cuisine, and he was "Uncle Jansen" to their kids. Over time, the obvious love in the Gonzalez household, and the strength of their ten-year marriage, had helped wipe out the bitter taste divorce had left and opened Jansen's heart to again believe in love.

"There is this little feline. . . ." Jansen finally said.

"Ha, I knew it!" Alberto made sniffing sounds.

"Stop it, fool! It's not even like that. This is a girl from back in the day. Michael's little sister. I've known her since she was a baby."

"But she's not a baby no more."

"Not at all."

"So . . . what's up with it?"

"We're hanging out for a minute. She's staying at the house."

"Damn, you got chicks hitting on you every other block, and now you get poontang delivered to your doorstep? You make me want to be single again."

"Okay, you do my bid, and I'll be the family man. Tuck in your babies every night and then crawl into bed with—"

"Careful, homey. You can have *los niños* for a minute, but don't you mess with *mi corazón.*"

The dispatcher's voice interrupted their camaraderie. "One-Adam 85, one-Adam 85, immediate assist on a

four-five-nine now in the 3600-hundred block of La
Brea Avenue. Two suspects believed to be still in the
building: black male, approximately twenty to twenty-
five years old, six feet, one hundred seventy-five
pounds. Black male, same age range, five eight, one
hundred fifty pounds. Suspects may be armed."

Both men immediately went into the zone: Alberto
flipped on the siren, Jansen reached for the radio. "This
is Black Four responding. We're in the vicinity, responding westbound on Martin Luther King Boulevard. . . ."

More sirens could be heard as Alberto made a sharp
right into a strip mall. He zoomed to the end of the lot.
Tires screeched as he rounded the corner to the back of
the building. A black van, facing in their direction with
its motor running, immediately raced past them. Both
Jansen and Alberto noted that the driver, a light-
skinned black male in his late teens to early twenties,
was talking on his cell phone. A millisecond later, two
young men exited the back of a clothing store carrying
several large garbage bags. They immediately dropped
the goods and ran in opposite directions.

Without a word passing between them, Jansen
jumped out of a still rolling car and gave chase to the
taller suspect with cell phone in hand who'd run south
on La Brea toward Coliseum Street. As a rule, officers
didn't split up, but Jansen McKnight and Alberto Gonzalez hadn't become one of the best special-teams units
in burglary suppression by always following the rules.
They relied more on instinct and the uncanny syn-
chronicity that shaped their professional actions. Alberto whipped the squad car around, peeled out of
the strip-mall parking lot, and barreled down La Brea

to aid Jansen's pursuit by blocking the suspect on the other side while simultaneously radioing information about the fleeing van to the coordinator of the tactical unit.

Jansen jumped a four-foot fence as the chase left La Brea and continued down Coliseum. Jansen knew the suspect was trying to get to an area known as the Jungle, a dense maze of apartment complexes long known as a drug and gang haven. The suspect lost a few precious seconds when he dared look back to see Jansen hot on his heels. He bolted over a car, knocked over two trash cans, crossed the street, and began running down a side street.

Shit. With his peripheral vision, Jansen saw a blur of black and white proceeding through the intersection. *Stay with me, Alberto. Come on, man!* He heard a screech of tires and knew Alberto had spun on a dime and was now on point, racing ahead of the suspect to block him in. More sirens blared as additional cars joined the chase, and residents came out of their houses to watch this real-life episode of *Police on Your Ass.* With increased speed, Jansen whipped through brush and under trees as the suspect cut into a residential area and began zigzagging between houses. Jansen knew the suspect was winded. *That's right, asshole. I'm in the kind of shape that can run with you all night long.*

"Police! Freeze!" The suspect broke out into open space only to see Alberto kneeling behind the opened door of his squad car, his gun aimed squarely between the *t* and the *l* of a T-shirt that read THUG LIFE.

"Down on the ground, now!" Jansen yelled, drawing his weapon as he spoke. The suspect let out a string of expletives but immediately complied. Jansen handcuffed the suspect and dragged him to his feet. "The wrong day to go shopping before the store opens, son. You're under arrest."

After spending more than four hours investigating the suspect and his potential link to the Baldwin Hill burglaries or other crimes in the area, Jansen's body was tired and his heart heavy as he drove home. He thought about the young man he'd arrested—a boy, really, as it turned out, barely seventeen—who reminded him so much of himself at that age—cocky, angry, and feeling invincible. If not for sports, the love of his grandmother, and his uncle's firm hand, Jansen's road could have been much different. He had lost his dad to cancer when he was fourteen and become an angry young man, blaming the world for his loss. For a while he mixed with the wrong crowd, participated in petty crimes, smoked his share of weed. But one day his uncle Jeff showed up at the front door with more swagger in his big toe than young Jansen possessed in his whole body. They'd gotten into a heated debate after Jansen had talked back to his mother.

"You're not my daddy, old man. You can't tell me what to do." He'd found himself against the wall with a large, strong hand around his neck before he could blink.

"I may not *be* your daddy," Uncle Jeff had calmly whispered, "but after the ass whoopin' that happens if you disrespect your mama again, you'll think I am."

Uncle Jeff had eased his hand away from Jansen's neck after that but stared him down as they'd remained toe-to-toe. From them on, Uncle Jeff quietly and unobtrusively became Jansen's role model, attending sporting events, inviting him on male-bonding outings such as fishing and golf, giving him "the talk" about women—the ones to respect and the ones to avoid. Jansen's begrudging respect grew into open admiration. They remained close to this day.

That young blood sitting in jail tonight doesn't have an Uncle Jeff. He might not have anybody at all. Jansen released a sigh as he entered Baldwin Hills. This was one of the tough parts of the job, staying emotionally detached from his professional duties. He tried to do his part in the community: handed out turkeys at Christmas; participated in the LAPD EXPLORE program, which was designed to mentor youth interested in law enforcement; and headed a basketball clinic held twice a year. But he was only one man, and with 70 percent of black children being born to single mothers, he knew there were thousands, if not millions, of hardheads needing a firm, guiding hand . . . and not getting one.

Jansen pulled into the driveway, behind Eden's Acura. Unconsciously, his shoulders relaxed, and the knot in his gut began unraveling. *She's a diversion, nothing more. A way to pass the time for two weeks.* Jansen had thought about it and knew there was no way he'd get away with casually screwing his best friend's sister unless she was totally down with it herself. The very best position for him would be if she initiated the act. "Yeah, good luck with that happening, brothah," he mumbled as he exited the car and pushed the lock button. *Still, nothing beats a failure but a try.* Jansen bounded up the steps with renewed energy, unlocked the door, stepped inside, and announced, "Honey, I'm home!"

8

After their tense discussion about the military, Eden had sworn she'd keep her pro-peace opinions to herself. But it was hard to do because she was in the dining room sorting out almost a month's worth of unopened mail, and Jansen had the living room television world news blaring like he needed a hearing aid.

He's just pissed off because I didn't respond to his flirting. "Can you please turn that down!" Eden yelled.

Jansen lowered the volume.

"Can you turn it down a little more?" *So that I can't hear about every murder, accident, and police chase that occurred over the last twelve hours? Or that the entire world is going to hell in a handbasket behind wars, economic collapse, and global warming?* Eden attacked a large envelope with a letter opener; then, angry that a piece of thick tape was impeding her progress, ripped the paper with her bare hands.

Seconds later, Jansen entered the dining room. "What's wrong with you?"

"Nothing, I just . . . . don't like to watch the news."

"You weren't watching it. I was."

"I don't like to *hear* it, either."

"What are you, like the three monkeys—hear, see, speak no evil?"

Eden gave Jansen a look. "Let's not get into it, okay?"

"Why not? You can't formulate your opinion into words?"

Eden resisted the urge to growl. *This man can be so exasperating!* She rose to her full five feet six inches and took a deep, calming breath. "I don't watch the news, because I believe that thoughts become things and that the more one thinks about something, the more likely it is to happen or continue happening. So when one fills their mind with negative situations and circumstances, more of the same is perpetuated. Likewise, when one focuses on the positive, with what is going right in one's life, or the world, more of *that* is generated."

Jansen adopted his familiar, wide-legged stance and crossed his arms. "So you're saying that if everybody just turned off the TV, ate tofu, and practiced yoga, the world would become a big kumbaya?"

"I'm saying there are plenty of good things that happen every day, and I think society would be better served hearing about those *good* things."

"Look, bad things happen. That's just a fact of life. It's not going to change because you close your mind and act like it doesn't exist."

Eden eyed Jansen for a moment and then began gathering her papers. "I'm not going to get into this with you."

"It's best not to. Because it's an argument you won't win. I'm on the streets every day, baby. I see how it goes down."

Eden almost bit her tongue off to keep from responding. When Jansen wanted to, he could be as stubborn as an ox and, when it came to his opinion, as immovable as an oak tree. She haphazardly stacked up the bills and other correspondence she'd just meticulously separated and headed for the stairs.

"Is that why you're moving to Santa Monica? Because you think it's an oasis from the real world? Think if you get out of the hood you'll flee danger? Well, I've got a news flash for you. Crime is everywhere."

"According to you," Eden snarled, spinning around to face him. "But thank God yours is not the paradigm in which I operate. For your information, Mr. Know-It-All, I'm not moving to Santa Monica to escape anything. I'm moving there because it has a vibe that makes me feel good. It's clean and vibrant, and the people are friendly. I can ride my bike to the beach and walk to vegetarian restaurants and, yes, yoga studios. Is there some rule book that says all people of color have to live in the same place, and if we don't, we're 'escaping'?" Eden used air quotes to emphasize the word. "That's pretty narrow-minded, Jansen. Even for someone like you."

"Someone like me? What the hell does that mean?"

Eden narrowed her eyes and hissed through gritted teeth. "Figure it out."

"Oh, I get it," Jansen said as Eden stomped up the stairs. "I'm not in your class, huh? I represent the common folk, regular joe, the masses. You can drop the bougie act because at the end of the day you're just an ex-hood weed looking for a safe place to grow. And there ain't none!"

The sound of a slamming door resounded throughout the house.

"Ooh, that sounded pretty *violent,* Eden!" Jansen shouted, sure he could be heard through the wooden door upstairs or, at the very least, through the floor vents in Michael's room. "Where's the kumbaya now? Where's that warm, fuzzy Kodak view of the world? Uh-huh," he continued, mumbling to himself. "I thought so."

Eden tossed the pile of mail on the bed and grabbed her cell phone. She was more furious at herself than at Jansen. He'd gotten under her last nerve since they were kids, knew just how to push her buttons, and was known to argue just because he could. *Still, how dare he question my integrity, love of community, or where I want to live?* Eden's temper rose another degree. "I'm going to go back down there and give homeboy a piece of my mind!"

The cell phone vibrated in her hand and stopped Eden in her tracks. She looked down at the caller ID. "Hi, Mom," she said with a hint of attitude, pushing over the pile of papers and plopping down on the bed.

"Who peed in your cornflakes?"

"Jansen, who else? I can't stand him!"

Phyllis chuckled. "Don't tell me y'all have picked up where you left off almost twenty years ago."

"I'm afraid so."

"You tell Jansen don't make me come up there."

Eden smiled and let her shoulders relax. Only now did she realize how tense they were. "I will."

"You heard from Michael?"

"Yes, last night. He finally sent a quick e-mail saying he was fine and would be in touch soon. Sorry I didn't call you," Eden rushed on, effectively cutting off her mother's retort. "But I told Michael he needed to phone home. He promised to call you today."

"How's he doing?"

While the convo between mother and daughter continued upstairs, the home phone rang. Jansen checked out the caller ID; his face broke in a smile.

"Big Mike!"

"J-Dog, what's poppin'!"

"You're the world traveler, brothah, you tell me!"

"Oh, it's all good. Getting ready to make this dirty money, son."

"Big ballah!"

"How's things at the house? You holding it down?"

"Things are cool. Except I just pissed your sister off."

"Now why doesn't that surprise me?"

Jansen laughed.

"Y'all always did get along like oil and water," Michael continued. "But like I told Eden, y'all should be able to act civil to each other until her place is ready."

"Truth be told, I think it's all just an excuse for her to hang around. You know how irresistible I am when it comes to the ladies."

"Uh, do I have to remind you that this is my little

sister we're talking about? The one I love and would guard with my life?"

"No, man, you don't have to remind me."

"I'm serious, Jansen. Don't play with Eden's emotions. She's been through enough."

Jansen paused at those words. "What do you mean?"

"If you find out, Eden will be the one to tell you. But I'll say this. She doesn't need to be dealing with any bullshit. Especially from you."

9

Eden turned down the soothing sounds of Jennifer Lindsay, the Enya-style singer with an angel's voice she'd stumbled upon online. She felt much better, thanks to thirty minutes of yoga and meditation, her second set of the day. There it was again, the sound she'd ignored earlier—Jansen knocking at her door.

Go away! They'd argued more than an hour ago, and while she'd calmed down, Jansen's comments had reminded Eden of things she'd rather forget.

"Little garden, can I come in?" Jansen's voice was soft, gentle.

She softened a bit at one of the nicer childhood nicknames he'd given her. "I'm busy."

"Come on, Eden. I've got something for you."

Silence.

"Can I come in?"

Eden walked to the door and cracked it open. Jansen pushed inside a single, perfectly formed red rose. Its fragrance wafted up to Eden's nostrils so strongly it was as if the scent had been sprayed on artificially.

"I'm sorry for being a jerk," Jansen said, his voice dripping with sincerity. "I had a hard day, but that's no excuse."

Eden reached out and took the rose. "Apology accepted."

Jansen blocked the door when Eden would have closed it. "Are you hungry?"

"I'm fine."

"I cooked dinner. Some vegetarian stuff."

Skepticism was written all over Eden's face. "What kind of *stuff?*"

"That's what you'll have to come downstairs to find out." Jansen tilted Eden's chin and ran a rough thumb over her soft lips. His eyes darkened as he stared at them. Eden swallowed, tried to breathe, and removed his hand from her face. "Don't take too long. Dinner's ready."

Later, Eden would ponder why she'd felt the need to change clothes before joining Jansen downstairs, but she had. Nothing fancy, just a long, print dress she often donned when she wanted to look casually chic. Its slinky, no-wrinkle fabric and comfortable cut made it one of her favorites. She'd never thought it sexy. But the way Jansen looked at her when she came down the stairs had her rethinking that opinion.

"Something smells good." Eden started for the kitchen, but Jansen reached for her hand and directed her to the dining room instead. She turned the corner and stopped short. "Jansen, you didn't have to do this."

"I know. But I wanted to."

The dining room table had been set with plates, silverware, wineglasses, and folded napkins. A dozen roses—or eleven, as one was resting in a mini vase upstairs—was the vibrant centerpiece, and a bottle of red wine stood next to it, uncorked and breathing. It had been years since anyone had treated Eden special. Her heart expanded, but she quickly tried to banish the flame. This was Jansen McKnight, her tormentor from high school, the lady-killer and basketball player who'd scattered broken hearts from the Valley to Orange County. *And don't forget the double-dog dare. Jansen is the ultimate competitor and always plays for keeps.*

She pulled her hand from Jansen's and walked to the other side of the table. *The best defense is a good offense.* Aware that his eyes were probably trained on one of her best assets, she swayed her hips seductively and lowered her voice to a soft, husky tone. "This is nice, Jansen." She turned and cocked her head. "Is it part of your seduction?"

An unreadable look scampered across Jansen's face, but before Eden could analyze it, she was met with his cocky smile. "I guess we'll see." He stepped forward and poured wine into the stemmed glasses.

"What? You're having some of this sissy drink?"

"A nod to my sensitive side," Jansen replied with a wink. He handed Eden her glass and lifted his in a toast. "To peace offerings."

Eden raised her brows. "Peace? Hear, hear."

Jansen's eyes never left Eden's as he took a tentative sip. He grimaced as it went down.

"You don't like it?"

"It's all right."

"It's an acquired taste that gets better over time."

"Many things do. . . ." The look Jansen gave Eden

before leaving the room suggested he wasn't talking about the merlot.

Moments later, he returned with two piping-hot plates. A tantalizing aroma tickled Eden's nostrils as soon as the food was set before her. "There's no meat in these dishes?" she asked.

"Nope."

"No beef or chicken stock, no bouillon cubes or lard?"

"The only meat on this table is the chicken on my plate. The sausage in the dressing is that fake stuff y'all dare call meat."

"The soy sausage must have covered the smell of the chicken you cooked."

"I picked up a rotisserie chicken at the market— figured I'd already made you sick enough for one day."

"Wow, you did think of everything."

"I'm admittedly a knucklehead sometimes, but I know how to come correct."

Eden picked up her fork and tasted the soy-sausage dressing. It had a perfectly crispy crust while being moist and flavorful in the middle. She kept herself from moaning aloud, but just barely. Next, she tried the vegetable medley of carrots, pearl onions, snap peas, and corn, surprised to taste fresh herbs amid the creamy sauce. Lastly, she took a bite of fluffy mashed potatoes. Had Jansen really prepared this dinner, or was one of their grandmothers in the kitchen?

"Well?" Jansen asked, preferring fingers to silverware as he finished off a crispy chicken leg.

Eden finished chewing and took a sip of wine. "At the risk of having this thrown in my face for the rest of her life," her smile belied the sarcasm in her words, "it's delicious."

"What happened between you and your ex-husband?"

Eden stopped in midchew. The abrupt change in subject caught her completely by surprise. She swallowed her food and wiped her mouth. "Where'd that come from?"

"From wanting to know. It's true that we mix like oil and water most of the time, but you know I care about you."

"My marriage isn't something I often discuss."

Whoever this fool was, he must have hurt her bad. Jansen's muscles flexed involuntarily. Aside from being a classic alpha male, Jansen was proficient in the martial arts. His hands were classified as lethal weapons, and one would not want to cross him in the wrong way on the wrong day. In that moment, a wave of protectiveness rose up, and Jansen recognized the vulnerability behind Eden's feisty facade. *Don't play with Eden's emotions. She's been through enough.* As Michael's words ran through his mind, Jansen figured that "enough" had come at the hands of her ex. He shifted in his chair to hide the discomfort that came from this unexplainable need to make sure no one hurt Eden again.

"I can understand you wanting to keep the door closed on bad memories," Jansen said, feeling Eden might open up if he first talked about his own failed marriage. "I surely could go the rest of my life without seeing my ex-wife."

Eden relaxed against the back of the dining room

chair and picked up her glass of wine. "Well, I'd sure like to meet the woman who caught the cougar."

Jansen smiled at Eden's reference to the Crenshaw High mascot.

"How did you two meet?"

"In the service, initially. We were both part of the peacekeeping mission in Somalia, back in '93. She was in the army, and when her platoon got reassigned, we lost contact. Later, we met again in Chicago."

"How you'd end up in the Windy City?"

"A friend of mine recruited me to be a part of a special-units team on the south side. I didn't have anything in particular calling me back to LA, so I joined him there. Maybe subconsciously I remembered that was where Yolanda was from." Jansen shrugged. "We ended up running into each other at a party and were married six months later."

"Wow. The attraction must have been intense."

"Physically, yes. But I quickly learned that good sex isn't enough to hold a marriage together."

"Any kids?"

Jansen sighed. "No. I wanted to, but . . ."

"You still want to be a father?" Eden softly asked, intrigued by this side of Jansen she was seeing for the first time.

Jansen shrugged again. There was only so much of one's sensitive side an alpha male could reveal in one night.

"Gregg was my college sweetheart," Eden began into the silence. "Met him in my sophomore year. I thought he was my soul mate, the father of my children, and the one I'd swing with on the porch when we got old." She looked at Jansen with a bittersweet smile. "We dated for five years before getting married. I thought I knew him. But he changed."

"What happened?"

"That's a long story, but the short version is that behind his well-crafted, gentlemanly image was a closet asshole."

"He hit you?"

Eden's nod was almost imperceptible.

"More than once?"

"Does it matter how many times I was assaulted?" she snapped before continuing in a calmer voice. "Actually, the verbal jabs hurt more and lasted longer than the physical ones. I was one of the most highly respected aides on Capitol Hill, yet my self-esteem was in shreds by the time my marriage ended." Eden visibly swallowed and drained the rest of her wine.

Jansen rose and walked around to Eden's side of the table. "I'm sorry you went through that, little garden," he said, placing his hands on her shoulders.

Eden tensed. "That's all right, Jansen." She started to rise.

"Whoa, relax, it's okay. You're as tight as a drum. You've been tense all evening. And for the part I played in that, again, I apologize."

"I've endured worse. I'll be all right."

Jansen's firm fingers kneaded the knot at the nape of Eden's neck and were surprisingly gentle as he massaged her temples. He ran his fingers through her hair and massaged her scalp as if he'd been born to do it. Eden didn't try to stop the moan this time. Jansen's manhood twitched at the sound, but he ignored it, kept his attention on the task at hand. "Trust me when I tell you, baby girl. You're nobody's weed. You're the rarest of flowers, whose fragrance and beauty is beyond compare."

Eden closed her eyes and allowed herself to relax under Jansen's expert ministrations. This beautifully orchestrated evening may well have been designed as part of his seduction plan. But at this moment, with the warmth of the wine in her belly and Jansen's hands on her skin, Eden simply didn't care.

10

"I love the ocean. The vibration is simply *amazing!* Isn't it?" Bright green eyes, sparkling and animated, turned in Eden's direction.

"Yes, Ariel." Eden laughed. "It's amazing."

Ariel Sun was the name that former Nebraska native Betsy Meeks had adopted as part of her transition from meat-eating farm girl to new-age vegan psychic nymph. She and Eden had met at the yoga studio where Eden had purchased a membership, and—after discovering they both loved art films, rice cream, and Egyptian singing star Amr Diab and had both spent time living in DC's world of politics (Betsy's uncle had worked in the House of Representatives)—a friendship was born. To others, Ariel may have been viewed as, well, an airhead, but to Eden she was a refreshing breeze. While the days since her last argument with Jansen had been relatively peaceful—a truce of sorts—his was still a commanding, domineering presence, his very physique that of unyielding brute force. And then there was the gun Jansen insisted on keeping close to him, even in the house. He'd told her it was a habit born out of his years in the military and time spent in law enforcement. "Guns don't kill people, people kill people," he'd told her when she'd asked if the offensive piece of metal could stay in his room and out of her sight. "People with guns kill more people than those without them," Eden had retorted. And then she'd thought of some of the things she'd seen and heard in hallowed political chambers. *Well, maybe not,* she'd thought but not voiced.

Eden came out of her reverie and realized Ariel had asked her a question. "I'm sorry, Ariel . . . a lot on my mind."

"No worries, my friend," she replied, the singsong quality of her voice at once festive and calm. "Everything is always in divine order, even that which appears chaotic."

"Yes, well, my life will be much calmer once I move into my place. One week to go. I can't wait." They found a bench and sat down. Eden watched a flock of seagulls glide effortlessly over the sparkling blue water. They formed a near-perfect *V* and flew with the freedom of not having a care in the world. Eden watched them until they seemed to fly into the sun. *I want to feel as free as that.*

"Why is your life not calm now?" Ariel asked. She effortlessly crossed her ultra-skinny legs into the lotus position and turned to face her.

"My temporary roommate isn't woo-woo," Eden answered, using her favorite word to describe people who lived holistically, or some semblance thereof.

"And that affects your peace because . . ."

"Because he's a gun-toting, meat-eating, classic alpha male I've known since childhood—my brother's best friend."

"What a beautiful place to shine your light, Eden—to cast your positive thoughts in and around his energy field, viewing not the illusion of his rough personality, but the perfect essence of his highest self."

Eden picked at a splinter of wood on the table and pondered Ariel's words. Jansen's "illusive" personality was so in-your-face it was hard to ignore. Yet she'd seen flashes of another being inside him, the one who'd thoughtfully prepared a vegetarian meal, rubbed away her tension with caring hands, and bought her a copy of *House Party* because he remembered her crush on Kid 'N Play. "If I'm too nice to him, he'll take it the wrong way," she finally said.

"We're responsible for only our actions, not someone else's reaction. Are you afraid of your love for him?"

Eden's head jerked up. "Love?" she asked incredulously.

Ariel's laugh was light and melodic, floating on the air like crystal chimes. "Don't worry, Eden. Your secret's safe with me."

"It's not like that at all, Ariel. Jansen is like a brother to me, so of course I love him. But not in the way you mean."

"Well, then," Ariel sang, an impish smile on her face, "you can shower him with lots and lots of *brotherly* love and not worry about a thing."

Later that night, when Eden entered the house to find a shirtless, barefoot Jansen reclined on the couch like an African god awaiting palm fronds and grapes, she recalled Ariel's statement and Cheshire–like grin. Eden tossed out a hurried "hello" and escaped up the stairs, knowing that as long as that six-foot-four-inch candy bar was anywhere near her, and that damnable dare was still on the table, there'd be plenty of worrying to do.

II

Jansen hadn't intended to play the role of voyeur. He'd waited until eight-thirty, and when he still heard no sounds coming from Eden's room, he'd knocked on the door. No answer. Again, a little louder. Still nothing. He'd almost pounded his fist against the wood, but something stopped him. A memory. And then more. With a wicked smile on his lips and a twinkle in his eye, Jansen had eased open the door and crept inside with the stealth of a panther, intent on scaring the living daylights out of Eden as he'd done countless times in their childhood. He'd almost laughed out loud as he'd eyed Eden's fully covered body in a round heap near the center of the mattress. She still slept as he'd remembered, with the sheet pulled all the way over her head, even in summer, as it was now. It had felt like he was seven again, when he'd placed the plastic eyeball in the bottom of her oatmeal, or ten, when he'd played the prank that had almost made his grandmother pull a switch off the tree. With the observational development honed when one's life depended on it, Jansen quickly scanned the room and took in the reason for Eden's deep slumber—a near-empty wine bottle standing next to a partially eaten bowl of popcorn. An *O* magazine shared space on the nightstand, its cover partially hidden by an open DVD case. *Boyz in the Hood.* Jansen smiled. *Oh, so you're going down memory lane, too, huh?* The menacing smile returned as he took one step toward his prey, and then another. Then something happened. Eden turned over.

The delectable picture she painted stopped him in his tracks. Her thick black hair lay splayed across the stark, white pillows, a hint of something soft and pink peeking out from the top of the sheet while a long, darkly tanned leg peeked out from the bottom. Long eyelashes formed a shadow on her upper cheeks, and when she moved her head and licked her lips, years of abject discipline through his years of martial arts were the only reason Jansen didn't grow hard. He knew he needed to break the spell she seemed to be weaving around him, knew he should shout her name or clear his throat or in some way make his presence known, but Jansen couldn't seem to stop staring at her. Usually when they encountered each other, it was among a swirl of activity or argument. Now, with Eden quietly uninhibited, he was able to study a face that for years he'd all but ignored, surprised and awed that he could have missed something so exquisite growing up in his own backyard. Jansen knew it was time to wake Eden before he did something he wanted to do even though it was totally irrational—run his tongue up the length of her creamy, dark caramel leg to the treasure that lay hidden beneath five hundred threads of Egyptian cotton.

"Eden!" Jansen barked as if he were preparing to issue a military order.

Eden frowned, moaned, and turned over.

"C'mon, now. Off your butt and on your feet!"

"Go away," Eden growled while pulling the sheet over her head.

"Not a chance," Jansen replied as he headed to the window. Waves of sunshine poured into the room's east-facing glass. "No one told you to play the wino role last night," Jansen scolded as he yanked the sheet away from Eden's face.

"Boy, I'm not playing." Once again, Eden disappeared under cotton. "You have no business in here. Get out of my room!"

Jansen adopted his trademark wide-legged stance. He scowled down at the prone form that dared defy him. "Last week I let you off easy. We ran only one mile. You promised that this week you'd give me two."

Silence.

"You've got three seconds to take that sheet off your face, or I'm picking you up and dumping you into a cold shower. One . . ."

Eden stifled a groan. She knew he would do it.

"Two . . ."

"Jansen, get out of my room. I'm not running anywhere."

"Maybe not next week, but you're running today. A promise is a promise."

Eden released the groan this time but didn't uncover her head. "Fine! I'll be down in a minute."

"Uh-uh. I remember your minutes. Like when me and Michael had to wait to walk you home because Tanesha Brown was gonna beat you up for talking about her mama. You told us you'd be out in 'just a minute,' and we almost missed practice waiting on your scared behind." Without further warning, Jansen closed the distance between him and the bed, scooped up Eden, and headed to the shower.

"Jansen!" Eden screamed, fighting to release the left arm entwined in the sheet while her right arm flailed awkwardly against a hard-as-steel chest. "Put me down!"

Jansen allowed Eden's feet to touch the floor but still held a firm arm around her waist as he reached over and turned on the water. He tried not to focus on the softness of the body squirming against his hard, lean frame, tried not to feel the silky hair brushing against his bare skin.

Eden finally worked her arm out of the sheet, but the cotton bunched in and around her legs—not to mention Jansen's viselike arm grip—still made quick flight impossible. She focused all her attention on his long, thick fingers, trying to pry them away from her waist. In the tousling that ensued, the pink strap of her lingerie top worked its way off her shoulder.

Jansen was secretly amused at Eden's valiant attempts to free herself. "You might as well quit squirming, girl, and get ready for this cold sh—" The rest of the words faded from his lips as Jansen turned to Eden. His eyes were quickly drawn from her face to the black, hard, perfectly formed areola that, with each deep breath, peeked out of Eden's top. In a matter of seconds, he took in the creamy caramel skin surrounding this flawless rendition of a chocolate kiss, allowed his eyes to travel to the indentation of her collarbone, to the slightly parted lips that had tempted him for days. His gaze moved to Eden's darkened eyes, and he knew that she, too, had felt the shift—that the mood had gone from playful to passionate. He wasn't even aware that his arm was moving until his finger reached out and lightly flicked Eden's nipple just before his mouth covered hers in a searing kiss.

Eden barely had time to breathe, much less think. At first, all she could do was feel—Jansen's solidly sculpted body pressed against hers, the long, thick evidence of his desire pressing into her stomach. His other hand slid down and cupped her derriere, pressing her into his hardness. Her mouth had opened of its own accord and welcomed his tongue, swirling, probing, claiming . . . once, and again. A slight whimper escaped when Jansen deepened the kiss while teasing Eden's nipple into further hardness with his thumb, mimicking the same swirling motion of his tongue in her mouth.

Oooo, Jansen. This feels so good, your tongue in my mouth. Slowly thoughts began to seep through her haze of desire. *Jansen's tongue in my . . . wait! This isn't supposed to happen. This can't happen!* It took all the strength she could muster, but Eden broke the kiss and pushed away from the chest that she could feel forever. "Stop. We can't. . . ." Eden took in deep gulps of air, still reeling from the intensity of her body's reaction to Jansen's touch.

Jansen was trying to recover as well. His heart was

pounding as if he'd run ten miles, and one very specific
muscle was aching for a release that even a marathon
couldn't provide. In this moment, Jansen knew there
was only one thing, only one person who could give
him what his body craved, and her name was Eden.
And in this moment of stark realization, he swore to
have her.

Jansen thought these thoughts even as he sought to
diffuse the current tension. The time for the inevitable
would come soon enough. "What, baby girl? Can't
take the heat?"

"I can't believe you did that," Eden snapped, thankful she could breathe again. "I haven't even brushed
my teeth!"

"It's a good thing my breath is fresh enough for the
both of us then, huh?"

"Move out of my way. You're disgusting." Eden
pushed past Jansen and tested the water still running
into the tub.

"If you're not downstairs in ten minutes, I'm
coming back up here." Jansen's eyes narrowed as he
gave Eden the once-over from head to toe. "And if I
do, I promise you we'll still get our workout on, but
running won't have anything to do with it."

12

"You still got a crush on Morris Chestnut?" Jansen asked. He and Eden were in the living room, eating on TV trays and checking out the movie she'd rented last night but hadn't watched.

"Naw," Eden answered before putting a forkful of the fluffy vegetable omelet she'd prepared into her mouth. "He hasn't been my main squeeze since *The Best Man.*"

"I remember you cried like a baby during that scene from *Hood* when he gets shot," Jansen teased. "You would have thought the brothah really died."

"I was heartbroken, that's no lie. It even took me a while to warm back up to Ice Cube. Even though his character's finger didn't pull the trigger, it was because of Doughboy's thuggish behind that Ricky took a bullet."

"Boo-hoo," Jansen mimicked, clutching his heart and leaning sideways. "They shot him! Why'd they have to shoot him! It was you and . . . What was your friend's name?"

"Who? Oh, Chandra. Chandra Brockman. Wow, I

haven't thought about her in years. Wonder where she is?" Eden sipped Jansen's freshly squeezed orange juice while she pondered the whereabouts of one of her former best friends.

Jansen bit into a tender sausage. He'd been pleasantly surprised when Eden didn't make a big deal about his pig consumption, though she had warned him not to fry the links in her newly purchased stainless steel. "I'm surprised y'all didn't stay in touch."

"Me, too. We were thick as thieves until she and her family moved to St. Louis. We kept in touch for a while. Then she got pregnant and—"

"Chandra had a baby?" Somehow Jansen just couldn't see the fly-girl chick with the sassy mouth taking care of a child.

"At least three, from what I heard. She and I lost contact, but I ran into another classmate around my sophomore or junior year of college and found out she was married with children, and a preacher's wife at that."

"You're lying!" Jansen exclaimed. It was no secret that half the basketball team had slept with Chandra, and the other half had wanted to. Jansen wasn't proud of the fact that both he and Eden's brother, Michael, had been on the receiving team, on more than one occasion. He wondered if Eden knew this but quickly decided against asking her. Some things, he deduced, were best left in the past. "Wow, I guess anybody can change," he finished, an opinion formed by firsthand experience. He'd given up his player card when he got married and hadn't renewed it since getting divorced.

Between scenes of Furious Styles teaching life lessons to his sons, and the streets conducting classes

of their own, Jansen and Eden took another stroll down
memory lane. Eden learned things she'd never known,
like how Jansen's grandmother had "cured" his stutter-
ing by forcing him to take a breath between each word
when he spoke to her. Jansen laughed, recalling how it
would sometimes take him five minutes to ask if he
could ride his bike to the store for chips and candy.
One day, he explained, he woke up and simply didn't
stutter anymore. Another surprise was the fact that
Jansen had actually been a preemie baby, and spent his
first couple years in and out of hospitals. Eden took
in the picture of health sitting next to her, the well-
defined this and ridiculously buffed that, and found it
impossible to put *Jansen* and *frail* in the same sentence, even one describing a premature child.

The credits rolled, and Jansen and Eden enjoyed a
companionable silence. Neither wanted to acknowledge how right it felt spending time together and
how much they enjoyed each other's company. Jansen
clicked the screen from DVD to TV. A woman's hands
swam onto the screen, rubbing parts of her body as she
advertised a lotion that was "soft as satin." *Eden's body
is as soft as satin, and as rich as silk.* Jansen remembered how good she'd felt up against him, even as his
fingers itched to once again squeeze her round booty.
Eden's thoughts were similar, recalling the swirl of
Jansen's tongue in her mouth, and imagining how it
would feel on her nipple . . . and elsewhere. . . .

"You know what?"

"Hey, remember that time—"

Both spoke at once and then broke out in nervous
laughter.

"What?" Jansen asked.

"No, you go ahead," Eden encouraged.

"All right. I was just remembering you and the frog." Eden picked up a pillow from the couch and flung it at Jansen's head. It caught the side of his ear before sliding to the floor. "C'mon, now! I apologized for that!"

Eden picked up another pillow and this time held it in both hands as she playfully pummeled him. "I'd never been so scared in my life! You almost made me have a heart attack!"

Jansen couldn't defend himself for laughing. "Girl, I never saw anybody move so fast in my life. You ran out of your bedroom, barefoot, through the living room . . . and I think you were halfway down the block before your dad finally caught up with you to find out what was wrong. You woke up half the neighborhood that night."

"Thanks to you. I'll never forget the feel of that slimy creature on my leg. I'd just gotten that baby-doll nightie, feeling all grown up with my legs bare, a departure from my cotton pj sleeping attire."

"That's why I knew it would work so well. You came prancing out of the room, thinking you were cute."

"Knowing I was."

"Me and Michael had found the frog earlier that day, came home, and made a little cage with some grass and a shoe box."

"I knew something was going on, but when I tried to come into the room—"

"We'd put it on lockdown!"

"I knew y'all were up to something."

"And I knew that if I bided my time, and played it cool—"

"I'd drop my guard. By the time I went to bed that night, I'd forgotten all about your sneaky behavior."

"Mama! Daddy!" Jansen screeched, in the high-pitched voice of panic he remembered Eden using. "It's in my bed! Something's in my bed! Argh!" Jansen began to laugh so hard it became difficult to breathe. "That scream rivaled those you hear in horror movies. And all you could see was this blur of pink, yellow, and braids fly through the house!"

"I felt like I was in a horror movie, believe that," Eden said, her own laughter threatening to erupt. "I was barefoot, but I don't remember my feet touching the ground."

"They probably didn't!"

Finally Eden couldn't hold it any longer, and soon her chortles joined Jansen's guffaws. "You know what," she continued, wiping away tears. "I never got you back for all that stuff you did to me. And just so you know, payback can happen at any moment."

"And just so you know, a J-styled prank can happen at any time. You might want to check between the sheets before getting into bed at night."

"You wouldn't dare."

"Wouldn't I?" Jansen's smile was brilliant and totally mesmerizing.

"No, you wouldn't." Eden stood, reached for their dishes, and walked into the kitchen. Her thoughts were definitely of something—correction, someone—being in her bed that night. This thought alone almost made her run screaming out of the house again.

13

"Yeah, man, I'll substitute for you. The practice lasts for how long?" Jansen turned off Imperial Highway onto Crenshaw, his eyes critically surveying the surrounding area even though he was off the clock. He subconsciously took in an old lady pushing a shopping cart, and two skimpily dressed teenage girls who laughed as they sauntered past a group of teenage boys. The group paused in their trash talking to ogle the goods on display before one began his plea to "get with that." He then noticed another older man talking on his cell phone, standing off to the side, surveying the area every bit as carefully as Jansen watched him. Jansen was 80 percent sure that, if searched, the man would have a supply of drugs on his person. This assessment had nothing to do with the man's skin color or loose-fitting wardrobe, but rather came as a result of an intuition honed through years on the streets of Chicago's south side and the last four Jansen had spent in south LA neighborhoods.

"Hey, dog, you there? I need to know for sure you're

down with this. For a lot of these boys, the league is all
they have to look forward to."

"I'm here, man. Got sidetracked while observing
some suspect activity, that's all."

"Where you at?"

"Crenshaw District."

"Oh, well, I heard that. But like I said, practice starts
at one o'clock and lasts for two to three hours. The
boys have to present their reports to you before they're
allowed to suit up. And by the way, one of the teams
still needs a coach. We've been searching ever since
my super's early and unexpected retirement. I still say
you'd be perfect, even though I know your game is
shot."

"Aw, here we go."

The two men who'd known each other for more
than a decade talked another few minutes before his
colleague had to take another call. Jansen continued
toward his destination, thinking about his friend's last-
ditch plea to get Jansen to coach the tenth citywide
basketball team. Volunteering had always been an important component of Jansen's life. He regularly participated in EXPLORE and in Chicago he'd mentored
a young man, Cameron, whose single mother, Nicki,
struggled with keeping him on the straight and narrow.
When he'd told the teen he was relocating, the boy
asked if he could move to Los Angeles with Jansen.
Telling him no was one of the hardest things Jansen
had ever had to do. In the back of his mind, getting too
close to the young men in this league was something
Jansen feared. And Jansen Darrell McKnight didn't
fear much.

* * *

Eden stood in the middle of her bedroom, second-guessing what a couple hours ago had seemed like a great idea. The plan had hatched itself in her brain after she'd finished a yoga workout at the Santa Monica studio and then decided to browse a mall and look for summer-clothing sales. Twelve years in DC had left her wardrobe heavily weighted on the forty-and-below side. Now that she was back in seventy-five-and-sunny-every-day LA, Eden realized she needed to cool down her clothes. She'd purchased a couple sundresses, short sets, and matching sandals and was on her way out of the mall when she passed Victoria's Secret. A cotton-candy-pink number in the window caught her eye. She'd immediately thought of Jansen. Now here she stood in her bedroom, feeling ultra-feminine, fairly feisty, but more than a little fearful, in a lacy top with satin boy-short bottoms, wondering if she really wanted to go through with the idea. The sound of the front door closing caused her to jump. *He's home.* Eden's hand went to her mouth as her heartbeat increased. *I'm not going to go through with this! What in the #$@! was I thinking?* But Eden knew what she'd been thinking—about this morning, and the kiss. The feel of Jansen's lips against hers, his tongue probing, claiming, hadn't been far from her thoughts all day. Sure, they'd regained their casual comfort while eating brunch and watching the movie. But Eden had sensed sizzling heat just under the surface of their calm demeanors. And she thought Jansen had sensed it, too.

The refrigerator door closed. Eden turned and stared

at the closed door. She knew Jansen's routine. When he came home, he walked straight to the refrigerator, pulled out a soda or beer, and drank it while watching some form of news: CNN, MSNBC, even FOX. After that, he'd head upstairs to take a shower. *That's it. I must have been crazy to even consider such foolishness.* Eden eyed the stretch yoga pants and strappy top she'd discarded before she'd taken a shower. She took a step toward the bed and a saner wardrobe choice but stopped as Jansen laughed at something he saw or heard on TV. His was a deep, rumbling chuckle that resonated through to one's bones and, in some cases, their punanas—a deeper version of the same laugh Eden had heard many times after Jansen had embarrassed her in one way or another.

And then she remembered why she'd thought her little scheme was a good idea—the dare. Even though she knew they'd both enjoyed the kiss, Eden also believed that at the end of the day Jansen's seemingly spontaneous come-on was actually a thought-out part of his plan to seduce her. And win. Again Eden thought of Jansen's competitive nature. She knew that during the few remaining days she was in Michael's house she couldn't let her guard down, even for a minute. *You'll come to the shooting range with me, learn how to handle a firearm, and I'll get to put my handcuffs on you . . . at a time that I design.* Remembering Jansen's prize if he won the dare spurred Eden into action. There was no way that she'd ever touch a gun, much less shoot one. Eden hurried out of her room and into madness. Just as she got into position, she heard

Jansen's hard-soled shoe land on the first stair to the second floor. It was too late to turn back now.

Jansen entered the guest bedroom and stopped short. He planted his feet wide, crossed his arms, and looked around. His eyes narrowed, looking in the direction of Michael's room, where Eden spent her nights. With one more look around the room, he sat on the bed, took off his shoes, and then walked into the master bath.

She heard the shower turn on, and Eden let out the breath she'd been holding. Again she wondered about her sanity as she huddled behind a row of sweatsuits in the guest rooms' walk-in closet. It had been pure accident that she'd hid behind the rack that held Jansen's clothes. Her tough luck; the woodsy, musky scent she'd smelled when he'd hugged her that first night now filled her nostrils. Eden took one last deep breath, slowly turned the knob, and exited the closet. She blinked several times, her eyes readjusting to the indirect yet bright sunlight that spilled in through the open blinds. *He's gonna know something's up, but I've got to close them.* Eden hurried over to the windows, closed the blinds, and then climbed into the bed that had been made with military precision. And, again, the smell of Jansen enveloped her. She tried to tamp down her nervousness, as well as the excitement building between her legs. But it was as if her body had a mind of its own. All she could think about was the fact that Jansen was mere feet away from her—wet, hard, and buck naked.

The water stopped. And so did Eden's breathing.

Willing herself to breathe again, she took a deep, calming breath through her nose, slowly releasing the breath out of her mouth. *Ah, that feels better.* She took another one, and again. Eden imagined Jansen wrapping the towel around his waist, imagined his shock when he'd exit the bathroom and find her in the center of his bed. She almost giggled, but then movement behind the half-closed doors stopped her. *This is it! Remember, girl, you're in control. You're seducing him. Get him hot, and hard, and then run for the border. Five minutes, tops. You can do this.*

Seconds later, Jansen emerged from the bathroom, drying his still wet head with a towel. Which was why he didn't see the look of shock and awe in Eden's eyes before her hand clamped over her mouth. Too late, it didn't stop the gasp that sprang forth at the sight before her. By the time Jansen heard the sound and removed the towel from his face, Eden had scampered off the bed, run out of the room, and slammed her bedroom door. Jansen's deep, throaty laughter rang out, piercing the wooden door where Eden rested, willing her heartbeat to slow down. *Girl, what in the heck were you thinking?* "I wasn't thinking," Eden whispered. She closed her eyes and viewed the image of what she'd seen, etched like a painting in her mind's eye. She'd often wondered what Jansen was working with, and whether he was all of what she'd heard other females brag about. Well . . . now she knew. And he was. Eden still didn't want to handle a gun. But Jansen's more personal weapon? *That* was another matter altogether.

14

"Eden." The big smile on Jansen's face could be heard in his voice. He waited. Nothing but silence from the other side of the door. "Found a snake instead of a frog this time, huh, little girl?" Still nothing. Jansen tried the door. Locked. He wasn't surprised. Eden had run out of his room like her pants were on fire, but real-life flames couldn't have covered the creamy brown cheeks that winked from the bottom of those shorts. Nor could any fireman's hose douse the ardor that now hardened his shaft. His hastily donned shorts couldn't hide his desire. Jansen didn't care. Dare be damned, he wanted Eden Anderson. At this moment, in his mind, all bets were off.

Jansen leaned against the door. "Eden, open the door." His voice was low and silky. He mindlessly massaged nine inches of pulsating flesh. "C'mon, now, baby girl. Quit playing." He waited a beat. And another. "We're not kids anymore, Eden. And this isn't about the dare either. Let's stop denying what we both want. Did you hear me, Eden? I want you, too, all right?"

Eden sat in the middle of Michael's bed, chin resting
on the hands that cupped her knees. They might not be
children anymore, but right now Eden was feeling
rather childish. Here she was, a grown-ass woman of
thirty-four, acting out a dare, only to have her seduction plans blow up in her face. But one look at Jansen's
glorious dick, swinging between his legs like a
Louisville slugger, and rational thought had fled Eden's
head, along with what she thought had been a well-
thought-out plan. In her mind, the scenario was supposed to have played out a different way. . . .

Jansen would walk out of the bathroom, the towel
secured firmly *around his waist. He'd see her sitting in
the middle of the bed and stop, shocked. He'd take in
her silky hair, loose and hanging around her shoulders, the creamy orbs teasing above her lacy pink top,
and be mesmerized.*

*Eden had planned to run her fingers through her
hair while looking at Jansen seductively. "You want
this," she'd purr.*

"Yes," he'd whisper.

"Well, come and get it."

*She envisioned Jansen taking one step and then an-
other, crawling onto the bed from the end of it, invok-
ing images of the panther he reminded her of. And just
when he reached her, and closed his eyes for a kiss,
she'd scamper out of the bed. "I'm not seducing you,
am I?" she'd ask, flinging the question over her shoulder as she sauntered to the door. She'd give Jansen a*

*peak of her goodies before walking to her room, falling
across her bed and reveling in her victory.*

The reality of what happened hadn't resembled her
vision at all.

"Eden." Jansen waited a couple more seconds and
then walked away. She heard his footsteps as he walked
downstairs.

After waiting a few more seconds, Eden got off the
bed, shed the skimpy pink short set, and donned jeans
and a cotton blouse. At six PM, it was still hot outside.
Shorts and a tank top would have been more appropriate. But after being exposed to Jansen's bedroom eyes
(and by the teasing manner in his voice, Eden knew he
had seen a fair share of her backside), she wanted to
cover up as much as possible. Right about now, she
would have worn a Quaker's dress if she'd had one.
And put on the bonnet, too! Eden put on earrings,
slipped into her sandals, and reached for her purse. She
didn't know where she was going, but she was definitely putting some distance between herself and her
temptation. *I can't wait to get out of here. That's it. I'll
go to the house. If the gods are kind, the contractor will
tell me it's ready and that I can move in tomorrow.*
Eden was filled with optimism as she bopped down the
steps and out the door.

Four hours later, Eden eased into Michael's driveway, feeling much better after dining at her favorite
eatery, RFD, and taking in an art flick at Laemmle
Theatres. She'd thoroughly enjoyed the Swedish flick
with English subtitles from Stieg Larsson's best-selling

Millennium trilogy. The movie provided a perfect escape—getting caught up in the thrill of the chase as the heroine in the movie worked to clear herself of a murder charge was exactly what she needed. But thinking of the movie title, *The Girl Who Played With Fire*, reminded Eden of how she'd done the very same thing just that morning and had almost gotten burned.

Jansen's SUV wasn't in the driveway. *Good, he's gone.* Eden smiled. Then she thought of where he could be. Visiting his mother? Hanging with the boys? Or was his snake languishing in someone else's garden? Eden's smile faded. She didn't even want to think of someone else licking on that gigantic Tootsie Roll. "It's none of your business," Eden mumbled to herself, opening the door and then locking it behind her. "A few more days, and you're out of here." Eden ignored the fact that this thought didn't make her feel better.

Eden fixed herself a smoothie, went to her room, and pulled on the pair of safe, cotton pajamas she'd purchased between her home visit and the show. Then she pulled out her phone. She knew she'd missed a couple calls while in the theater and had gotten caught up in an NPR talk show on her way home. Even though it was the weekend, she hoped one of the calls was a potential employer. She'd sent out several résumés over the last few days but so far had no responses. She'd planned financially to handle four to six months without employment, but Eden knew that getting back to work wasn't just about the money. It was about reestablishing a life for herself and not having so much time on her hands.

After scrolling through the missed messages, she hit her phone's fave list. "Hey, Mom."

"Hey, Eden. What's up?"

"Nothing, returning your call."

"Oh, I didn't want much; just checking in. Is Jansen still staying there with you?"

"Yeah, why?"

"Because I want to know, that's why! Don't get all huffy with me, girl. You're too grown and too far away for me to put on punishment, but I'm still your mother." Phyllis chuckled, reveling she wasn't half as mad as her words implied.

"I'm sorry for snapping, Mom. It's been a long day."

"What's been so long about it?"

Jansen's snake. "Oh, just preparing to move into my place. I went by there today. Overall it's looking good, and the new kitchen and master suite will be fabulous. I can't wait to move!"

"Why, so you can use your new gourmet stove or so you can get away from a different kind of heat?"

Eden pulled the phone away from her ear and looked at it, puzzled. What was her mother implying? Phyllis Anderson always did have that thing her grandmother called "mother wit"—what others called intuition. As much as she tried to hide her feelings, Eden's mother always seemed to know what was going on—like when Eden had called, crying, to tell Phyllis she was getting divorced. She couldn't get the words out. But her mother knew. "You're better off without him," she'd said amid her daughter's tears. Eden's healing began in that moment.

But there were moments when Eden didn't want

her mother all up in her business. Now was one of those times. "You're going to love my range, Mom! It's self-cleaning, with a grill in the middle, all stainless steel. In fact, my whole kitchen is stainless steel, and my cabinets are this deep red cherry wood. The countertops are black granite. That seems dark, huh? But it really isn't because the walls are ivory, and there is track lighting. It looks like a kitchen you'd see on HGTV!" Eden knew she was rambling but hoped mentioning one of Phyllis's favorite shows would throw her off the Jansen track.

"Sounds like you might be planning some romantic meals for two," Phyllis continued in that calm, I'm-your-mother-and-I-know-it-all voice. "Do I know him?"

"Okay, Mom. Obviously you're getting at something. Out with it."

"I talked to Kathryn today. She said Jansen stopped by the house and mentioned how fine you'd gotten over the years. Told her you weren't the weed he used to tease back in the day. Kathryn said he had that look in his eye when he was talking about you, like he was digging you or something. Is Michael's best friend getting ready to be my son-in-law?"

"Mom! Are you serious? Jansen tells his mother I'm cute, and you think it's time to shop for a dress with a veil?"

"For something that's no big deal, to hear you tell it, you're getting pretty riled up."

"I am not."

"You are, too."

Eden bit her lip to end the argument. She was getting riled up, and she knew why. She was trying to convince herself that Jansen was just an old acquaintance who happened to be her brother's best friend. A guy with whom she had no personal feelings or romantic connection. The guy from whom Eden would be glad to put some distance, except Eden knew it was closer to, not farther from, Jansen that she'd like to be.

"I'm kinda surprised you and Jansen never dated," Phyllis continued in the same casual tone as one would use to discuss the weather. "He's always been a good-looking boy. And while I know he was wild back in the day, I always thought he had a good heart. It's been almost five years since your divorce, Eden, and in that time I've rarely heard you mention a man's name. Now, maybe Jansen isn't the one, but I think it's time you entertained the idea of having a serious relationship again."

"Mom, I—"

"I know, Eden. It's hard to put your heart out there again, to risk being hurt or rejected. But the possible rewards outweigh those risks. You're still young, vibrant, a lot of life ahead of you. Don't you want to spend it with someone? Have children? I never thought I'd be almost sixty years old and still waiting for my first grandchild!"

"Michael's older than me," Eden readily countered, jumping at the chance to take Phyllis's mind off her daughter's single status. "I think he's the one you should be talking to about settling down."

"When he gets back here, maybe I will. But it's you on the phone right now. I want to see you happy, baby. And while it's true that you don't need a man to enjoy life, they can be pretty nice to have around. Especially a caramel candy like Jansen."

"Mom!"

"Kathryn e-mailed me a recent picture of him." Eden listened, speechless. "Honey, if I had a little cougar in me, I'd go after that boy myself!"

"Mom! Okay, really, this is too much information . . . okay?"

"Okay, baby," Phyllis said, laughing. "I guess I've shocked my daughter enough for one day. But because your mouth is already open, let me drop one last tidbit before you close it."

Eden closed her eyes. "I'm almost afraid to hear it."

"I've met a man. We're dating."

Eden's eyes widened. Had she heard correctly? As far as she knew, her mother hadn't dated anybody since her divorce years ago. Her father had gotten married two years later to the woman with whom her mother believed he had been having an affair. But Phyllis had seemed content to work, hit the casinos every now and then, and take care of Grandma. Phyllis Anderson? Dating? It was all too much.

"Eden, are you still there?"

"Yes, Mom, I'm still here. I guess you can tell I'm shocked."

"Me, too!" Phyllis chuckled and shared a bit about her beau with her daughter.

Eden relaxed as her mother recounted how she'd met Larry Bates and how their meeting for coffee at Starbucks had turned into a date that lasted five hours. Eden walked downstairs as she listened, laughing as her mother described trying to get into a Spanx Bodysuit for their second date, and how her refrigerator was now full of Jenny Craig, Lean Cuisine, and flavored water.

"You sound happy, Mom," Eden said sincerely as she leaned against the counter and munched on a bowl of grapes.

"I am, Eden. Maybe that's why you and Michael have been so on my mind lately. I want you both to find your mates and be happy, too."

Eden's response was interrupted by the sound of the front door opening.

"Is that Jansen?" Phyllis asked as if she could see through Eden's eyes.

"Yes." All the tension that yoga had worked out of her body came back full force and settled around Eden's shoulders. *It's just Germy Jansen,* she told herself. *No big deal.*

"Then, baby, I'd better let you go."

"No, that's all . . ." The rest of the sentence died on Eden's lips as she realized the call had ended. She turned to find Jansen staring at her and knew for certain that things between the two of them were about to change.

15

"Hey." Jansen breathed the word into the atmosphere. His deep brown eyes were almost black with unveiled desire, drinking her in like water. There was no teasing in his tone. Instead the word held warmth and promise. Jansen noted that striped cotton pj's had replaced the lacy pink number he'd seen earlier that day. But it didn't matter. Changing the wrapping didn't stop Jansen from imagining what was underneath. What he'd seen . . . and felt. . . .

"Hey." Eden's voice was low and soft. She felt shy and vulnerable, like the fourteen-year-old who used to watch with puppy-dog eyes as he strode up and down the basketball court. She used to stare at his picture in her brother's yearbooks and even daydreamed about their being together, married and everything. But those were fantasies, nothing more. Eden knew it would do her well to keep this in mind. Especially since Jansen stood there looking like "oh, my goodness" and "Lord, have mercy" rolled into one. The black jeans hugged his legs and emphasized their length, while the beige silk shirt caressed his muscles and brought out the bronze tone of his skin.

"I think we need to talk."

"Me, too."

Jansen walked to the refrigerator and grabbed a beer. "You want some water or juice or something?" he asked over his shoulder.

"No, I'm good." Eden took her bowl of grapes into the living room and sat in the black leather recliner that sat adjacent to the couch.

Jansen plopped down on the couch, unscrewed the cap from his bottle of beer, and took a long swallow. "Dang, Eden, I'm not going to bite you. Why don't you come over here so I can hear you?"

"This room isn't that big. I'm fine right here."

Jansen shrugged his shoulders and took another swig of beer. Then he sat up and put the bottle down. "Okay, little garden, it's like this. I'm digging you. And this isn't about the dare, or me being competitive, or none of that. This is about me acknowledging that I have a thing for you, and that I'd like to take you out."

"A date?"

"Yeah, you know—dinner and a movie, concert, or stroll on the beach."

Eden had been prepared to discuss the little tryst that had happened that morning, even seeing Jansen à la nude. But she hadn't expected declarations of "digging her," much less to be asked out on a date. And how had her mother been so on the money with her suggestion to consider going out with him? Either Phyllis Anderson was turning into Miss Cleo, or Jansen had told his mother more than Phyllis had shared.

"Jansen . . . you know that's not us."

"Oh, here we go with the you're-like-a-brother-to-me routine?"

"Well . . . you are!"

"Am I really, Eden? You have the same thoughts about Michael that you have about me?"

"Hell, no!" The outburst happened before Eden could stop it.

The merest of smiles scampered across Jansen's face. His eyes sparkled. "So what kind of thoughts do you have about me that are different than ones you'd think for your brother?"

"I've never seen my brother's . . . I've never seen Michael naked before, for one. Well, not since we were, like, six and nine years old and both had the chicken pox."

"I've seen you naked, too, you know."

Eden's head shot up. "Excuse me?"

"I have," Jansen said laughing. "Now, I wasn't a peeping tom or nothing, but one time I saw you getting out of the shower. You must have been twelve, thirteen years old."

"What? I don't believe you, Jansen. There's no way you would have seen my booty and not teased me about it."

"Yeah, well, believe it. I'd come into the house looking for Mike. I called out, but nobody answered. That's when I heard the shower running. I thought it was Mike and started to walk into the bathroom. You'd just gotten out of the shower and were toweling off.

I caught myself before saying anything and backed out of the room."

"You. Are. Lying."

"Swear to God, Eden. I didn't tease you, because it messed with me, to be honest. Here I was a fifteen-, sixteen-year-old player, or so I thought, getting turned on by my friend's kid sister? That shit surprised me, I'm not going to lie. But you were standing there, all smooth and creamy, little dimples winking from the top of that round backside. . . ." What Jansen didn't tell her was that he'd had to go home and relieve the hard-on that instantly resulted from seeing Eden's ass. He'd had to do the same this morning.

"Jansen!" He *had* seen her. Eden did have dimples just above her rump, dimples that the boy shorts had covered. "You pervert!"

"You were beautiful then," Jansen replied, once again serious and sexy. "And you're even more beautiful now."

Eden studied the handsome face of the man in front of her, a man she'd known almost her whole life. "How do I know you're serious, that this isn't some standard line you've used a million times to talk women out of their panties?"

"Because I'm not going to take anything you don't want to give. We're both adults here, Eden. And we both know what's up. I'm just suggesting we stop denying the attraction and let nature take its course. I don't know about you, but since getting divorced, I haven't had too many women. Now, I know that's hard for you to believe," Jansen said hurriedly, continuing on before Eden could object, "but it's true."

"You're right, it *is* hard to believe."

Jansen shrugged. "Guess I've become more discriminating in my old age. And, to be honest, the divorce did a number on my emotions a little bit. Separating was my idea. I wasn't a saint during our marriage, but Yolanda having an affair was the final straw."

"Were you always faithful to her?"

Jansen shook his head. "I messed up once when my comforting a grieving coworker, who'd lost her son, got out of hand. I'm not proud of it either, believe me." He stood and walked to the window. The street was quiet, the darkness broken up only by a streetlight nearby.

"So what was good for the goose wasn't for the gander?" Eden's voice was soft, questioning. There was no sarcasm or condemnation there.

"Made me ashamed all over again. I'd been cheated on before, knew how it felt." Jansen looked away from the window, turned to stare at Eden. "Which is why I'd never step out on a woman again, wife or otherwise. I know how it feels. And it doesn't feel good."

Seeing this caring, sensitive side of Jansen made Eden uncomfortable. She tried to diffuse the building intensity with humor. "Well, don't worry about me being the wifey you step out on," she said, forcing a laugh. "Been there, done that. Single is good."

"Single is safe. I don't know how good it is." Jansen walked over and knelt by Eden's chair. "Look, if you just want to hang out, not take the relationship to an intimate level, I'll respect that. But I've enjoyed getting to know you again, spending time together. I think what we've discovered is worth exploring . . . don't you?"

"I don't know what you think we've discovered, but I think you're at least worth a date."

"Ah, okay, it's like that, huh?" He stood, pulled Eden up with him, and wrapped her in his arms.

"Yes, it's like that." Eden basked in his musky manliness for mere seconds before pulling away. She didn't want him to feel how rapidly her heart was beating.

A semblance of their casual camaraderie returned after that. Eden joined Jansen on the couch, where they finished off Eden's bowl of grapes before giving in to something a little more decadent—chocolate peanut-butter ice cream . . . shared from the same bowl. Jansen watched as Eden slipped a spoonful of cream into her mouth and pulled it out empty. He imagined her tongue savoring the chocolate—knew that that would be him later on. Eden watched in fascination as Jansen licked an errant drop of chocolate from his finger, watched his thick, firm tongue against smooth caramel skin before returning to its hiding place behind soft, cushiony lips. Suddenly Eden wanted to lick something besides ice cream. She wanted to lick what they hadn't discussed earlier, what she'd seen of Jansen's that had sent her scurrying away from him faster than a roach from a can of Raid.

"Be ready at seven tomorrow night," Jansen commanded into the silence. "Dress to impress."

"Why? Where are we going?"

"That's for me to know and you to find out." The familiar cocky smile, with a hint of added devilishness, returned to his face.

16

Had she slept at all? Eden wondered because half the night she'd tossed and turned, her body refusing to sleep on command. She tried to tell herself it was the ice cream she'd eaten, but that lie didn't sound good even to her own ears. She was excited. About Jansen, and their first official date.

Eden stretched, rolled over, and looked at the clock: eight-fifteen. *I probably got three hours' sleep in the last eight.* She remembered looking at the clock at midnight, and then again at two, three-thirty, five-fifteen and seven. Had Jansen's night been as fitful as hers? She doubted it. She hoped so.

After quick ablutions in the bathroom, Eden pulled on a pair of navy yoga pants and a powder-blue T-shirt. She wanted to get out of the house before Jansen awoke or, if he was already up, escape while he was out on his morning jog. She pulled her hair back into a ponytail, slipped into a pair of lightweight tennis shoes, did a last check for earrings, watch, and keys. *Check.*

Eden grabbed her phone from its charger, her purse from the dresser, and was out the door.

Jansen couldn't stop smiling, and he had enough energy to run all day. *Admit it, dog, you're excited.* More excited than he thought he could ever be over a female. And Eden Anderson, of all people. *When did it happen?* he wondered. When did he go from loving her like a sister to being in love with her?

Jansen stopped in his tracks, a scowl on his face. *Wait, I'm not in love with Eden. Am I?* He started running again, turned the corner, and purposely chose to run up a hill. He instantly felt the pull of the incline in his calves, relished the feel of muscles clutching and releasing as his feet pounded pavement. He worked his arms, using them to propel him forward. His fists clenched as he neared the top of the hill, his body straining under the taxing climb. He reached the top of the hill, but instead of leaning over and panting the way a mere mortal would, Jansen pranced on the balls of his toes, like a boxer, working the kinks from his neck, with a few jabs at an imaginary opponent thrown in for good measure. Only then did he stop, put his hands on his waist and twist this way and that. He did a couple lunges and massaged the muscles in his thighs and calves. He looked at his watch, surprised. Had he really run for an hour straight? Jansen pondered his options and then decided to take a shortcut that would put him back at the house in thirty minutes. He did one last stretch and began to run.

Just three more blocks to go. Jansen increased his

speed, ready to get home, take a shower, and eat. He'd promised Reggie he'd coach the boys again and wanted to get there early in order to hang out with them a bit before practice. He'd already practically decided he'd coach one of the summer leagues full time next year. Truth be told, he'd missed his time spent with young, impressionable males, missed the feelings that came from steering one away from negative choices and toward the good ones. After practice, he'd make a couple more stops before returning to the house and getting ready for the evening. *With Eden*. And, again, came the smile. . . .

The scream was weak but audible. Jansen stopped, all senses put on red alert. He quickly scanned the area, straining to hear anything, see anyone. It was a relatively quiet Sunday morning. He'd seen a couple neighbors walking their dogs, had waved to Mr. Johnson, who'd sat on his porch, doing his weekly ritual of enjoying the Sunday *Times* and several cups of coffee. A jogging couple had passed him several blocks back, and a few teens here and there were going about their business. Activity, to be sure, but scarce in the span of two hours.

Jansen slowly retraced his steps, not making a sound. He casually felt the small of his back, and the small Smith & Wesson hidden there. That was when he heard it again, an attempted yell cut off in midshriek coming from the second floor of the house in front of him.

Jansen wasted no time. He ran to the door and banged furiously. He had no time to think or try to surprise the assailant. Somebody's life was at stake. He had to interrupt whatever was in progress. "Police! Open up!" He banged again. "Police!" Jansen scanned the door quickly. *Solid wood. Dead bolt.* He had no doubt he could kick in the door, but it might take a while.

A yell, louder this time. Whoever was being assaulted had at least temporarily escaped her attacker. "Get him!" the woman yelled from inside. "He's running out my back door!"

Midway through the sentence, Jansen heard the bang as the rear screen door slammed back into place. He rounded the corner in time to see a blur of blue jeans and a black, hooded shirt of some kind round the bushes and sprint down the alley. Rather than give chase, Jansen reached for his cell phone as he hurried inside the house. "Ma'am? It's the police. Are you okay?"

"Here," came the ragged reply. "I'm up here."

Jansen quickly provided a description to the 911 operator and then took the stairsteps two at a time. He walked into a bedroom, and his heart stopped. On the floor was a woman Jansen guessed was around seventy years old. Her dress was torn, and her hair was askew. She was balled up, almost in a fetal position, rocking herself. "Thank you, Jesus," she kept saying over and over. "Thank you, Jesus, for sparing my life."

Jansen rarely got emotional on the job, but he felt his eyes grow misty as he helped the small-boned woman to her feet. Jansen guessed she was around five-foot-one or -two and a hundred pounds soaking wet. The woman reminded him of his favorite great aunt. It was probably a good thing he hadn't caught the perpetrator—he may have pummeled him senseless.

"It's going to be all right," he whispered to the woman. He led her over to the bed and sat her down.

She was still murmuring her thanks to God and clinging to Jansen as if he were a lifeline.

"The Lord sent you," the woman whispered, her watery brown eyes staring at Jansen in wonder. "I prayed for God to save me, and here you come. An angel. . . ."

"I'm just an officer doing his job," Jansen replied, touched by her kindness.

"You don't look like no police I've ever seen. You're one of those tall, strapping types, and a handsome one, too . . . though my eyesight ain't what it once was."

Jansen laughed even as he remained in police mode. "Do you think you could identify the man who attacked you, say, in a lineup?"

"Wouldn't have to do no lineup, I know'd who it was." Jansen waited. "It was Odette's grandson, a friend of mine's daughter's boy. I used to have him over to do odd jobs, cut the grass and thangs. Then, as he got older, he started hanging with those gangbangers, smoking that crack, and getting all funny acting. The last time he borrowed fifty dollars and didn't pay it back was the last time I invited him into my house. Until today. He begged me to let him in, said Odette had sent me something. Something told me not to open that door, or at the very least to call and confirm she'd sent him. But I didn't listen.

"You saved me," she said again, her eyes watery as she caressed Jansen's cheek with an aged hand. "You're an angel, and you saved me."

* * *

Eden felt great. She'd been primping and getting pampered all day long. After an hourlong workout of yoga and pilates, she'd splurged on a massage and body wrap at Burke Williams. Then she'd gone for a mani-pedi and finally to the hair salon. By the time she arrived back at the house, she fairly floated toward the front door, carrying a dress she hoped would drive Jansen wild. She knew how disciplined he could be, how he liked to be in control. Tonight Eden wanted to lead the dance, from the time he saw her in her silk, to the time he took it off her. That's right, the end of the evening had already been decided. By Eden. She and Jansen McKnight were going to make love.

She opened the door and immediately felt that something was wrong. This feeling was confirmed as she rounded the corner and saw Jansen sprawled on the couch, some cop show blasting. *Oh, no.* She ignored his mood and placed a smile on your face. "Can you hear it?" she yelled with a smile.

Jansen reached for the remote and clicked off the TV.

"I didn't mean for you to turn it off, but it was pretty loud."

"That's okay." With barely a glance in her direction, Jansen lay back and closed his eyes. "I don't need to be watching that shit anyway. I live it every day."

"Even on your off days?" Eden eased a little flirt into her voice.

"*Especially* on my off days," was Jansen's gruff reply.

"Well, that's all the more reason to get up and shake a tail feather. You've only got an hour until our date."

"Look, Eden," Jansen said, settling deeper into the couch. "We probably should hook up some other time. I don't feel like going anywhere."

"Hook up"? Is that how he defines our evening— a hookup? Eden felt immediately defensive, but she didn't let it show. "Fine," was all she said before she calmly climbed the stairs.

17

Exactly thirty minutes later, Eden walked back down. Her scent preceded her, tickled Jansen's nose before she'd taken the second step from the top. A sensual aroma of vanilla and something . . . floral maybe? Jasmine? Gardenia? Jansen couldn't tell. He just knew he'd walk on hot coals if it meant being able to smell this flower in Eden's garden. The scent immediately made you want to wrap your arms around the person wearing it. Jansen sat up.

But was glad he was sitting down. A vision of sheer loveliness hit the middle landing before proceeding down the remaining seven steps. *Stunning* was the word that came to mind as Jansen watched Eden walk, or, rather, glide, down the stairs. The simplicity of the dress was its best feature, a breezy pale yellow number for which Jansen felt Eden needed to wear a flashing neon sign—DANGEROUS CURVES AHEAD. The vee-neck dipped down to show enough cleavage to tantalize, but not enough to embarrass. Jansen's mouth watered. Shapely calves were accented by strappy jeweled sandals, their sparkle teasing him, taunting him, begging him to massage the feet they encased. Jansen wanted to do that and more. Now.

"Where are you going?" Jansen asked as Eden reached the door without looking in his direction.

"Out," she replied, opening the door.

Looking like that, there's no way in hell she's going anywhere without me. Jansen was off the couch and by the door in a flash. He firmly grabbed her wrist. "I'm going with you."

Eden looked down at her wrist and then up into Jansen's eyes. The look on her face conveyed that she was not impressed or amused. "You will kindly remove your hand from my wrist."

Jansen's smile was easy, his mood unfazed by Eden's brashness. "Yes, I will. There are several other places I can see to place it."

Eden jerked her arm away and walked out the door.

"Give me thirty minutes!" Jansen yelled after her. "I made reservations."

"When?" Eden asked, turning around.

"Earlier, when I was in a better mood."

"Where?"

"Don't worry about that." Eden frowned her skepticism. "Someplace nice."

Eden looked at her watch. "I'll give you fifteen minutes. And then I'm leaving."

"When you leave, it will be in my car, and it will be at seven PM, the way we planned it. Now move your car from behind mine so we can roll on *time*." Jansen paused, eyed Eden with a smoldering look. "Then get back in here before somebody swoops up your fine ass." Without waiting for an answer, Jansen walked inside and bounded up the steps.

Most fibers of Eden's being wanted to leave Jansen hanging just because she could. *Who does he think he is, ordering me around? Like I have to wait for his moody behind. I don't!* But that was most of the fibers of her being. Those other pesky threads, like the ones that formed her heart and lower parts, wanted nothing more than to have that fine hunk of manliness by her side. Eden moved her car, then went back into the house. She forced herself not to smile. There was no way she'd get giddy over going out with someone she'd known for three decades. Still, she had no doubt that even with her four-inch heels, sparkly tennis bracelet, and diamond studs, Jansen would undoubtedly be her most valuable, and hottest, accessory of the night.

At precisely seven PM, Jansen opened the passenger door and helped Eden inside his black Navigator. Eden wasn't surprised to find it spotless. He kept his temporary quarters the same way. She watched Jansen stride around to his side of the car. He looked amazing in black, light wool slacks, a stark white shirt, and polished black loafers. His jewelry was simple: silver watch, silver cross chain, and a two-karat diamond stud in his left ear. Truth be told (though Eden would never tell Jansen this truth), he could have thrown on a T-shirt and khakis and looked just as good.

"Thanks for waiting," Jansen began as he eased the car out the driveway.

"You're welcome."

Silence ensued as Jansen headed north on La Brea.

These two who'd known each other since back in the day had spent countless moments together, shared dozens, if not hundreds, of conversations. But this felt different. This . . . was a date. A current of attraction fairly sizzled between them; the air was dense with anticipation. Jansen turned on the iPod that was connected to the car stereo. Tupac's signature smoothness oozed through the speakers, telling everybody it was him against the world.

Jansen glanced at Eden. "You like Tupac?"

Eden shrugged. "He's all right, I guess. I'm not much into hip-hop."

"What do you like?"

"Mellow music: jazz, new age." Eden cast a side glance at Jansen to gauge his reaction. When she didn't see any, she went on. "I like some of the neo-soul sound. Love some of the sounds coming out of England."

"Your musical tastes have definitely changed. You used to like rap."

"Um, not really."

"Yes, you did." They reached a stoplight. Jansen breezed through his playlist, pressed a button, and soon a flow of rhymes about summertime filled the air.

"Ha! DJ Jazzy Jeff and the Fresh Prince!" Eden said, laughing, immediately beginning to move from side to side and bob her head. "But this was a different kind of rap—positive, made you feel good."

"Looks like it's making you feel good now!"

Thanks to the DJ and Fresh, the uncomfortable atmosphere between Jansen and Eden dissipated. By the time they arrived at the seaside Italian restaurant, they were once again laughing and chatting like the old friends they were. Between their delicious antipasti and main course, they shared the day's events.

"She was shaking like a leaf when I reached her," Jansen finished. "Just a few minutes longer and . . ."

Eden put a hand on Jansen's forearm. "You arrived just in time," she said softly. "And thank God you did." They were silent a moment. Jansen toyed with the few remaining bites of his homemade ravioli with a lobster ragout, while half of Eden's cannelloni remained untouched. "Is that what had you in such a mood when I came home?"

Jansen nodded. "That and the fact that one of the boys I coach didn't show up."

"Coach?"

"Yeah, I'm doing a little basketball coaching for a city league, substituting for a friend whose mother-in-law is seriously ill."

"That's a nice way to give back to the community."

"It's not just that. But for the grace of God, and my uncle, I could have been one of these kids." He told Eden about his former neighbor Nicki's son, Cameron, and how mentoring the boy had been a positive experience for both of them. "The league is one of the few safe hangouts these kids have, and the coaches are sometimes the only positive role models. One of the boys—"

Jansen was interrupted by the waiter who came with dessert options. Eden was glad for the interruption. Her intense study of the dessert menu was actually a chance to tamp down the emotions that Jansen's heartfelt observations elicited. This tender, sensitive side was the one she most loved but rarely saw. However, she was starting to put two and two together. She felt that his sometimes brash exterior was simply the armor that protected a very big heart.

"You were saying?" Eden prompted after the two decided to split a dish of tiramisu.

"Never mind that. I want to talk about us."

"There's no *us,* Jansen."

"Not yet."

His voice was effortlessly sexy, and the fierce attraction that always lingered just under Eden's skin rose to the surface. But she hid it behind teasing. "Is this the part of the evening where seduction begins?"

"You've got a lot to learn, baby girl." Jansen reached out for Eden's hand that toyed with her water glass. He rubbed her pulse point with his thumb, noticed the fast pitter-patter. "I've been seducing you all evening."

"Oh, really?" Eden used the pretense of picking up her water glass to disengage herself from Jansen's touch.

"I don't want to play games anymore, Eden. Do you want to be together or what?"

"What do you mean by 'be together,' exactly?"

Jansen's long stare made Eden nervous. His face was an unreadable mask. A fine, perfectly sculptured, nana-wetting mask. "You know exactly what I mean, Eden," he finally said.

Had the air gone out in the restaurant? Eden suddenly felt hot in all the wrong places. The years slipped away, and once again she felt like the thirteen-year-old bookworm with a crush on the star jock. "No, I don't," she shyly whispered.

At that moment, the waiter delivered a mouthwatering, layered concoction of spongy cake and mascarpone smelling like coffee and looking like heaven.

"Make that to-go," Jansen told the waiter, his eyes still fixed on Eden's face. "And bring me the check."

"Why?" Eden asked.

"You said you didn't know what being together meant. I figure I can show you better than I can tell you."

18

"Where are we going?"

Jansen glanced over at Eden. He continued down Pacific Coast Highway without answering her question. He'd hardly said two words since the valet attendant had brought their car around.

"Jansen?"

"Will you just relax, Eden? I'ma take care of you, all right?"

"That's what I'm afraid of," she mumbled under her breath.

But not far enough under. Jansen pulled the car to the side of the road, put the gear in park, and turned to face her. "Do you want us to call it a night?"

Yes! No! I don't know. . . . Eden looked at Jansen, saw the smoldering desire just beneath the determined glare. *Okay, no. Definitely, no.* "I'm scared," she whispered. Even before her true feelings were out, she wanted to snatch back the words.

"Of what, me?"

"No. Of this. . . ."

"Little garden, don't you know that I've got you? I would never do anything to hurt you. I know this nice little stretch on the beach. Quiet. Isolated. I thought it would be a great place to talk and enjoy this beautiful evening. Talking is all we'll do . . . if that's what you want."

A short time later, Jansen turned off onto a side street and pulled into a private parking area.

"Can we park here?" Eden asked, noting the private-property/tow-away signs. Then she realized what she was doing—not letting Jansen handle things. In this moment, she realized just how independent and self-contained she was. Not that these weren't good traits, but with a man like Jansen, she could release the reins a bit. It would take some effort on her part. The last time she'd let someone else take control, it had ended badly.

"Those shoes are hella sexy, baby, but not much use in the sand, I'm afraid." He'd already taken off his loafers and was removing his socks.

"I don't know about going barefoot, Jansen. I can't see what's out there."

"Girl, I remember a time when you didn't mind dirt on your soles. Besides, this area is very clean, which is why I like it. It's a private stretch of beach. I know the owner." Jansen reached back for the dessert from the restaurant, exited the car, and walked around to Eden's side of the car. He reached for her hand as they strolled toward the water. His large hand engulfed her smaller one.

Indeed, Eden felt safe and protected. She realized she could get used to this feeling and, for the first time, forced herself to not run away from the idea. The two remained silent as they continued walking near the shoreline. The brilliant reflection of the night's full moon was magical, and the sound of the waves crashing against the shore was the perfect lovers' soundtrack. Jansen released Eden's hand, put his arm around her shoulder, and pulled her to him. Eden's arm found Jansen's waist. They continued walking, listening to the night's promise.

Jansen turned away from the water at the same time Eden noticed a small stone bench perched several feet from the sand. She imagined that in the daytime it provided one the ability to stare for hours at what she knew was a stunning view, and at night provided the perfect place for lovers to connect. Eden wondered how long Jansen had known about this spot and how many other women he'd brought up here.

His next comment was as if he'd read her mind. "I was just turned on to this place," he said, sitting down and guiding her to sit right next to him. "A couple weeks ago. The owner approached me in a mall, said I looked liked the bodyguard he needed. I told him I wasn't interested, that I had my hands full with police work, but he gave me his card and asked me to meet him here anyway. It was a pretty generous offer, one I might jump on one of these days. In the meantime, he told me to feel free to come here whenever. The first person I thought about bringing here was you." Jansen turned and placed a light, tender kiss on Eden's mouth. He then opened up the box of tiramisu, picked up a forkful, and placed it near Eden's mouth. She took the bite and immediately closed her eyes to enjoy the flavors. They came together like a perfect symphony, the coffee bursting against her taste buds while the creaminess of the brandy-infused mascarpone melted on her tongue.

Jansen waited until Eden opened her eyes and then offered another bite. "Is it good?"

Eden nodded. "It's amazing. Taste it."

"Okay." Before she could react, Jansen's soft, cushiony lips had covered hers, and her mouth, opened in surprise, welcomed his tongue. Immediately, the squiggly feelings he often elicited came on full force. Her kitty throbbed with desire. Eden had never been so turned on in her life . . . especially from a simple kiss.

Except, this one was not so simple. Jansen turned her to face him more fully and deepened his exploration. His tongue dueled with hers even as he lifted his head just enough to lick her lips and kiss the sides of her mouth before delving back inside. The tiramisu forgotten, Eden became Jansen's sweet treat. He came away from her mouth, only to lick a trail to her ear and nibble her earlobe. His free hand scanned the top of her dress before his fingers reached inside and released a full, heavy breast from its confines. He rubbed his thumb over her already hardened nipple, hardening it more. His touch was feathery, bolstered by the feel of the soft ocean breeze against her skin. Eden shuddered under the assault, feeling herself grow wet. She reached up and put her arms around his neck, pulling him in closer. She'd fought the inevitable as long as she could but was now ready to have what she'd wanted for more years than she dared admit. She was ready to ignore her fears, lose the dare, do whatever it took to feel this man inside her. It had been four years since she'd made love—four long, lonely years. And now that her body had been fully awakened, she didn't want to wait a moment longer.

"Jansen, please," Eden panted when Jansen finally pulled away from her mouth.

"Mmmm, you taste so good," he whispered, lifting her off the bench and onto his lap. "You feel so good."

"It's been a long time for me," Eden continued as her breathing returned to normal.

"How long?"

"Since my divorce."

Jansen was surprised but didn't let it show. Yet it made the moment even more special, that after what she'd endured from her jerk of a husband, she would dare take a chance and share herself with him. He looked into her eyes, brushed errant strands of hair away from her face, and reached for the fork. While finishing the dessert, Eden opened up a bit more about her tumultuous marriage. Jansen listened, and his desire to protect Eden from ever being hurt again increased.

"Let's go back to the house. This isn't the right setting for what I have in mind." Jansen reached for Eden's hand, and they walked to the car.

"Jansen," Eden said, once he'd helped her into the car and then slid into the driver's side. "I have to ask. Are you seeing anybody else right now?"

"No. And I won't be as long as you and I are kicking it."

"Is that what we'll be doing—just *kicking* it?"

"What do you want me to call it? Going steady?" When Jansen's offbeat comment failed to lighten

Eden's suddenly somber mood, he continued. "Look, baby. I'm feeling you in a very real way. I want us to explore what's happening. But remember, you're not the only one with relationship scars. I have them, too. Which is why I will always keep it one hundred with you, Eden—no empty lies, no false promises. For now, that's all I can offer. Is that enough?" When his question met with silence, Jansen continued. "Like I said earlier, we'll go at your pace. But from here on out, just know that every time I look at your lips, or that body, I'm going to be thinking about how many ways I can make love to it, and for how long."

Conversation ceased after that. Jansen turned on the stereo and let Maxwell help glide them home on pretty wings. He'd said all he could say. It would be on Eden to make the next move. That move came a block later when she placed a light hand upon his thigh. Jansen's dick twitched its excitement and began to harden. He pressed on the gas.

"So, what's the first one?" Eden asked softly.

Jansen placed his hand over the one that rested on his thigh. "The first what?" he asked, barely able to think of anything but Eden, naked and wet beneath him.

"The first way you'll do it . . . make love."

Jansen smiled. He lifted Eden's hand to his lips and first kissed, then licked her palm. "The first way," he began softly, "will be to spread your legs wide so I can take my time and acquaint myself with your lovely petal. Then we're going to flow into whatever position allows me to bury myself the deepest into that flower."

Eden shuddered and shifted positions to try to calm the fire that raged between her legs. Jansen must have been burning, too, she thought, because he exited the freeway at La Brea and sped through the neighborhood into Baldwin Hills like a man on a mission. He whipped into the driveway, turned off the car, and drew her into a mind-altering kiss. "Mmmm, let's go inside. Let me get inside your paradise." He unbuckled her seatbelt and was reaching for the door when he looked up at the house. He frowned. "Did you leave your light on?"

"I don't remember," Eden responded, not knowing or caring whether every light in metropolitan Los Angeles was on at this moment. It was taking all her restraint not to rip his clothes off in this driveway. She would screw this brothah's brains out in broad-open daylight!

Jansen shook away the uneasy feeling and reached for the door again. Just then the porch light came on and the front door opened. Both he and Eden looked up, shocked at what they saw. Her verbal reaction was a question; his, a resigned statement.

"Michael?"

"Michael."

Eden's brother, Big Mike, had come home.

19

Michael Anderson came bounding off the steps and down the walkway. A huge smile was spread across his face as he reached the passenger side of Jansen's SUV. "Little sis!"

Eden had recovered from the initial shock of Michael being home (the same shock that had instantly cooled her ardor) and warmly returned his smile. Even with his reprehensible timing, she was still glad to see the older brother she adored. She stepped out of the opened door and onto the sidewalk into Michael's big bear hug. "Mikey!"

Michael lifted Eden off the ground and twirled her around. "Hey, weed," he said, putting her back down. It was only then that he noticed how dressed up she was. He looked over at Jansen, who remained standing on the other side of the car. What Michael didn't know was that something else was standing at attention, and Jansen couldn't move until this something was at ease.

Michael's look was speculative and slightly confused as he gave a hand to his best friend. "J-Dog."

"Big Mike," Jansen responded rather woodenly. This was his best friend in all the world, but right now Michael Anderson was the last person Jansen wanted to see. He finally came around the car and grasped Michael's hand as they did the standard brother-to-brother bump-shoulder hug. Jansen crossed his arms, his stance intimidating, even though, at five feet eleven, Michael was a bulky two-fifty. "This is a surprise."

Michael slowly looked from Jansen to his sister. "I see," he said slowly, eyeing Eden from her French-manicured toenails to her bone-straight hair. When he looked back at Jansen, he wasn't smiling. "What's going on, man?"

Eden could feel the tension and didn't want anything to get out of hand. She knew these two men were closer than brothers, and they acted like it. She'd also witnessed plenty of arguments between them— a couple that had turned physical. She did not want now to be one of those times. "What's going on, big brother," Eden said lightly, linking her arm in his and turning him toward the door, "are two friends calling a truce after getting on each other's nerves all week. We just came back from dinner."

"Damn, where'd y'all eat? The White House?"

Eden laughed, but she was the only one. Michael again looked at Jansen, who did not return his stare. The three entered the house and walked into the living room. Michael and Eden sat on the couch, while Jansen occupied the oversize chair on the other side of the room. "Is that right, Jansen?" Michael asked him after they'd sat. "Y'all just having a little casual dinner that doesn't look so casual?"

Jansen gave Eden another of his trademark unreadable expressions before looking at Michael. "If she says that's what it was . . . that's what it was."

Eden wanted to walk over and slap Jansen upside the head. *Geez, men and their egos! Why couldn't he just follow the script?* "What's going on?" Eden sang jokingly. She playfully punched her brother. "Can we stop with the interrogation, Michael? You're acting like I'm twelve years old!" She scooted over and twirled one of his locs in her hand. "Wow, your hair has grown a lot in the past six months! I bet they loved you over in London."

Michael saw how much Eden wanted to change the subject and went along with it. There would be time enough to make sure Jansen hadn't crossed the line with his baby sis. "I did all right," he answered with a crooked smile. He looked over at Jansen. "How were things over here, dog? Any information on who might be robbing folks in the neighborhood?"

The atmosphere calmed, and the three slipped back into their familiar friendly flow as Jansen recounted the event with the elderly neighbor who lived on the block behind Michael.

"You talking about Sassy? Miss Mayleen Smith?"

Jansen smiled. "She told me everybody called her that. I thought she was teasing."

"Naw, that's what we all call her. Damn, man, I'm glad you jogged down her block. She's the nicest woman you'd ever want to meet—never meets a stranger and would give you the shirt off her back."

"Yeah, being nice almost got her raped, or worse."

"I think I know the punk you're talking about," Michael said after a pause. "Short, bulky, dark-skinned dude, bald?"

"Not too bulky, and he was wearing a hooded shirt, but it could be who you're thinking about."

"I think they call him Pookie or Sookie or something. Him and some of his boys hang out by the 7-Eleven down the street."

"His name is Terrell, Terrell Ford. He's the grandson of one of Sassy's best friends." Jansen almost broke protocol and shared what he'd learned when he'd called the name in to the station—that Terrell had spent time in jail for attempted robbery and had been arrested on suspicion of sexual assault. The charges had been dropped after the woman refused to testify. "He probably won't come back around for a while, and I told Miss Smith I'd check back in on her, but now that you're home, try to keep an eye out also, if you can."

"For sure, man." All three were quiet a moment, absorbed with thoughts of surviving in an imperfect world. Michael got up and walked into the kitchen. "You want a beer?" he yelled.

"No, man, I'm good."

"What about you, sis? You want one of these froo-froo drinks you have in here? What is this . . . colored water?"

"It's healthy water, with vitamins and other stuff. And, yes, I'll take one."

"So," Michael continued when he came back into the living room, "this punk is the one responsible for the break-ins?"

Jansen shrugged. "Could be, but more than likely there are others." Jansen thought back to the arrest they'd made the week prior off of La Brea. "It's probably a burglary ring of eight, ten people. Or even more. You never know."

"Gang related?"

"Maybe."

Eden took off her shoes and curled her legs beneath her. "All right already! Enough about crimes, gangs, and negative stuff. I want to hear about your trip, Michael. And this new group you're managing."

As Michael talked and Eden became absorbed in his tales of celebrity, Jansen became absorbed in her . . . remembering the silky feel of her dress and her even softer skin. His eyes traveled from her exposed knees and calves to the dark, thick nipple he now knew resided behind a lacy black bra. These thoughts had been diverted for a minute, but they slammed back into his consciousness with the force of a tsunami. He wanted Eden Anderson more than he'd ever wanted anyone in his life. Nothing was going to tamp down his desire. Not even distance. But right now distance was what he needed to have, or else he'd swoop up Eden like a caveman, throw her over his shoulder, place her soft cheeks into his car, and whisk her to his house so they could finish what they started. He stood abruptly and strode toward the stairs.

"Whoa, where are you going, dog? I'm just now getting to the good part—the night I hung out with Corinne Bailey Rae."

"While some are living the high life, brothah, others have to prepare for a regular *J-O-B.*" Jansen mounted the stairs. In less than fifteen minutes, he came back down with two garment bags and a medium-sized suitcase.

"Hey, man. You don't have to leave tonight. I can sleep in the weight room," Michael said, rising.

"You know there's nothing like your own bed," Jansen answered. "I may have left a few things, but I'll stop back through tomorrow." He looked over at Eden. "Later, weed." Michael followed Jansen out the door.

Eden's heart sank with each step Jansen took away from her. Their conversation grew faint, and Eden wondered if Michael was once again questioning what had happened that evening. Then she heard Jansen's rumbling laughter and knew that all was well. At least for now. But Eden also knew that nothing would totally be well in her world again until the "weed" Jansen had referred to upon leaving had her petal licked with passion and her flower deeply plucked.

20

Every minute, every hour. I'm going to inhale the scent of your flower.

Fill your heart with my love power in the garden of love.

Eden turned this way and that, convinced she was dreaming. Who'd Jansen given these lyrics to, and when did they have time to record a song? But then her eyes snapped open, and the pounding bass over which the smooth-sounding singer sang still beat its incessant tune. But for the fact that she knew better, she'd swear the drummer had set up shop in the living room downstairs. And then it all came rushing back to her. Michael was home. And so was his bad habit of playing music at the highest volume possible. She looked at her clock. It was barely nine AM. *Some things never change,* she thought as she got out of bed. When they were kids, their mother had had to constantly hound him to turn the sound down, often threatening him to within an inch of his life before her order was obeyed.

Eden didn't have the "mama fear factor," but she was going to give her search for silence the old college try.

"Turn that down!" she yelled as she stomped down the stairs and over to the stereo. "Dang, Michael. Do you know what time it is?"

"Yeah, baby, it's time to come up! This is my band, Eden. They're the hottest thing happening in London right now. Listen!" He walked over to the stereo and turned up the music to almost as high as it was before. He then danced around the room as he sang along with the chorus: *"Fill your heart with my love power in the garden of love."* A rapper's staccato delivery then cut in about how he was going to take the girl and show her the world, and then more about Bentleys and Hypnotic and other expansive promises delivered at a pace too fast for Eden's listening ear to absorb. "This is the stuff right here," Michael exclaimed, bobbing his head to the beat. "You can't get with this? Girl, this is the next number one!"

"It's all right," Eden conceded. She walked back over to the stereo. "It sounds even better at this decibel level." Once she'd turned down the volume, she swayed to the beat in exaggerated fashion. "Ooooh, I really like it now," she said. She danced over to and up the steps.

After showering and brushing her teeth, Eden returned downstairs. She walked into the kitchen, looked over at the breakfast booth, and was immediately reminded of the cozy moments with Jansen sharing laughter and ice cream. She'd started to call him last night, only to realize that in all the time they'd spent together, they'd never exchanged cell-phone numbers. She fixed a bowl of fresh fruit and wondered if he thought of her as much as she thought of him, if he ached for his touch the way she did for his. And what was up with the song that had awakened her, the song recorded by her brother's band? The lyrics were so much like Jansen's words of the previous night it was scary.

"Who wrote that song?" Eden asked as she entered the living room.

"Kory, the lead singer," Michael replied. "The brothah's from London, that's how we initially hooked up with the contact over there. And he's the real deal. After he sang it for me, I told him about you, how we used to call you "little garden" and "weed," and what-not. He's a pretty cool dude, wants to meet you. Although you might be a little old for him. You're pushing what, forty?"

"Whatever, fool! Only if you're forty-three! And I look twenty-three. You'd better recognize."

"You look all right."

"What's the name of the band?"

"Reign—like the dynasty, not water."

The two continued to listen as the song played. "He sounds like Usher," Eden said.

"Please, Usher wishes he could throw down like Kory. You just heard one song! This dude is bad. He can sound like Prince one minute and Barry White the next. His range is phenomenal."

So is Jansen's tongue. Eden went down memory lane so quick she didn't even realize it had happened until Michael repeated her name.

"Eden."

"I'm sorry . . . what?"

"I was saying did you . . . Never mind that. What's up with you and Jansen?"

Eden's fork stopped in midair before she answered nonchalantly, "Nothing."

"Didn't look like nothing last night. I don't have to remind you about J-Dog, right?"

"Gosh, Michael. He's your best friend. If he's a dog, what does that say about the company you keep?"

Michael eyed Eden with brotherly concern. "Being a best friend is one thing; being a boyfriend is another. Jansen's a good man, Eden, has had my back every day of my life. But he's also got a history and a track record. I've seen him in action and . . . I don't want to see you get hurt."

"A man can change, Michael," Eden said testily.

"Wait—y'all fuckin?" Michael's question came out more like an accusation.

"Not only was that crass and uncalled for, Michael," Eden replied with forced calm, "but it's none of your business."

"Well, I guess that's my answer. And just so you know, anything that affects you is my business."

Eden's heart swelled with love for her brother. He'd been her protector from the time she was born. "No, big brother," she said, her voice filled with kindness, "it's not. I know I'll always be your little sister, but I'm way past grown. I'm a thirty-four-year-old divorcee who's navigated places in relationships I hope you never experience."

Michael got up and turned off the music. "I know, sis. Which is why I don't want you hurt again. You never would open up about Gregg's punk ass—"

"Because I never want to have our conversations reduced to only between visiting hours with a sheet of bulletproof glass between us."

"Oh, he's still got an ass whooping coming if I ever see him, trust me on that."

"Gregg will get what he has coming to him, Michael, one way or the other. I've forgiven him and moved on. I want you to do the same. Anger and unforgiveness are unproductive emotions, Mikey. They take years off your life."

"Yeah, well, kicking that nuckah's ass will add back a few."

Eden laughed, and soon Michael joined her. They spent the next two hours catching up on each other's lives and then another half hour on a call to their mother. After they'd shared a lunch of grilled-cheese sandwiches and fresh tomato soup, one of their childhood favorites, Eden prepared for her yoga class and to run errands afterward. She'd enjoyed the morning with her brother. And had almost forgotten how much she missed Jansen.

"Here you go," Michael said as Eden headed to the door. He gave her a copy of his band's CD, *Silent Reign*.

"How's a band going to call a CD silent?"

"Not the band, fool—everybody who's listening. Our reign is so tough it will have the listeners unable to do anything but groove to the beat—spellbound and speechless."

Eden didn't know about all that, but she knew she liked at least one of the CD's tracks. "I'm proud of you, Mikey," she said with a hug.

As she made her way to Santa Monica and the

serenity of the yoga studio, Eden put the fifth track, "Garden of Love," on repeat and listened to it the whole way there. In her mind, Kory's fateful lyrics mixed with Jansen's heat-producing promises from the night before: *... acquaint myself with your lovely petal ... bury myself the deepest into that flower.* Last night, Eden's feelings about whether or not she wanted to be with Jansen had been mixed. Today her mind was clear. She wanted to be Jansen's flower garden, and she was ready for him to help her bloom.

21

"Oh, my goddess, this is *amazing!*" Ariel took another bite of her guacamole and cheese burrito—which was actually a raw, vegan concoction made with nut cheese, salsa, and vegetables rolled up in a collard green. She'd been singing the praises of her new, 80 percent raw diet ever since starting it the previous week. It was early evening, and she and Eden had met back up after both ran errands. They were eating at Ariel's new favorite Santa Monica restaurant, Planet RAW. "How is your burger?"

"Well . . . I think it would work better for me if they didn't call it a burger," Eden honestly answered. At that moment she thought of Jansen and how he'd react to trying something so different. She'd been doing way too much imagining of Jansen trying things—especially those positions he'd described. She forced those thoughts away and refocused on the food in front of her. "Seeing the words *bacon western double* sets up a certain expectation, even for someone who's only eaten veggie burgers for the past four years. But for a dish made solely with nuts, grains, and vegetables, it is a respectable nod to its namesake." Eden took another bite of the burger, topped with macadamia-nut cheese, heirloom ketchup, and fig mustard. "You know, Ariel, the more I eat it, the more I like it. It's different, but good."

"That's exactly what happened to me. When Travis— oops!" Ariel's face turned red, even as her green eyes sparkled.

"Oh, no—too late! Who's this man that has you as red as a beet?"

"He's just . . . the guy who told me about this place," Ariel said, trying without success to regain her composure.

"Uh-huh," Eden answered. She crossed her arms while leaning back in her chair.

"Okay, he's just the most gorgeous, most amazing man I've ever met in my life," Ariel gushed. "But I wasn't going to mention him to anyone. It's all so new and magical—I don't want to jinx it."

"Then my lips are sealed."

"Thanks, Eden."

"So if you weren't going to mention the guy we won't mention to me, then what is the good news you said you'd share later?"

Ariel clapped her hands together. "I got a job!"

"That's great, Ariel!" Looking for employment was another thing in common Eden and Ariel had shared when they met. "From the look on your face, it's obviously one you wanted."

"Absolutely. I'm going to be working at a new healing center in Venice—the Zen Den—with an absolutely fabulous shaman."

"Shaman?" For the most part, Eden embraced the new-age lifestyle, but some things were still a bit much for this ex-government worker.

"Yes! He's a fifth-generation healer, and he's so amazing. His name is Om. He combines his natural gift of spirit communication with energy healing. He's a master, and I get to be his assistant!" Ariel drained her bottle of Kombucha, a fermented drink for which Eden hadn't developed a taste. Ariel drank it like an ambrosia. "And the Zen Den?" she continued. "Oh, my *goddess*, Eden. It's filled with gorgeous green plants and serenity fountains. There's a meditation garden behind the facility, along with a labyrinth and a sweat lodge."

Sweat lodge? "Okay, girl, you've lost me now."

Ariel placed a hand on Eden's arm. "Trust me, Eden. It's exactly where you need to be."

"Me?"

"Yes! That's part of the good news I want to share with you. I think they have a position with your name written all over it."

Eden raised her brows but remained quiet. So far she couldn't see herself anywhere near the Zen Den.

"I don't officially start until next week, but I've gone every day since being hired and, Eden, there is something special about that place. When I learned that they are looking for a managing director to run the facility, I immediately thought of you."

"I don't know, Ariel."

"Why? With your organizational skills and attention to detail, you'd be perfect!"

"Yes, administrative management is a strong suit of mine, but, quite frankly, it sounds like this may be a little too different from the world I left. I'm thinking more like working in a yoga studio or one of the alternative-medicine facilities here in Santa Monica. I've even thought about a job at Whole Foods."

"Uh, earth to Eden, come in, please! The Zen Den is the epitome of a holistic center and more! We're offering every modality imaginable to balance and heal one's mind, body, and spirit."

There's no denying your passion, little sistah. Nor had Eden missed the possessive "we" with which Ariel aligned herself to the center.

Ariel continued, counting on her fingers. "There's yoga, pilates, acupuncture, reiki, and other forms of energy healing. There's a western-trained medical doctor on staff who's spent the last ten years in China and India practicing alternative medicine, an herbalist who's a master of Chinese medicine, plus several practitioners trained in a variety of spiritual healing. I have a very strong feeling about this, Eden. This is where you're supposed to be." When Eden remained silent, Ariel decided she'd pressed enough for now. "So, Eden . . . how's your roommate?"

Eden looked up to see Ariel's sparkling green eyes boring into hers. The knowing look on her face dared Eden to try to act as though she didn't know to whom Ariel was referring. She resisted the urge to fidget, instead returning Ariel's intense gaze, sans the devilish smirk. "Jansen? He's fine, but he's no longer my roommate. My brother arrived back from Europe last night, and Jansen went back to his place."

"Ah, so that explains the energy I was picking up from you earlier during yoga. I noticed how quiet you were when you came in. I had a feeling you were thinking about your guy, but—"

"Jansen's not my guy—"

Eden was interrupted by the sound of Ariel's tinkling laughter. "You are so funny, Eden! No, please, let's not do this." Ariel sobered for a moment. "Whatever we share stays strictly between us. As an intuitive, I often know more about people's lives than what they're comfortable with. You and Jansen were together in a past life, and you're destined to be together again. The less you both fight it, the more beneficial the partnership will be for both of you." Ariel paused, gauged Eden's reaction, and saw that she definitely had her friend's attention. "If you'd like more detailed information, I can perform a tarot reading for you."

"No, thanks, Ariel," Eden responded, thinking that the only taro she was comfortable hanging out with was the root vegetable used in her casserole dish. "I don't need any cards to tell me what's up. I already know." She took a sip of water and continued. "You're right, I'm attracted to Jansen, and the feeling is mutual. We went on our first official date last night."

"That's exciting!" Ariel exclaimed. And then, in a lower voice, "How was it?"

"What, the food? Oh, it was good."

"Ha! Yeah, I bet. So how was *dessert?*"

"You know what, Ariel Sun, no one should let your

airy demeanor fool them. When it comes to getting information, you're like a pit bull! I should tell you, however, that I'm equally as determined to keep my business to myself." Eden's smile dissipated the sharpness of her words.

"Sure thing, Eden. But I bet that's not what you told Jansen last night!"

"Girl, let me get out of here. I'm moving on Wednesday and still want to hit a few stores before they close."

"Okay, but promise me you'll visit the Zen Den this week. I want you to meet Om, maybe have him do some energy work on you, balance your chi."

"I promise I'll visit the facility. We'll see about . . . anything else once I get there."

Once outside the restaurant, the two women hugged. "Thanks for dinner," Ariel said.

"You're welcome." Eden started toward her car.

"Oh, and Eden?" Eden turned around. "Jansen's thinking about you. He's hungry, and not for anything in his fridge."

Ariel winked and was gone before Eden could reply. Eden pulled out her phone and tapped her brother's picture. She'd rather call someone else, but Michael was the easiest way to get Jansen's number. Eden smiled, thinking that for all her talk of stardust and fairies, there was definitely something to Ariel's psychic gift. Eden's mind had gone to Jansen just before Ariel had called out to her. She'd been wondering what he was doing at the very moment Ariel had said he was thinking about her, had been thinking of one of his last statements before arriving to the surprise of Michael back home. *If dessert is what you want, Jansen McKnight, dessert is what you'll get.* Eden headed to the mall, mentally planning the rest of her evening and how a silk-wrapped caramel-chocolate surprise was going to end up on Jansen's doorstep.

22

Eden had just left the mall and was on her way to Michael's house when her phone rang. "Hey, Michael."

"Hey, sis. So check this out. The man just finished installing my new alarm system."

"I see you didn't waste any time implementing Jansen's suggestion."

"Of course not! When it comes to thieves and protection, Jansen knows his stuff. Anyway, I need to give you the code. I'll show you all the other details tonight, or tomorrow if I get back too late."

"Oh, you're going out?"

"Yeah, going to meet up with a little honey I left simmering before my trip."

"What happened to the chick you were seeing when I came here house hunting six months ago?"

"Bridgett—that's who I'm talking about."

"All right, now! She's passed the six-month mark. When do I meet her?"

"Maybe this week. I'm heading back to London

soon for an extended stay. I'm thinking of taking her with me."

"Wow, sounds serious. You know how Mom's been talking about grandkids. You're almost forty, big brother. It's time for you to settle down."

"You may be right."

Wow, he's for real. There was only one other time Eden could remember Michael talking this serious about someone, which was also the one and only time she could remember him getting his heart broken—when his fiancée had broken their engagement because, as she'd put it, she was "revisiting her sexuality."

Michael gave Eden the security code and prepared to end the call. "All right then, Eden, later."

"No, Michael, wait. I need to get something from you." Eden hesitated, nervous as to how Michael would react to her request. *There's only one way to find out.* "What's Jansen's number?"

"You mean homeboy is hitting it, and you don't even have his number?"

"I never said Jansen was hitting it, Michael. That was your assumption. And, no, I don't have his number because I didn't *need* his number. We were staying in the same house, remember?"

"I would think that if Jansen was that interested in keeping in touch, he would have gotten your number."

"Look, Michael, I have a daddy, and you aren't him. If you don't want to give me the number, don't. But don't give me advice I didn't ask for either, because I don't need it!"

"Fine. I won't." The click in Eden's ear was Michael's good-bye.

Eden gripped the wheel, frustration flowing to her very core. *How dare Michael try to run my life!* "We're not kids anymore!" she hissed aloud. At the end of the day, she knew Michael was just being Michael. He had tried to tell her what to do from the time he rocked her cradle, and most of the time she'd let him. Come to think of it, this was the first time she'd truly gone against his opinion or not taken his advice. But there was a first time for everything, and when it came to Jansen, Eden appreciated her brother's concern but knew she had to follow her heart. She thought of the silky gold nightie she'd found that came with a matching thong. "Oh, brother, why do you have to be the hitch in my giddyup?" Eden sighed as she exited the freeway, wondering if she should stop and get a video, because unless Ariel's tarot cards or intuition could provide her with Jansen's telephone number, it looked like it would definitely be another long night.

An hour later, Eden felt better. She'd come home, poured herself a glass of woodsy pinot noir, and was now enjoying both it and the CD Ariel had suggested she download, while soaking in a tub of bubbly hot water. The near-constant tension she carried in her neck and shoulder area (her mother said this came from Eden trying to carry the weight of the world) eased as Eden sank deeper into the baby-oil-infused water. She reached for her wineglass, repositioned her bath pillow, and closed her eyes. If she couldn't be in Jansen's arms, she'd bask in this paradise of her own making.

Her cell phone rang. *Oh, please, not now.* Eden knew it was her mother calling, and she didn't want to move. But then she remembered that Phyllis had called earlier, when Eden was in a checkout line at the mall. She'd forgotten all about calling her back. Eden thought about switching off the call but then changed her mind. She and her mother talked almost every day. "Make it quick, Mom," Eden said after allowing the call and pushing the speaker button. "I'm enjoying a delicious soak, and you're an interruption."

"Then that's all the more reason to make this break worth your while."

Jansen! Eden almost dropped her wineglass into the tub. As it was, the water sloshed from side to side from her abrupt change in position. "Jansen! Hey! How'd you get my number?"

"After enduring an interrogation that would make the FBI proud, your brother gave it to me."

Eden smiled. "Oh. So what's up?"

"You even have to ask?"

Was it just her, or did her hot water just get hotter?

"Looks like my timing is perfect. After you finish your bath, just wrap yourself in a towel and head straight to my house. That'll save me a step or two."

"Who says that, one, I'd even come over to your house and, two, if I did, that there would be any un- dressing involved?"

Jansen chuckled. Eden grew wet, and the water in the tub was not the reason. "Baby girl," he answered, his voice low and soft, "I could barely do my job today for thinking about finishing what we started. I called Mike last night, but I guess he was asleep. I called him again as soon as I got off work. Nothing was more important to me than getting your number. Of course,

I felt like an ass for not having it in the first place. And
then to have to go through your chaperone . . ."

"Michael means well."

"I know that."

The sound of sloshing water could be heard as Eden
lifted herself out of the tub and reached for the large,
fluffy white towels she'd purchased that would accom-
pany her to her new home.

"Mmmm, baby, I can just imagine how you look
with those rivulets of water running down your body
between those soft titties and that nice and trimmed cat
I'm going to lick tonight."

Eden's legs almost buckled, even as her face broke
out with a smile. "Stop talking nasty."

Jansen stretched his legs in front of him to accom-
modate his growing erection. "Talking isn't the only
nasty that's going to happen tonight."

"Oh, is that a fact?" Eden purred.

"No, baby, that's a promise. Now key my address
into your phone and then get over here before I have to
put out an APB for my stuff."

23

The air felt warm, almost moist against Eden's bare skin. Tendrils of hair swung close to her nose, teasing her with a whiff of the vanilla-and-gardenia-infused perfume she'd sprayed in it after deciding to let it hang loose and free. Eden felt wanton and sexy as she neared Jansen's front door. She wore the barely there gold nighty as a top, paired with wide-legged pants—shear, paisley-print fabric flecked with black and gold. At the last minute, she'd slipped out of her flat leather sandals and into a pair of four-inch shiny black stilettos.

Eden reached her destination and rang the doorbell. Almost instantly the door opened and Jansen pulled her into his arms. Kicking the door closed, he immediately assaulted her mouth, plunging his tongue deep inside, rubbing her back, arms, and butt with his large, strong hands. "Damn, baby. . . ." Jansen broke the kiss but kept his arms securely around Eden's body. She'd wrapped her arms around his waist and now luxuriated in his protective embrace. He smelled so clean and fresh and . . . male. Both of their hearts beat wildly. Jansen squeezed Eden's luscious butt cheeks while she turned her head to place a kiss on his bare chest. It was hard and soft at the same time—hard with muscle and perfectly placed sinew, soft with skin that was warm to the touch. The merest hint of hair lay across his chest, a trail of it continuing down his stomach and into his crotch.

"Little garden, let me look at you." Jansen stepped away from Eden and eyed her from head to toe. Eden grew warm under his perusal but met his stare head-on. There was no place for a shrinking violet anywhere among what she'd envisioned for the evening. Jansen licked his lips, and her nipples hardened. "You're looking even better than the last time I saw you."

"You look good, too," Eden answered as she did her own quick head-to-toe. Jansen's dress was simple: a pair of black, pull-on pajama pants that rode his hips. No shirt, no shoes. The attire gave Eden an unobstructed view of perfection and caused the now familiar squiggle to begin its dance.

"Mmmm," Jansen began, pulling Eden farther into his home. "You make a brothah forget his manners. Are you hungry? Want something to drink?"

"I've already eaten, but maybe something to drink."

A few minutes later, Jansen came back into the living room with a bottle of beer and a glass of wine. "I knew this is what you'd want," he said, handing her the stemmed glass.

"Ah, thanks for thinking of me." She took a small sip.

"I told you that is all I've been doing since last night, when our date was rather rudely interrupted.

After talking with you earlier, I ran out real quick—bought some wine and some . . . healthy junk."

"Ha! And what, pray tell, fits your description of that?"

Jansen reclined against the couch. "Some salad, nuts—I even bought some of those nasty patties you fix."

Eden was touched and impressed. But she hid suddenly vulnerable feelings behind a jokey facade. "Dang, Jansen, I appreciate the gesture, but it's not like I'm moving in."

"Maybe not," Jansen answered, pulling Eden into his arms. "But we're getting ready to work up quite the appetite."

Eden nestled into Jansen's embrace. They shared a companionable silence as they sipped their drinks. "I like your place."

"You haven't even seen it yet."

"Well, what I have seen, I like. It looks like you and doesn't have that bachelor-pad vibe I envisioned. You know the look: black leather, wild-animal prints, and a nude painting or two thrown in for good measure."

"Nah, all that is upstairs," Jansen joked.

Eden looked around and took in the understated elegance of a room designed to be functional yet warm. The tan sofa sectional dominated the space, a dark cherry wood bringing balance with the large square coffee table and dining room table beyond it. A sleek entertainment center dominated one wall, its doors accented with large bronze knobs. The other wall in the room was bare except for a metal carving of Chinese symbols and two complementing abstract paintings.

Eden's perusal was interrupted by a hand reaching into her top and gently squeezing her nipple. "Let's go upstairs," Jansen whispered. She nodded. He stood, reached for hand, and led the way.

The master suite was at the end of a short hallway. Eden could see the glow of candles before they entered the room. Once inside, her eyes immediately went to the king-size platform bed that dominated the space, made up with fabrics in chocolate and gray. The headboard was tall, almost to the ceiling, and seemed to be made out of the same wood as the tables downstairs. Eden was vaguely aware of the pewter candle holders from which the flames danced, but then Jansen turned around, and her eyes were for him alone.

"Come here." Jansen looked massive and majestic, his authoritative voice matching his stance.

Eden complied. When she reached him, Jansen buried his hands in her hair, gently pushed her head back, and rained kisses down on her face and neck. While he claimed her mouth, branding each crevice with his tongue, Jansen reached underneath her top, felt the elastic band around her pants, and eased them downward. He went down with them, easing himself into a kneeling position as he silently commanded her to step out of the material now pooled on the floor. He pulled her close to him, buried his head in her heat, and inhaled deeply. "Mmmm . . ." His tongue was stiff and forceful as he licked her there through the wispy fabric of the thong. Eden shivered, placing a steadying hand on Jansen's shoulder.

"Spread your legs." Again, Eden complied. At the moment, Jansen could have told her to turn a flip from the top banister to the floor below—and she would have complied. Jansen eased a finger between the flimsy thong material and Eden's hot skin. He looked up and into Eden's eyes as he slowly stroked her rectangular patch of hair. He ran a finger along the folds to her treasure. She looked at him for a moment before her eyes fluttered closed. For this reason, she didn't see when Jansen's tongue replaced his finger, only felt the wet tip as it slid inside her heat and flicked her petal, just like he said he would. The apex of her thighs felt the void as soon as Jansen raised his head and ran his tongue up to her navel. He squeezed her lush booty as he placed feathery kisses across her waist and then reached for the thong's string and pulled. He eased the triangle of fabric down her legs and then stood, picked up Eden, and walked to the bed.

Eden's breath caught as she was whisked up in Jansen's arms. She felt the evidence of his desire while pressed against him, which was only for a moment. Jansen reached the bed and placed her at the center of it. He stepped back and released the drawstring on his pants. Nine inches of throbbing masculinity danced before her, like a fencer's sword or a ballplayer's slugger. His dick was thick and perfectly formed. With her ex-husband, Eden hadn't been too into oral sex, but at this moment her mouth watered with anticipation. She wanted to taste Jansen the way he'd tasted her.

But not yet. Jansen had other plans. He eased onto the bed, reached for Eden's top and pulled it over her head. His eyes drank in the body he'd viewed with new eyes ever since seeing Eden again after so many years. "You're even more beautiful than I imagined." He slid

his body next to Eden's as his lips grazed hers. He
continued his assault, on her neck and shoulders, all
the while flicking and rubbing one nipple and then
the other with his thumb. By the time he covered the
hardened peaks with his mouth, Eden was on fire. Her
body writhed this way and that. Jansen was driving
her crazy, and after four years without intercourse,
she wanted to feel his hard, thick flesh inside her, and
she wanted to feel it now.

"Jansen, now, please . . ."

"Baby, I want to take my time with you. You taste so
good. . . ."

"Please . . . I need it. . . ."

Jansen placed his hand between her legs and slid
his middle finger in deep. "You need *it,* or you need
me. I want you to need me, baby . . . only me."

"I need . . ." Eden couldn't think, much less talk,
with Jansen's hand causing such delicious sensations
throughout her body.

Jansen slid down farther, and soon, once again, his
tongue replaced his finger. But this time his strokes
were deep and aggressive, branding her with his hot-
ness, driving her over the abyss with the sweetest
torture.

Just as Eden felt the tremors of an oncoming orgasm,
Jansen stopped, rolled over, and reached toward his
nightstand. "No, don't . . ." she whimpered.

Jansen quickly unrolled the condom and shielded
his sword. "Eden, do you want me? Do you need me?"
He placed his shaft at the tip of her entrance, taunting,
teasing. . . .

"Yes!" Eden gasped.

"Then say it."

Eden reached for his hips, tried to force him inside her.

"Say it," he murmured, grinding his hips and slipping in just a bit more.

"I want you," Eden murmured. "I need you, Jansen. Please, I need you now!"

"And you are going to have me, all of me, for as long as you can stand it."

Jansen inched his way inside her, giving her body time to adjust to his size. And then, for the next hour and a half, their hot, impassioned lovemaking was the only conversation.

24

"Damn, man! What's up with this whistling?" Alberto closed the passenger door of the police cruiser and buckled his seatbelt. "Did you win the lottery or something?"

Jansen went through a quick check of the radio, mirrors, and laptop. "I don't know what you're talking about."

"Jay, if I didn't know better, I'd think you were on the rag. Yesterday you barely said two words and then almost snapped my head off when I made the observation. Now today you're whistling and grinning like . . . Wait a minute. Of course! The feline!"

Jansen shot a quick glance at Alberto. "You're reading too much into my good mood. You need to get out more, son."

"From the way you're acting all chipper after a little *cho cha* . . . you don't need to get out more, you just need to *get* more."

"You might be right," Jansen agreed, refusing to say more about how one night with one woman had turned his world upside-down. In the past, it wouldn't have been unusual for Jansen to kiss and tell, to rehash with Alberto a night of freaking some lovely. But nobody would hear about what he and Eden had shared. The beauty of that was special and for them alone.

Jansen turned off Crenshaw onto Slauson Avenue, headed toward the scene of a recent robbery. This crime had turned ugly because, unfortunately, on this day that the store was closed to the public, the owners had been in their office at the back of the store when the would-be burglars had come in. The man had pulled out a weapon and tried to defend his property and had gotten shot for his troubles. His wife, who'd stepped out of the office to use the restroom, had heard the confrontation and jumped into a large utility closet to hide. From there, she'd viewed the surveillance camera and gotten a stellar view of her attackers. Jansen and Alberto were on their way to interview her.

"You think it's the same dudes trying to rob this spot?" Alberto asked, changing the subject. It was clear that whoever had Jansen as giddy as a schoolgirl would remain his secret. For now. But Alberto was sure he'd learn the details eventually. There was very little about the Gonzalez family to which Jansen was not privy. That's just the way these partners rolled.

Jansen nodded. "Probably."

Alberto flipped through a stack of papers. "I got a report on her old man. He's out of intensive care but still in serious condition. The bullet missed main arteries by inches but is still lodged in his back. They're waiting until his organs get a bit stronger before making the final decision on whether to try to remove it."

"His wife was smart to do what she did," Jansen said. "If she hadn't hid, she would have been shot, too."

"Hell, yeah, they would have got her. No doubt about that. They probably thought they killed her husband. That's—hold on a minute." Alberto reached for his cell phone. "Yeah, *mami*," he answered. "Probably the same time I always get home. Why?" Jansen could hear Delphia's animated voice from where he sat, though he couldn't make out her words. "What is it? Just go ahead and tell me." Alberto frowned. "Why did you even call me then? Damn, girl, you trippin'." He ended the call.

Jansen waited a beat before speaking. "What was that about?"

Alberto sighed. "Delphia's pregnant."

"What? That's what she just told you?"

"No. She wants to tell me tonight in person."

"So how do you know she's pregnant?"

"The same way I knew she was pregnant the first two times. My ass gets morning sickness before she does."

Jansen laughed. "Right! I remember that time we stopped and ate some Louisiana Chicken, and you got sick as a dog! Seven months later, your son was born."

"Yeah, I thought I was going to get to retire after suing the restaurant, and then I found out it was little Alberto making me sick!"

"So number four is on the way, huh? Is this the last one?"

"It could be as far as I'm concerned, but not if Delphia has anything to say about it. That woman loves being pregnant."

"Well . . . congratulations, man."

They neared the jewelry store that had been robbed. As they turned into the parking lot, Jansen thought about how it might be to have a family, and how cute a certain female would look if she were carrying his child.

"Her name is Eden," he said to Alberto as the two exited the vehicle.

Alberto nodded, a big, knowing smile on his face. "I know a *cho cha* whistle when I hear one."

25

"Where do you want this box, ma'am?"

Eden checked the label. "That one goes in the kitchen." Two other moving guys entered her condo. "Guys, all the boxes are marked. Please put them in whatever room is written on the white label."

Two hours later, Eden paid off the last day worker and dropped the four men back at the Home Depot parking lot. Whatever one felt about immigration, Eden was thankful these men had been available to help her move, and they'd expressed their gratitude at her generosity. She believed in honest pay for honest work and had paid each man an extremely fair wage for the five hours they'd spent with her. Not only did she feel her moving mission had been accomplished, but tonight a group of hardworking men had money to feed their families.

While she was driving home, Eden's phone rang. *Shoot.* "Hello? Hey, Mom, hold on, let me grab my hands-free." After unwrapping the wire from around her purse, she was finally able to plug it into her ear.

"Sorry about that, Mom. I just dropped off the workers who helped me move."

"So you're finished?"

"I've just about gotten everything into the house, but that's just the beginning. I'll be unpacking boxes and arranging furniture for weeks."

"Not if I know you. Miss Organized can't stand for things to be out of place. You'll have that house turned into a home in no time."

"Well, that time won't be tonight. I'm exhausted."

"That's what you said when we talked yesterday. What's going on with you, girl?"

Eden smiled. Jansen McKnight was what was going on with her. After leaving his house at three in the morning on Tuesday, she'd gone back for seconds last night, and this time birds were chirping when they'd kissed good-bye. "Just . . . trying to get everything organized," she finally answered. "I've stepped up the employment search, so on top of the move, I'm job hunting."

"Remember that Rome wasn't built in a day, Eden. You left the roller-coaster lifestyle behind in DC, right? Don't get back on it, girl."

"I won't, Mom." Eden's headphone beeped. "Mom, I have to take this call. Talk to you later, okay?" She didn't give Phyllis time to respond before clicking over. "Hey, handsome."

"Uh, if you say so," Phyllis drawled sarcastically. "Personally, I prefer pretty, beautiful, or even cute to handsome."

Dangit! "Oh, sorry, Mom. Bye!" Eden rolled her eyes as she pressed the button again. "Hello? Hello?"

Just great. Missed your call and busted myself to my mother. Eden reached a stoplight, quickly scrolled through missed calls, and dialed Jansen. "Hey."

"Hey." Eden's heart swelled at the sound of Jansen's voice. She wondered when she'd get used to him, stop reacting over a single word he'd spoken. "I want you, baby. I want to squeeze that juicy asset of yours and pick my favorite flower."

Eden's vaginal walls clenched of their own accord. *Guess I won't stop reacting any time soon!* "You're welcome to visit my garden, Jansen. But you'll have to come to Santa Monica."

"You're all moved in?"

"Yep, just finished moving in the last boxes. The place is a mess, but you're welcome to come over."

"Is your bed set up?"

"It's about the only piece of furniture that is."

"Have you eaten?"

"No, I was going to pick something up on my way home."

"Don't worry about that. Just give me your address and clear a pathway to your bedroom. I'm on my way."

26

By the time Jansen buzzed Eden's intercom, she'd showered and changed. When she opened the door, she could tell her faded short-short jean cutoffs and strappy blue-and-white-striped tee, worn braless, had been a good idea. "Welcome to the garden of Eden."

"Girl, that's a corny line." Jansen leaned in to give her a kiss. "You can only get away with that because you look so good." Jansen stopped just inside the door and looked around. "This place is bigger than it looks from outside."

"It's not bad. Not as big as yours or Michael's homes, but it's just right for me." Eden noted the bags Jansen carried. "P.F. Chang's! Good choice."

"I was going to grab some KFC, but they weren't serving any vegetarian chicken."

"Hardy-har-har—now who's spouting the lame jokes? Come on over to the dining area. I cleaned off the table so we could eat here, and washed up a couple plates and silverware." Eden went into the kitchen and returned with the dishware and a roll of paper towels. "Thanks for dinner."

The two continued chatting as they fixed their plates and began eating. Eden talked of the relatively easy moving day, and then Jansen filled her in on his day. "Me and Alberto don't usually sit in on the general meetings," he concluded. "And now I remember why. Man, I don't miss the days when I was trying to make quota, messing with hardheads and being glad when they resisted arrest just so I could get my count."

Eden stopped eating and placed down her forkful of vegetable chow fun. "Excuse me?"

"What?" Jansen was oblivious to anything wrong, as evidenced by how he continued to devour his Mongolian beef, followed by a crunchy bite of pork-filled egg roll. "Oh, no, baby, am I eating with my mouth open? Crunching too loud?"

"Jansen, you don't find anything wrong with what you just said?" When Jansen kept looking at her with a blank stare (and kept eating), Eden continued. "You guys have a quota to meet, arrests you're required to make?"

Oh, hell. "Yes, there are certain numbers to meet, but trust me, Eden. It's not hard to do."

"And if it is, I bet you guys still find a way, huh? How many of those young men have I seen on television, butts on the curb, hands cuffed behind them, who are part of this quota some zealous cop was trying to meet?" Eden's shock was replaced by anger. She tried to calm down by eating again, tried to focus on how garlicky the spinach was that Jansen had brought her. But her appetite had all but disappeared.

"Look, Eden, I was just trying to share a bit about my day. I'm sorry I mentioned anything about it."

Eden took a deep breath and a sip of tea. "And I'm sorry I reacted the way I did. If we're going to be to-gether, I need to make peace with what you do, no matter how I personally feel about the profession."

Jansen nodded. "I'm not going to lie about the rogue cops that give us men in blue a bad name. But we're not all like that, Eden. As quiet as it's kept, most of us are not that way. But doing good deeds rarely makes the news. There was no video rolling the day I saved Sassy from being raped, or when I act as a stand-in father to many of the boys I coach. Yes, there are some bad apples in the bunch, but, trust me, neighborhoods would look quite different if the police weren't around."

Yes, and some look different because the police are there. Eden thought back to her friend in DC, more of a work associate, really, Renee Newton. Renee had also worked on Capitol Hill, and after finding out she was semivegetarian, eating fish only, they often met for lunch. It was during one of these meetings that Renee had shared a tragic family secret, one that haunted Eden to this day.

"Have you listened to Mike's CD? Your brother's group is pretty good."

Eden nodded, glad for Jansen's change of subject. "You've heard it?"

"Yes, and was especially intrigued with the song, 'Flower of Love.' I'd almost demand royalties, except there's no way a brothah in London would know he's copping the words meant for you alone. Wait," Jansen said, a slight frown interrupting the handsome on his face. "Did Mike tell this dude about you? The one who wrote the song?"

Eden laughed. "Not until after Kory had written it."

"Kory—how do you know his name?"

Jansen's possessiveness could have been irritating, but it wasn't. Eden felt good knowing it mattered to Jansen if other men were interested in her. "I had the same reaction to the song you did, felt it ironic, considering the conversation we'd had the night before."

"It's just fate, baby," Jansen countered, his countenance once again unruffled. "We're meant to be."

The topics stayed safe and relatively neutral—Michael's band, life in Los Angles, the upcoming Labor Day weekend. By the time they walked back to Eden's bedroom, the earlier friction between them had dissipated. Once again, they let their bodies do the talking. Jansen slowly undressed Eden, his fingers playing a symphony on her body as he deftly slid the straps off her shoulders. A nipple winked its pleasure at being released, and Jansen flicked it with his finger. The bud hardened, and Jansen pricked it, lightly running his fingernail over its ridges. His mouth watered, and he leaned forward, lightly brushing his tongue over her nipple once, and again, before suckling her breast like a thirsty man. He gave the other breast equal attention before slowly removing his shirt, muscles ebbing and flowing as he did so. Eden's hands acted of their own accord and slid themselves over his washboard abs, tickling the hairs that dotted his chest and formed a nice, neat line into his crotch. She followed the line with her fingers, but just as she reached the band on his boxers, he stopped her, placing his large, strong hand at the nape of her neck, pulling her to him and crushing their lips together in a mind-boggling kiss. He prodded her mouth open with his tongue: forceful, owning, taking no prisoners. Eden opened her mouth wide, welcoming the taste of him, her tongue dueling, dancing, searching. Jansen rubbed his muscled chest against Eden's soft globes and hardened peaks, the friction causing an instant wetness between her legs and a hardening of his shaft. She moaned, and he swallowed the sound, answered back by the wrapping of his arms more tightly around her, crushing their bodies together.

"Jansen," Eden cried, feeling she was losing herself in his firm grasp.

"I'm here," he whispered, walking them to Eden's queen-size sleigh bed. She sat when they reached it, her legs incapable of holding her up one minute longer. He knelt before her, his eyes boring into hers, his hands on her knees, gently prying her legs apart. He kissed the insides of her thighs, a probing finger quickly deducing she wore no underwear beneath her shorts. "No panties? Nice. . . ."

"Well, actually I . . . ah!" Eden's reply was cut short by Jansen's fingers skimming the hem of the denim and finding her treasure. He leisurely stroked the nub to attention while leaning in, capturing Eden's mouth, and mimicking this agonizingly pleasurable swirling with his tongue. His breathing increased as he pulled her closer, spread her wider, and sank a finger to the hilt, then another, and another still. Just when Eden felt she could take no more pleasure, he nipped her nipple, blew and sucked, until she exploded in an unexpected orgasm that left her legs shaking and her insides quivering.

Jansen licked his fingers, as if he'd just enjoyed a gourmet meal, before reaching for the band on her jeans. In his haste, the lone button flew across the room, the zipper zinged with the urgency of his mission. He quickly rid her of clothes, anchored his arms around her thighs, and lowered his head between her legs. His tongue was sure and steady, focused, parting her folds with leisurely licks before feasting in her heat. Eden screamed his name, tried to push away from the agonizing pleasure. He gripped her thighs, held her in place and increased the blessed torment, nipping sensitive skin, thrusting into the length and breadth of her being.

Eden felt like molten lava—hot and burning—all the way to her soul. The climax into bliss left her whimpering and reaching for her man. "Please," she whispered, her hand on his leg, precariously close to his engorged manhood. "I want to—" Her breath caught as Jansen placed one last kiss at the top of her still pulsating mound.

Jansen was ready for her to return the favor. He stood, quickly pulled off his boxers, and released the beast that bobbed and weaved for attention better than a boxer ever could. He sat on the edge of the bed, leaned back, and closed his eyes. Eden went to work straight away, lovingly grasping his massive shaft, licking her appreciation from the base to the tip, swirling her tongue around its smooth edge before taking him fully into her mouth. A loud and sustained hiss told her she was on to something. Smiling, she continued, tickling his sac with her fingers even as she repeated her previous ministrations over and again. She didn't think it was possible for him to grow larger, but he did. That she was responsible for this physical transformation turned her on immeasurably. She became a wanton nymph, concerned only with her lover's pleasure. She opened her mouth wide, took him in deeper, lavished unspeakable love on a man she'd been infatuated with since forever. Jansen moaned and writhed beneath her, exciting her further. She lightly brushed his inner thighs with her fingernails, and he grew bigger still.

"Now, woman," he growled, his body shuddering from her actions. "I want what belongs to me . . . my garden. . . ." He reached out, in seconds had flipped them over, and now hovered above her.

"Wait, I have to—"

"Already done." Jansen seared Eden with a kiss, hot and filled with promise, even as he reached for his shorts and pulled a condom out of the front pocket.

Eden's eyes fluttered open as she watched him protect them. The move was at once ordinary and amazing, his sword making "Magnum" work hard to live up to its name. Once covered, he moved to the middle of the bed, bringing Eden with him.

"Do you want to go for a ride?" he murmured as he lifted her onto his lap.

She figured she could show him better than she could tell him and did so by aligning his tip with the entrance of her love and slowly joining them together. She snugly clasped him within her walls before rising slowly and sinking down again. She increased the pace, up and down, and then swirled her hips, the gyration as playful as it was nasty. She braced herself against his broad shoulders, rocked back and forth. Jansen took advantage of her mouth's proximity. The kiss was wet and steamy, broken when Eden reared back her head and closed her eyes, her body rocking, hips grinding as she strove to ride him harder, feel him deeper. Ever the leader, Jansen grasped her hips and began to command the dance, his eyes glazed and darkened as he watched Eden's movements. He took a jiggling globe into his mouth and increased her pleasure. Just when she thought she could take no more, Jansen lifted her off him, silently commanded her to her knees, and entered her once again with one powerful thrust. The new position touched parts of her body, and her soul, that heretofore Eden hadn't known existed. He ran a finger along her crevice, kissed her neck and shoulders, before straightening up and getting down to business for real. He grabbed her hips, pulled her body toward him as he pushed into her with stroke after powerful stroke. He shifted his body from side to side, his sword dancing along her inner walls, claiming every inch of her, melting every ounce of resistance she had ever felt. Over and again he pounded her, reaching for her hair and lightly tugging it while he slowed the pace, in and out, allowing her to feel every glorious inch. He released her, but only for a moment, moving them both to the edge of the bed. After positioning Eden exactly as he wanted her, Jansen stood behind her in that firm, wide-legged stance that was his signature and entered her once again, slow and easy. A few inches. Out. A few more inches. And out again. Eden rocked back, impatient with longing. Jansen smiled, grabbed her hips, and demanded she wait until he was ready, and she was even crazier with desire. In again. Four inches this time. Out, slow, steady. Eden wriggled back against him, her body shouting demands for which her discombobulated mind could not find words.

Finally, one word staggered through the haze of her mind and reached her mouth. "More!" she panted.

Jansen's smile was predatory, victorious, as he plunged into his garden with gusto, alternating between fast and slow, and side to side. "Is this what you want, baby?"

Eden moaned.

"Is this what you need, Eden?"

"Yes," she managed between gasps and groans.

He reached a hand around and fingered her paradise, doubling her pleasure. A light sheen of sweat broke out all over Eden's body, mixing with the moisture that made Jansen's body shine. The mating dance went on for over an hour, each partner taking and giving equally, wanting to please and to be consumed. By the time they mutually reached their last pinnacle of lovemaking, and called out each other's names, Jansen knew he'd protect Eden with his very life, and Eden knew . . . she was in love.

"I don't want to leave," Jansen said afterward as they both caught their breath in each other's arms.

"Me neither."

"I have to go."

"I know."

"I'm glad that little . . . conversation from earlier didn't throw us off track."

Eden nodded and placed a soft kiss on his lips. "No worries."

Shortly afterward, Jansen got up, dressed, and left. Eden took a quick shower and then returned to bed—

sore but satisfied. She lay awake thinking for a long time. She'd survived their conversation involving officers and quotas, and the sex had been otherworldly. Still, Eden worried. She wasn't sure how well or how long she could coexist with Jansen's worldview or, more importantly, what he'd deftly tried to conceal when he'd first entered her place—what he'd admitted was an extension of himself. Eden unashamedly adored his cock, but she absolutely, positively abhorred his Glock.

27

The next morning, Eden enjoyed a soy chai latte as she drove down Lincoln Boulevard toward Rose Avenue in Venice. Ariel had buzzed her first thing this morning and had launched into a sales pitch so filled with passion, Eden had capitulated and agreed to visit the Zen Den. Sure, Eden was curious about this newest new-age establishment, but even more so felt that Ariel would bug her relentlessly until she made an appearance. Plus, receiving no phone calls from the résumés she'd sent so far, she figured she at least owed a visit to the place. It did have some of what she was looking for in her next employment, even if it did seem a tad more alternative than Eden had experienced.

She turned from Rose onto Main Street, noting how dense was this area that had been popular since its inception in the early twentieth century. Bicyclists effortlessly vied with skateboarders for street space, undaunted by the rush-hour traffic that crawled between traffic lights. Eden noted how amidst the obvious luxury walked homeless men and women—their grubby clothing striking a discordant note against the designer-filled shops these residents passed. Eden thanked her parking angels when she spotted a space just three doors down from the address she wanted, deftly maneuvering into the tight space. She finished her drink, gave some change to a man who approached her, and headed toward the Zen Den.

Ariel was the first person Eden saw. "Eden! You came!" She leaped from her seat behind the modern reception area and came around to grip her unsuspecting friend in a tight hug. "I'm so glad you're here. Isn't this place amazing?"

"Uh, sure, from what I've seen in the five seconds I've been here." Eden laughed, disentangling herself from Ariel's exuberant embrace.

"But I sent you the Facebook link. It's amazing, if I must say so myself. I took all the pictures—a guided tour, if you will—and organized the descriptions of all our services, even writing a few myself. All that hard work, just for you," Ariel winked, "and you didn't look at it?"

"I'm not on Facebook," Eden said, turning to take in the airy, two-story lobby, lush plants, and bamboo flooring. The walls were painted a soothing light blue; a harp-driven instrumental played softly and added calmness.

"What?" Ariel's shriek resounded against the peaceful walls. "Oops," she stuttered, lowering her voice to a whisper. "You're not on Facebook? *Everybody's* on Facebook, Eden. It's like if you're not on it, you don't exist."

"Now, I would call that an *illusion,*" Eden replied,

using one of Ariel's common descriptions of anything she'd rather not acknowledge. For Ariel, poverty, war, and the like were all illusions to the truth of God being all there was. Even as Eden somewhat agreed with this position, in theory, she'd also felt an uncomfortable empathy with how Jansen must feel listening to her positive perspective.

"Ha! Maybe, but you need to get on it. It will help you become a part of the viable holistic community that exists on it, and once you're here, help you network with other areas of the country about the Den."

"You've already got me clocking in, do you?"

Ariel winked. "You're going to work here, and you're going to love it. The cards told me last night." With that, she gently grabbed Eden's arm and pulled her toward a hallway. "This is a general room, used for yoga and other stretching exercises," she said, beginning the tour. She showed Eden various rooms for the healing modalities offered, each bathed in calming nonfluorescent lighting, some with candles burning, others with fountains gurgling soft, liquid songs. Most of the offices were empty. "The practitioners work at various times," Ariel explained when Eden asked why. "By noon, most of these rooms will be filled with clients, but the atmosphere is always like this—quiet and peaceful."

They walked from that hallway back through the lobby area to the back patio. "This," Ariel said as they crossed a small bridge erected over a koi pond, "is where we conduct meditations. And this is the sweat lodge." Eden took a step forward. "Shhh, no talking," Ariel instructed, and they walked inside. The small square building was adorned with a mix of blankets and pillows on the concrete floor and a sunken fire pit in the middle. Various symbols were painted on the walls, and a Tibetan prayer flag was strung from one wall to the other. The place was embodied with serenity, but for Eden, there was claustrophobia as well. She was glad when they exited seconds later and walked back inside the center.

They came to an office with the door open, and a darkly tanned man, his hair long and unbound, sat inside behind a simple, wooden desk. His dark eyes were bright, his smile genuine. Uncanny, but it was as if peace radiated from the man's pores. For Eden, no introduction was needed. This had to be Ariel's boss, Om.

"Peace and blessings, my dear one," Om said, bowing slightly. "Welcome." He placed Eden's hands inside his, holding them loosely while looking into her eyes. She thought she was imagining the heat she experienced until it traveled up her arm and burst through her solar plexus.

"Oh!" she said, startled, pulling her hands from his.

"It is only Spirit, dear one," Om said, his eyes twinkling. "It is simply flowing to the part of itself already inside you, with desires to heal and make whole that which is broken. Some other time, perhaps, we can arrange a longer meeting, and a time of realignment with your source."

"Uh, sure," Eden said, suddenly overwhelmed with the urge to cry, though she couldn't figure out the reason. "I think I'd like that." She was still feeling out of sorts when they reached the last office, which sat directly at the end of the hallway. Here, too, the door was open. Ariel knocked lightly before entering.

"Dr. K?" Ariel's voice took on a fairy-dust quality, her admiration of this medical expert seeming to rival that which she felt for her sage. "If you have a moment, this is Eden, the woman I told you about."

Eden followed Ariel into the room, just as a tall, dark-haired man turned to face them. He was handsome, his facial features strong and defined, and his eyes the greenest Eden had ever seen. His eyes caught and held hers, darkening for an instant before a professional veneer was snapped neatly in place. "Alexander Kostopoulos," he said, coming forward with his hand outstretched.

Eden watched him approach her, trying to collect her thoughts. For as much as Ariel talked, and as much as she'd gone on and on about the center in general and Om in particular, she'd mentioned nothing about this man's good looks, obvious charm, or subtle accent she noticed with the uttering of his name. "Eden Anderson," she said, her succinct greeting adding to the corporate image she displayed in her navy pantsuit, ivory shell, and sensible heels. She knew it was an alternative center, but to Eden, an interview was an interview. When Ariel mentioned she might meet the doctor, who was also on the center's board, Eden had dressed to impress. But after taking in Ariel's pink tee and jeans, and the doctor's similar attire, she realized he might have been equally impressed with her yoga gear.

Ariel's eyes twinkled as she looked from Alex to Eden. "Can I get you two something to drink? Water or tea?"

Alex turned to Eden. "Ms. Anderson?"

"No, thanks, I'm fine."

"Thanks, Ariel. Could you do me a huge favor and bring one of the center's welcome folders in, please, along with an application?"

"Sure, Dr. K."

As soon as Ariel left the room, the doctor turned from his desk and headed to a love seat on the opposite side of the room. "Please, join me. It's less formal over here, a much better setting to get to know each other a bit." He waited until Eden sat and then sat on the other end of the love seat.

"I e-mailed my résumé earlier, but brought another one." Eden reached into her business clutch and pulled out the one-page document. "Should I call you Dr. . . . K?"

Alex smiled, revealing a perfect set of sparkling white teeth. He took the paper but kept his eyes on her. Eden noticed the crinkles that formed when he smiled and also took in the slight wisps of gray at his temples. Instead of making him appear older, the subtle white streaks made him look both distinguished and roguish at the same time. And again, she noted, she'd never seen eyes so green.

"Most of the staff and the clients prefer that to Kostopoulos," he answered, emphasizing each syllable. "You can call me that . . . or Alex."

"And please, doctor, call me Eden. Kostopoulos is Greek, correct?"

Alex nodded. "My father came from a small village near Piraeus, where much of my family still lives. When he arrived, he was encouraged to shorten his name to something easier to pronounce, more American sounding. But he refused. I was embarrassed by it as a child, but, in time, embraced it as well. Eden is a lovely name. As in the garden, I presume."

An image of Jansen's lust-filled eyes swam into her consciousness as she remembered how he called her his garden while pounding into her over and over again. She suddenly warmed, much as she had at the shaman's touch, and wished she'd taken Ariel up on her offer for water. "Um, not exactly. Though a Bible story is probably how my mom heard it, she said she simply liked the name."

"The Garden of Eden is said to be a beautiful place," Alex continued. His tone was cordial, not flirtatious at all, yet his eyes seemed to embrace her. He was the kind of man whose simple "hello" seemed a come-on, and whose "how are you" sounded like a promise.

Eden's response was interrupted by Ariel, who walked into the room with two bottles of water. "Just in case you get thirsty," she said cheerily with a nod to the doctor and a quick wink to Eden before she left the room. *That girl and her intuition. Thank you!* Eden reached for the water and took a long swallow, thankful that the slight discomfort she'd felt seconds before had dissipated. With years spent on Capitol Hill, she was used to being around attractive, affluent, powerful men. *It's just that this was so unexpected,* Eden reasoned. Another thought of Jansen chased away the last of her flutters. She squared her shoulders and got down to business.

"You'll see that while most of my work history is in government, my degree is in business administration.

I think that my skill set would lend itself beautifully to the running of this center. That and the fact that I am personally on a holistic journey could make this a wonderful opportunity for me."

Alex took a moment and scanned her résumé. When he looked up, there was an unmistakable twinkle in his eye. "Ms. Anderson—Eden—I think this could be a wonderful opportunity for us all."

28

Eden sat in front of her computer nibbling on veggies and sipping sparkling apple juice. She glanced down at her computer clock and was surprised she'd been online for two hours. No, more specifically, she'd been on Facebook for that long. *Now I remember why I hadn't joined this site.* Michael had told her how addictive it could be, how sometimes he'd click on, intending to respond to one message, and stay on an hour reading other people's mail, participating in various applications, accepting or turning down invites, and "liking" half the world.

Eden had done much of the same but also felt this was time well spent. She'd sent friend requests to several holistic practitioners or establishments, most of whom had been recommended by Ariel. She'd also connected with her brother's "like" page, browsed Jansen's female-heavy list of almost five hundred friends, and reached out to personal contacts, including childhood friend Chandra Brockman and Capitol Hill associate

Renee Newton. She was just getting ready to sign off
the Web site when a pop-up appeared on her screen.

It was an instant chat from Chandra. Girl, is this
really you? OMG, Eden, long time!

Eden responded. :-) Yes, sistah, it's really me. And,
yes, it's been too long. How are you?

I can't complain. Wouldn't do any good anyway. . . .

I heard that! Are you still in St. Louis?

Yes, we're still here. But you know what? We've got
too much to talk about for this chat box. Here's my
number. Chandra typed her number, and within seconds, she and Eden were talking on the phone.

"Oh, my God, Eden! I can't believe it, girl. After
all these years!"

"I know, girl, me neither. How long has it been—at
least ten years?"

"At least. My oldest child is ten, and the last time I
talked to you, I didn't have any!"

"How many children do you have?"

"Too many! I'm just kidding, I love my babies. We
have two boys, two girls, a dog, and a cat, but I'm
drawing the line on this gerbil my youngest daughter is
demanding."

Eden chuckled. "Wow, Chandra. Out of all my
friends, you were the last one I'd imagined living a
more traditional life—you know, husband, kids, the
white picket fence. I thought you'd be in Hollywood
somewhere making a name for yourself, or married to
some rock star."

"Well, you know what they say. Life is what happens while we're busy making plans. It's not what I expected, but I'm happy with my life. I have a husband

who's loyal and dedicated to our family and kids I don't want to murder every other day. Instead of a white picket fence, ours is wrought iron. But I got one of the good ones, Eden. Ours is a happy home. What about you?"

Eden gave Chandra a brief rundown of her time in Washington, DC, and life with Gregg. "I've been back in LA less than a month, but it feels good to be here. The change is what I needed."

The two women continued chatting, catching up on each other's lives and families. After asking about Michael, Chandra remembered his best friend. "I wonder whatever happened to Jansen McKnight. That was one fine brother! I would love to know what he's up to now. Probably either married or has a string of exes and child-support payments. Oooo, but he was handsome. And talk about doing the do! He's one man I don't regret—"

"Actually," Eden interrupted, not wanting to hear Chandra's remembrances of Jansen's exploits, "Jansen is back here in LA as well."

"What? You've seen him?"

"Yes."

"How'd that happen? I bet you tracked him down the minute you returned home. I know I would have."

"No, I didn't go looking for anyone when I arrived here. Too busy. He and Michael are still close. I saw him when I was visiting my brother."

"Is he married? What's he doing there? Does he still look as good as I remember? Man, he probably looks even better. God knows I love my husband, but Jansen McKnight . . . unh-unh-unh."

The more Chandra rambled, the more uncomfortable Eden became. She began to second-guess her decision to reconnect "for old time's sake"—had forgotten the side of her former good friend who'd slept with Mike, Jansen, and probably a dozen or so more of their classmates. Eden knew Jansen had been around the track a time or two but didn't want to hear a play-by-play of any individual races.

She didn't want to pass on any information either. "Jansen is still Jansen," was Eden's succinct reply. *He's on Facebook. If you want to know more about him, look him up and ask him yourself.*

Eden was glad to have spoken with Chandra but was grateful when the call was interrupted. "I have to go," Chandra explained after a child's voice yelled something in the background. "Dinnertime here, and my husband just walked in. But let's finish catching up soon, okay?"

After ending the call, Eden took one last look at her homepage. She noticed that the doctor, Alex Kostopoulos, was online. She toyed with the idea of sending him a quick chat message, thanking him for his time during their earlier interview. *Would that be appropriate?* She clicked on his profile. Other than that he was a doctor located in Los Angeles, nothing personal was listed. No birthday, marital status, or other information that could tell her about the man who might become her boss. Again, she toyed with the idea of sending a quick thank-you by chat. *Or perhaps inboxing the note would be better.* She clicked to send him a message, and then her phone rang. "Hey, you."

"What have you done to me, woman? I need to be

focused on my job but can't stop thinking about what I'm going to do to you later on tonight."

"That sounds dangerous." There was a smile in Eden's voice.

Jansen's voice was low and smoky. "Oh, believe me, baby, you have no idea."

"Ha! No, I meant not being focused sounds dangerous. Yours is not a job where one wants to be caught off guard."

"You're right, which is why it's good I'm back at the station handling paperwork. What time are you coming over?"

"I hadn't planned on coming."

Pause. "And again I say, you have no idea. . . ."

"Jansen. You're such a bad boy."

"That's what you like about me. I'll be home around six. Will you meet me?"

"I will this time. But soon I'll be a working woman and not able to be at your beck and call."

"Oh, really? You got a bite on one of those résumés you've been sending?"

"Actually, this was a recommendation from a friend. I'll tell you all about it when I come over."

"Baby, that had better be a quick story. Because once you get here, my mouth will have more things to do than hold a conversation."

29

Eden awoke to soft, feathery kisses being placed at the nape of her neck. It felt good. She nestled back against him, spoon style, their bodies fitting perfectly. *I could get used to this.*

Jansen ran his hand along Eden's side, from her shoulder, down the valley of her waist, and over the crest of her hip. He squeezed a cheek and began the journey back over the skin he thought smooth as silk. Eden wiggled her buttocks against his hardness, wrapped his arm around her to snuggle even closer. It was all the invitation Jansen needed. He reached across her to the nightstand beyond, and after making quick work of protecting them, lifted her leg and sank deeply into Eden's heat. She moaned her appreciation, gyrated her hips to join in the dance. Jansen was focused, purposeful as he delivered thrust after powerful thrust. His fingers found her nipple, tweaked it once and again. Eden's whimpers became a song, Jansen's grunts the accompanying melody. They'd done the love boogie for hours the night before, but each acted as famished as a just-released priest. Jansen rolled onto his back, carrying Eden with him. He lifted her as if she were a feather, grasped her thighs, and went in for the thrill— harder, faster, rotating his hips, elevating himself off the bed to stamp his claim deep inside Eden's core. Eden cried louder, tears gathering at the corners of her eyes from the intense pleasure. Her insides quivered and legs shook amid a climax so powerful she thought she saw stars. Jansen followed her over the edge, a sustained shudder the final chord to their symphony. Breathing heavily, he pulled Eden into his arms, lying as they had at the beginning. He wrapped his arms around her, kissed her shoulder, and murmured two words: "Good morning."

Eden giggled. "Indeed it is."

"I could get used to this, little garden."

Eden didn't reply. The truth was, she was probably already more used to Jansen than she should be, and falling deeper in love every day. She knew it was dangerous territory she was treading, knew the potential pitfalls of risking her heart. *But the rewards* . . . She thought of their shared history, easy camaraderie, and physical compatibility . . . and knew this was a chance she'd have to take.

Jansen eased off the bed, groaning his displeasure at doing so. "Why don't you stay here today—be here when I come home?"

Eden performed the stretch of a satisfied kitty. "Right now it feels as if I could stay *here* all day, in bed."

"That's fine, too."

"No," she countered, sitting up. "I have some things

to research online and probably should send out a few more résumés, just in case this job doesn't come through."

"You never told me about the interview."

"Yeah, well, a certain someone had other things on his mind when I came over last night."

Jansen smiled. "Come take a shower with me and tell me all about it."

Afterward Eden climbed back into the bed and watched Jansen dress. He was very particular about his uniform and seemed to have a routine about putting it on. He started with his socks. *Interesting.* Then a pair of black Calvin Klein briefs, followed by the same brand black T-shirt. *Nice.* After splashing on a touch of cologne, he reached for the crisply starched and ironed navy blue pants hanging just inside the closet. Donning them was followed by sliding a thick Velcro belt holder through the belt loops and covering the hard, sculpted chest Eden relished with a navy-blue shirt. *Wow,* Eden thought as she admired him unabashedly. *Of all the LA scenarios I imagined, I never thought I'd be here . . . lovin' blue.*

Jansen walked to the dresser, strapped on a thick leather belt over the belt holder, and placed a radio, handcuffs, pepper spray, and extra magazine pouch in their respective holders. Lastly, with a quick look in Eden's direction, he reached for his gun and slipped it firmly in the holster. Normally, he would have loaded a full magazine clip, but given Eden's sensitivity where weapons were concerned, Jansen decided to do this downstairs.

"You going to be here for me?" Jansen's voice was a

whisper as he leaned over and planted a kiss on Eden's forehead. "You could use my computer downstairs in my office."

"Are you sure you want me in your home for eight hours? Not afraid I'll snoop through your things and find out your secrets?"

Jansen laughed. "Oh, so that's how it is. You're one of *those* women."

"Fortunately, no, thanks to Phyllis Anderson. She says women who go looking for doo-doo usually find it."

"Ha! I love your mama." Jansen placed a quick kiss on Eden's lips. "Let me get out of here while I still can, because as sexy as you're looking in my wife beater, I'm tempted to call in sick and sex you again."

After Jansen left, Eden fell back to sleep. When she awoke, she was surprised that she'd slept three more hours. Then she remembered the workout Jansen had given her and understood why. Her brow creased as she thought of Jansen protecting the public on barely six hours' sleep. She sent up a mental prayer to her angels to keep Jansen safe.

Preferring Jansen's tee to what she'd worn last night, Eden walked over to his dresser, found a pair of check-ered boxers, and put them on. Her hands lingered among his belongings, fingering his boxers, briefs, socks, and T-shirts, all folded with precision. She closed the drawer, smiled as she looked around the room, and wondered if it could work, if she and Jansen could last long-term. *How would it feel to be your wife?* "Whoa, girl," Eden said aloud. "It's way too early to go down that road."

To take her mind off things better left not thought about, Eden stripped the bed and went in search of the laundry room. Finding it just off the kitchen, she put in the load and then went to assuage a serious appetite. "Jansen, trying to keep up with your libido will have me as big as a house!" She laughed aloud when she opened the refrigerator and among other things saw salad fixings, a variety of vegetables, and soy meats. She took out a bag of muffins and orange juice, eyed a bowl of fruit on the counter and, next to it, two bottles of wine. "You're too much," she said, becoming increasingly impressed with her lover's thoughtfulness. Last night he'd surprised her with the music that had accompanied their lovemaking—a bevy of neo-soul artists he'd added to his iPod, along with a couple compilations of smooth jazz. This morning he'd surprised her with his stamina.

A ringing cell phone jolted Eden from her musings. She rushed to answer it, having totally forgotten to bring her purse up to Jansen's bedroom the night before. There was no telling who'd called or how many messages she had. "Hello?"

"There you are!" Ariel's high-pitched voice fairly floated through the phone. "I thought I might have to send out my fairies to find you."

"Sorry. I got tied up last night and haven't checked my messages."

"Sounds yummy!"

Eden laughed.

"Of course I was living to know how your interview went with the doctor."

"Ha! You mean, *dying* to know, don't you?"

"*Moi?* Never that, Eden. Death is an illusion. Everything about me is eternally *alive!*"

This girl, you've got to love her. "Okay . . ."

"Turns out, I already know. It must have gone well. You've created some great buzz around here."

"Oh really? More buzz than I felt go up my arm when Om shook my hand?"

Ariel laughed. "He gave you *shaktipat?*"

"Chaka who?"

"*Shaktipat.* It's the transference of spiritual energy. Your higher self must have requested it because it can't be given without consent."

"If you say so."

"It's good stuff, Eden. Look it up online. I think you'll benefit immensely from a session with him."

"I'll research it. That's all I can promise."

"Coolness! Om liked your energy. In fact, everyone seemed very impressed with your qualifications, especially Dr. K."

"Really."

"After you left, he asked me about you, how long we'd known each other, where we met, stuff like that. Of course I waxed poetic about your glowing attributes and what a great addition you'd make to our family. I know for a fact that they checked at least one of your references already, even though two other applicants are being interviewed today."

"Which means I shouldn't count my chickens before they're hatched."

"Those interviews are also part of the illusion. Visualize what you want, Eden. If it's your desire, this job is yours. Oops, call coming in. I have to run. Smooches!"

Eden walked to Jansen's office with Ariel's words ringing in her ears. *Visualize what you want. If it's your desire, it's yours.* After visiting the center and meeting the staff, Eden definitely wanted to work at the Zen Den. But that wasn't all she desired. She sat in Jansen's big leather chair, inhaled his scent, and visualized something else she wanted.

30

Jansen hummed along with will.i.am from the Black Eyed Peas. "Yeah, I have a feeling, too, man." He looked over at the roses he'd impulsively bought from the seller at an intersection on Hawthorne. Only in Los Angeles, he'd mused after the purchase, could one buy anything from fruit to nuts, to flowers to bean pies without leaving their car. He entered the gate, turned onto his block, and the song died on his lips. Eden's car was gone. It had been on his mind all day: coming home and having Eden there waiting for him, still wearing his oversize tee, perhaps the smell of something healthy yet delicious wafting from the kitchen. Eden had looked good in his home. It had felt right falling asleep with her last night and waking up pressed against her lusciousness.

He turned into his drive and, with motor running, dialed her cell. She picked up. "It had better be good."

"What?" Eden asked, already knowing the answer.

"The reason you're not at my house, woman!"

Jansen's tone softened. "Knowing I'd find you here is what got me through the day."

"Oh, baby, I'm sorry." And she was. Sorry that she'd looked into his top desk drawer to find screen cleaner and had found a handgun instead. Sorry that after jumping from the desk as if the semiautomatic could shoot, well, automatically, she took a good look around the room. A collection of handcuffs was framed on one wall, along with his college degree and various commendations from both his military and law-enforcement careers. On the other wall was a case housing an extensive gun collection. Eden was sorry that instead of leaving the house right then, she'd turned into the snoop she said she wasn't and found guns in a kitchen drawer, the laundry room, and inside the walk-in closet of his master suite. She was sorry she didn't make up the bed, didn't even take the linens out of the washing machine, but instead had dressed as quickly as she could and fled the feel of death.

"Why'd you go, baby? I want you here. I want you now."

"Something came up," she said, her mind grasping for an excuse to cover the truth. Eden didn't want to mess up the amazing vibe she'd felt with this man by mentioning the real reason. It would simply cause a debate, and Eden was not in the mood. All day she'd grappled with the reality of Jansen's chosen profession and its dichotomous position to her own truths and desired career path. How did one balance holistic living with weapons of destruction? Yet how could she judge Jansen's path when she didn't want anyone judging hers?

"I should have left you a key," Jansen said into the silence.

"It's okay, I had to come back to Santa Monica anyway to take a yoga class." *At least I can tell you the truth about that.*

"You still needed stretching after my workouts last night and this morning? Damn, I need to step up my game!"

"Trust and believe, Jansen, your game is top-notch."

Jansen felt himself relax for the first time since turning the corner and not seeing Eden's car. "So I'm headed to Santa Monica?"

"Sounds like a good idea to me."

"Should I bring dinner?"

"No, I'll whip something up."

Later, after a hearty dinner of lentil stew over quinoa, cornbread, and pie for dessert, Jansen and Eden once again struck up their familiar love song. Their bodies sang *I want you* better than Marvin Gaye and *whip appeal* better than Babyface. Jansen strummed her body like an instrument, made Eden sing soprano, and then begrudgingly made his exit. She clung to the sheets he'd just vacated, drank in his musky scent, her heart already missing the man who'd left just moments before. "What am I going to do?" Eden asked the darkness. With their differences, she didn't know how she could live with him, but with what they shared, she could no longer see her life without him in it.

31

"Why couldn't I reach you all weekend?" Michael walked over and turned down his stereo.

"Oh, no, you didn't," Eden retorted as she looked out and beheld a beautiful, if hot, August day. "Not admonishment from the brother who was MIA for a week before letting his family know he'd flown the country coop."

"Yeah, yeah, yeah, that was then, this is now. I tried to reach you all day Sunday and yesterday, too." Michael paused. "Couldn't reach Jansen either."

Silence.

"Are you and Jansen dating?"

Pause. "Yes." *Why do I feel like I'm talking to a parent instead of a sibling?*

"C'mon, weed," Michael said with a sigh. "Then again, on second thought, you know what? You're a grown-ass woman. You're no longer the little sister who needs protection from the bullies on her way home from school."

"Are you saying Jansen is a bully?"

"When it comes to J-Dog, I don't think it matters what I'm saying."

"Not as long as he keeps treating me the way he has, as a perfect gentleman."

"He'd better, 'cause I know where he lives. But, then, you probably do, too. . . ."

"Yeah, just like Bridgett probably knows her way around your house."

"You got me there."

"I know I do. I grew up with you, remember? She's probably there right now. So don't start none, won't be none, big bro."

"Ha!" Michael lay back on his couch and pulled a barely clad Bridgett down with him. "What are y'all doing for Labor Day weekend?"

"We're invited to a party at Jansen's partner's house."

"*El hombre* Alberto."

"You know him?"

"Met him once at a party. He seems like a cool dude."

"What are you doing?"

"Bridgett wants to barbecue over here, have a pool party. Cleaning the water regularly but still haven't been in it more than half a dozen times. We were going to invite you and Jansen over and a few more friends."

"Oh, dang, that sounds fun. Well, we can always party hop. I think Alberto's party is during the day. So if you could plan yours more toward evening, that would be cool. And I'd finally get to meet the woman with the track record on your heart."

"All right, then. We'll work something out."

They ended the call, and Eden walked to her laptop on the dining room table. She clicked on the Facebook icon, entered her e-mail address, and waited for the page to load. *Oh, my goodness. Renee responded to my request and sent me a message!* She was just about to click on it when the phone rang.

"Ms. Anderson?" a deep voice with a slight accent asked.

Eden's heart leaped. "Dr. Kostopoulos?"

Alex chuckled. "You'll want to call me Alex, or Dr. K. Pronouncing those four syllables repeatedly throughout the course of your day may become wearing after a bit."

"Through the course of my . . . wait? Are you calling to give me some very good news?" Eden couldn't contain her excitement. She jumped up from the table and then paced the living room and back.

"Yes, Eden. We are very pleased to have put together what we hope is a winning job offer. Can you come to the center today?"

"Absolutely."

"Good. Does three o'clock work for you?"

"Yes, Dr. Kostopou—I mean, Alex. Dr. K. Three sounds perfect."

"I look forward to seeing you then."

At 4:15 PM, Eden bounced out of the Zen Den with a glide in her stride and pep in her step. The 60K-a-year plus-benefits offer was twenty thousand more than she thought she'd receive and more money than was advertised. Dr. K had explained to her that because of her qualifications and diverse skill set, he'd gotten the board to combine two positions into one in order to offer a higher salary. As center director, Eden would oversee staff and operations and head up marketing as well. She'd signed a one-year contract and would be on a probationary period for ninety days, during which time either side could terminate the agreement, no questions asked. She reached her car, donned her earpiece, and retrieved her phone. Jansen had called, which did not surprise her. A picture of the gun in the middle of his top desk drawer floated into her mind. She closed her eyes against it. *What am I going to do?* Eden didn't know the answer to that question. But as she clicked on the link to redial his number, she knew one thing: not seeing him tonight was not an option.

"Hey, baby . . . I got the job!"

"That's great, little garden." Jansen's answer was quiet, his mood subdued.

"Jansen, what's wrong?"

Silence and then, "Got some bad news today."

"Want to share?"

"Not really." One second passed, and another, then several more. "Friend of mine died today."

Eden closed her eyes, once again trying to block out bad stuff. An ironic reminder that closing one's eyes to evil didn't make it go away. "I'm so sorry, Jansen."

Jansen snorted.

Eden fought not to take his reaction personally. "Someone you worked with?" Her voice was soft, nurturing.

"Used to. Back in Chicago."

Eden searched for words to say. Couldn't find any. "I'm sorry," she repeated finally.

"It's life, Eden. Shit happens. People die. It's fucked up."

Eden dared not comment on that one. What could she say? Instead she asked, "Do you want me to come over?"

"Not sure that's a good idea. I know you don't like to deal with the negative, and I'm not feeling too positive right now."

"Okay."

Jansen tsked again. "Later."

Eden sat for several moments, staring at the phone and into a situation that was impossible. Jansen McKnight was the man she loved, and this was his life—crime, death, navigating the bowels of hell every single day. The illusion, as Ariel would call it. The part of human existence with which Eden would prefer as little interaction as possible.

Eden started her car, headed toward Lincoln Boulevard and into the Whole Foods parking lot. She purchased beer, brown rice, and, for the first time in four years, a piece of farm-raised salmon. Then she got back in her car and headed toward Gardena.

When she reached her destination, she got out of the car quickly before she could change her mind. Part of her had wanted to go home and bask in the peace of her feng-shui environment. But Jansen wasn't just her lover, he was her friend. Eden wasn't the kind of woman who'd leave a friend hanging. She didn't know what kind of reception she'd get: anger, passiveness, rejection? At the very least, she'd prepare dinner and then leave. Jansen loved to eat, and she doubted he'd done so since hearing the news. *That's it. I'll just cook the food and leave.*

She rang the doorbell and then waited for what felt like an eternity. She rang again, and after another couple minutes, turned to leave.

The door opened. "Eden."

She turned around, looked deeply into Jansen's eyes. He looked into hers. She took a tentative step toward him, and then another, until she stood before him. He took a deep breath and wrapped her in his arms, squeezing her tightly. She dropped the bag and hugged him back, rubbing her hands across his taut back and stiff shoulders. Jansen took another deep breath and stepped aside so she could enter. Eden didn't leave until morning.

32

Eden looked down at her white shorts with resignation. They were ruined. Why had she thought it would be okay to wear such a color to an event with kids? Clearly, inexperience was written all over her choice, and now so was barbecue sauce, grass stains, and mud from Alberto Jr.'s midthigh hug. Eden guessed there had been twenty adults and double that number of children in and out of Alberto and Delphia Gonzalez's home in the two hours she and Jansen had been there. The backyard was crowded with plastic pools, card tables, and a bounce house. She hadn't known family life could be this much fun.

"Are you sure you have to leave?" Delphia asked, walking like a pregnant woman even though, at three months, she was barely showing. "We're doing old-school later on, complete with a *Soul Train* line!"

"Sounds wonderful, Delphia, but I promised my brother we'd come over. If not for that, you'd probably have to kick me out. I've had a great time."

"Well, don't be a stranger. And you don't have to

wait for knucklehead"—she cocked her head toward Jansen—"to issue the invitation. We girls have to stick together, and I'll give up the goods on that homey."

Eden eased closer. "Do tell."

Delphia leaned in. "You've got yourself a good one," she whispered. "In all the time he and my husband have been friends and he's come over, you're the first woman he's brought along."

"She's a hot tamale," Alberto was saying to Jansen on the other side of the yard. "No wonder you've been skipping to my loo, looking all goo-goo-eyed and shit."

"Man, why are you lying on a brother?" Jansen asked, laughing, looking over at the person who'd put the smile back on his face following the tragic loss of his former comrade. Later in the week he'd fly to Chicago and pay his condolences. But today he smiled.

"If I'm lying, I'm dying," Alberto replied. "You better keep an eye on that, dog, 'cause if you mess up . . ." Alberto raised his brow and then his beer bottle.

"Yeah, whatever," Jansen replied, clinking glass. "You handle your business, partner, and I'll handle mine."

After what seemed like a zillion hugs and *hasta luegos,* Jansen and Eden left Hawthorne and headed for Baldwin Hills.

"That was fun!" Eden exclaimed.

"That was crazy. That's my boy though. They're good peeps."

"I really like Delphia."

"Yeah, she's special."

"And so are you. Her using vegetarian instead of

traditional refried beans in the burritos, and no meat, was I'm sure your idea."

"Couldn't have you going into seizures on me, girl. You get nauseous smelling meat—no telling how you'd react to lard hitting your system."

"Ha! Thanks, baby. That could get ugly."

"If you say so. Me, I've never met a pig I didn't like."

Jansen pushed the volume button on his stereo and turned up Stevie Wonder's radio station, 102.3 KJLH. The deejays had been killing it all weekend, mixing today's hits with yesterday's favorites. TLC had gone creepin', and now Montell Jordan was explaining how we do it. Jansen and Eden bobbed and weaved in their seats—music blasting, sun shining, love everywhere.

When the song ended, Jansen turned down the radio. "Little garden . . . do you want to have kids?"

Eden stopped in the middle of her cabbage patch. "What?"

"Babies, children, *niños*—do you want them?"

Eden overlooked the abrupt change of subject and answered. "I always thought I'd have kids, but now . . ." She shrugged her shoulders.

"Now what?"

"I'm thirty-four, Jansen. If I had a kid today, I'd be fifty-two when the child turned eighteen."

"And?"

"And? When I turned eighteen, Mama was in her forties."

"You really think you're too old to have kids? Age is just a number, Eden."

"Easy for you to say. Men can be seventy and still shoot a tadpole into an egg, no worries. You don't have to carry it nine months and deliver it through your vagina."

"True, you're probably closer to the grave than you are the cradle." Eden scowled, Jansen smirked. "But I don't think you're too old to be a mother."

"Who asked you?" Eden huffed, rolling her eyes and crossing her arms for good measure.

Jansen simply smiled. He couldn't let too many days go by without getting under Eden's skin. As much as he cared for her, it just wouldn't be natural.

They arrived at Michael's to a nice but totally different atmosphere. Bypassing the front door for the back gate, Jansen and Eden walked in to see Michael and a few others in the pool, two couples playing Spades, and a tall, lean woman hovering over the grill. Jansen began peeling off clothes and within minutes was alongside Michael in the kidney-shaped pool. Eden walked up to the woman wearing a big smile, a short dress, apron, and heels.

"You must be Bridgett."

"And you must be Eden."

Eden stuck out her hand. Bridgett swatted it away and enveloped her in a hug. "Girl, we hug where I come from. My parents are Southern."

Eden liked her already. "Nice to meet you."

"You, too. You seem down-to-earth, and I like that. When it comes to men and their families, you never know what to expect. Michael thinks the world of you, sistah, so if we didn't like each other . . . there would be problems. 'Cause I love me some him, know what I'm sayin'? I'm not trying to go *nowhere*."

"As long as you keep doing what you're doing,

looks like you won't have to. I'm going to go change, get out of these dirty shorts. Then you can tell me what you need me to do."

"All you need to do is enjoy yourself. Food's almost ready."

Eden entered the house from the back door and walked through the kitchen. She passed bowls of green salad, spinach salad, green-bean salad, potato salad, macaroni salad, carrot salad, and yet another salad filled with avocado and corn. *No wonder she doesn't need my help. She has enough food here to feed . . . the Gonzalez family!* Eden climbed the stairs, changed into her swimsuit and cover-up, and joined the party heating up outside.

33

"Eden Anderson, so nice to meet you."

"Likewise, Eden. Welcome aboard."

Day one at the Zen Den had arrived. Ariel, over the moon that her friend had been hired, had volunteered to take Eden around and introduce her to the staff, referred to as "the community." Many of the part-timers worked in the afternoon. Still, in addition to Om and Alex, Eden had met the nutritionist, an herbalist, a couple exercise instructors, an acupuncturist, several energy healers, and two masseuses. By the time she and Ariel returned to the airy, modern kitchen/break room, she'd met almost half of the community's twenty-eight members.

Eden carried a steaming mug of green tea into her small yet adequate office located on the building's back side. Her favorite office feature was the large window that looked out upon the meticulously landscaped garden that was the two-story office's backyard. She gazed out upon the picture-perfect September morning and then turned and surveyed her new domain. The furniture was minimal, the walls not adorned. Dr. K had explained that this was so she could personalize the office to her liking. With that in mind, Eden sat behind the desk and began compiling a shopping list.

Her stomach growled, signaling lunchtime. Eden checked her watch and was surprised to see how quickly four hours had passed. In addition to completing the shopping list, she'd further familiarized herself with the community members by reviewing their résumés and Web sites and studied the various healing modalities offered at the center. Eden had discovered a lot about the holistic lifestyle and alternative methods of healing in the four years she'd ventured down this path. After three hours on her new job, however, she knew there was still much to learn.

A light tap on her open office door signaled company. "There are no brownie points for not taking a lunch break," Alex said as he entered her office. "In fact, while eating is not mandatory, it is highly recommended."

Eden sat back, smiling. "I totally agree with you, doctor, and so does my growling stomach."

"I thought perhaps we could grab a bite together, have a casual strategy session regarding the center's direction in these first six months. You've seen the mission statement and basic-goals outline, but I'm interested in having your input, given what you've learned so far."

"Sounds great." Eden powered down her laptop and

retrieved her purse from a side drawer. "Do you have a restaurant in mind?"

"Seed, over on Pacific Avenue. Have you eaten there?" Alex motioned for Eden to precede him out of the office, placing a light hand at the curve of her back as she did so.

"No, never heard of it."

"You'll love it."

They continued chatting as they walked to Alex's shiny black Prius. He hit the unlock button, opened Eden's door, and closed it once she was safely inside. Alex deftly navigated the dense lunch-hour traffic and the ever-present bicyclists, skateboarders, and dog-walking pedestrians. Soon they entered a small and bustling establishment, with a simple decor. They walked up to the counter, reached for menus, and perused the tasty-sounding choices. After a brief conversation with the man behind the counter, they placed their orders.

"You're vegetarian?" Eden asked, once they'd sat down.

"Mostly," Alex answered. "I still eat seafood and, once a year, on my birthday, I'll have one of my favorite Greek dishes—a lamb fricassee, for instance, or a pork-filled moussaka.

Eden looked up in surprise. "How's that work out for you?"

Alex shrugged. "Fine."

"You don't get sick from ingesting meat after three hundred and sixty-four days without it?"

"No, but that's probably because of the seafood in

my system. If Ariel or someone like her ate meat, they'd probably end up in the emergency room."

"You're probably right. I think Ariel has been pretty much vegan for ten years."

"What about you?"

"Four years without meat or fish, but I still eat dairy and soy-based products."

Alex paused as the waiter delivered their orders: an Italian "soysage" panini for Eden and a Thai coconut bowl for Alex. After taking a couple bites of his food, he continued, "What started you on this holistic journey?"

"Finding out that my ex-husband wasn't the only thing giving me indigestion."

"Ha!"

Eden laughed, too, but was a bit embarrassed. She couldn't believe that answer had come from her mouth, had wanted to keep her private life just that—private. "I reached a point in my life where I didn't feel as good as I thought I should. I went to a health fair that just happened to have an entire row dedicated to alternative-health modalities and became intrigued. A counselor at the event told me that while part of my lethargy was due to emotional fatigue, stress, and lack of exercise, she also thought part of it was due to diet. She made some recommendations, I followed them, and here I am."

"Looking fit as a fiddle!"

"I don't know about all that, but I feel good. What's your story?"

"I've always been somewhat of a health nut, always exercised and took supplements. But, like you, the more I delved into the world of holistic medicines and alternative healing, and learned the correlation between diet and good health, the more my food choices changed."

"Did you always want to be a doctor?"

"From the time I was ten years old. I went in for a tonsillectomy, fell in love with the doctor's stethoscope, and got spoiled by the pretty nurses." Alex's green eyes sparkled as he fixed her with a crooked smile. "And here I am."

He's a very attractive man. I wonder why he's not married. Eden thought this and then realized she didn't know his marital status. She wanted to, out of simple curiosity, but felt it an inappropriate question to ask during her first day on the job and first lunch meeting with her boss. Instead she steered the conversation back toward business, asking about Alex's studies in eastern and Chinese medicine, and how the center's community would be expanded to allow members well versed in these teachings. Conversation flowed easily, and the food was delicious. Two hours went by in a flash, and by the time the two returned to the office, they were both excited about the future of the Zen Den.

Eden returned to her office, fired up her laptop, and, based on the conversation she'd just had with Alex, began outlining both her personal goals and goals for the center for the next six months. Her body fairly hummed with satisfaction and joy. She felt *alive.* This was why she'd switched careers and relocated—to change the dynamics of her life. Eden laughed out loud, thinking about just how quickly those changes had come about. Her dream job landed; a fabulous man in her life. What more could a woman want?

* * *

Alex finished a call with a colleague, discussing the latest trends in his former profession, hematology-oncology. He still saw patients a couple times a week, and attended the conferences to stay up to date on the ever-changing technology in traditional western medicine. He wanted to stay current in his chosen field even as he embraced and incorporated his training in eastern healing modalities. He clicked on his computer and saw that Eden had sent him an e-mail. In it was an attachment, a skeletal outline reiterating what they'd discussed at lunch, and a timeline for incorporation of these ideas.

Alex leaned back, pondering his latest hire. He had no doubt that, by far, she was the best of the applicants interviewed—a perfect fit for the center. Job aside, he deduced, she was a very attractive woman. She intrigued him. Alex had dated only a handful of women since his divorce ten years ago, and only one of them had lasted longer than a year. His current liaison was casual, a mutual agreement for stimulating conversation and physical pleasure, without expectation. Alex led a busy life, traveled often, and hadn't met anyone who piqued his interest enough to consider a serious relationship. He also had a rule of not dating anyone in the workplace. But Eden Anderson had changed the game. As he clicked on the Internet to once again Google her name, he came to one undeniable conclusion: rules were made to be broken.

34

Eden exited the shower to the sound of her ringing cell phone. She quickly grabbed a towel and wrapped it around her as she dashed for the bedroom.

"Well, girl, how was it?" Phyllis asked after her daughter had answered the phone.

"I think I've found my dream job," Eden answered. She put her mom on speakerphone and dressed in stretch pants and an oversize T-shirt. "Everyone was friendly and helpful, and I think Dr. K and I will get along well."

"Hmmm, tell me about this doctor."

Eden had purposely avoided telling her mother of her and Jansen's burgeoning relationship. The last thing she needed was her mom, and her busybody friend Kathryn, Jansen's mom, putting their heads together and trying to orchestrate their children's future.

"His name is Alexander Kostopoulos. He's professionally trained as a medical doctor but is now combining his knowledge of alternative medicine, namely eastern traditions, into his healing solutions. He's the resident doctor at the center, even though he maintains patients at one of the local hospitals."

"Is he good-looking?"

"He looks all right."

"How does 'all right' look?" It was obvious that Eden's nonchalance hadn't convinced her mother.

"He's an attractive man, Mom. Around six feet tall, black hair, green eyes. But my interest in him begins and ends at the office. I'm not about to jeopardize what I feel to be an amazing career opportunity with an office fling."

"Oh, so he's available?"

"Mom! This was my first day on the job. I didn't ask the man for his personal résumé."

"Hmph. And I thought I raised you right." The women shared a laugh. "What about Jansen. Have you seen him lately?"

"On Labor Day. Michael didn't tell you he was at the barbecue?" Eden knew Phyllis's propensity for playing ignorant with one child to get info from the other, which was why early on Eden had asked her brother to remain mum on her and Jansen's dating status.

"Oh, yes," Phyllis said, nonplussed. "Now that you mention it, Michael did mention Jansen being there. He didn't say with whom, though. . . ."

"Speaking of dates, how goes it with you and Larry?" Eden felt it was time to get her mother out of her business and back into her own.

"So far, so good. I didn't know how much I'd missed having a man around until I had one around again."

The two women conversed for another few moments.

Eden looked at the clock, surprised that it was already eight o'clock. She was definitely going to have to get back into the groove of an eight-hour-plus workday. "Mom, let's finish catching up this weekend. I haven't eaten dinner and want to make it an early night."

"Dress to impress tomorrow, and learn your boss's marital status. Sometimes what you're looking for is right beneath your nose."

Instead of responding, Eden ended the call. "Love you, Mom. Bye." She immediately dialed Jansen. "Hey, you."

"'Bout time you called."

Eden ignored Jansen's possessive nature and continued to flirt. "You miss me, baby?"

"I'd ask you the same question, except if that were true, you'd have your sexy self over here instead of making me hard over the phone."

"Sounds tasty."

"You know it is. So are you coming here, or am I coming to you?"

Eden noted that Jansen's question assumed that getting together was a foregone conclusion. She couldn't blame him. Aside from the three days he'd spent in Chicago, attending his comrade's funeral and visiting with friends, they'd been together every night.

"Today was my first day at work," she began after a pause. "Considering the fact that I've been a lady of leisure for a month, it was pretty exhausting."

"I know it was your first day, baby. That's why I've got a massage with your name on it, among other things." Jansen's voice was low, sexy, causing squiggles in Eden's stomach and beyond.

"Your offer is extremely tempting, Jansen. But I won't get the eight hours of sleep I need with you beside me. Can I make it up to you some other time?"

"Some other time . . . like tomorrow, right? You know my appetite, baby. It's ferocious."

Memories of said appetite caused Eden to shudder. "Tomorrow, baby. My place, okay?"

Eden hung up the phone, ate a light dinner, and checked her e-mails. At a little after nine she changed into pajamas and climbed into bed, planning to watch a half hour or so of television and call it a night. She'd just settled into an episode of HGTV's *House Hunters* when her cell phone rang. She took a look at the number. It wasn't one she recognized. After a seconds-long debate about whether to answer, she accepted the call.

"Eden, it's Alex."

"Dr. K?"

"Forgive my calling after hours, but I have some quick thoughts on the outline you sent. Do you have a minute?"

"Sure." Eden listened to the easy lilt of his European accent, remembered the crooked smile and deep green eyes, and heard her mother's words echo in her head. . . . *Learn your boss's marital status. Sometimes what you're looking for is right beneath your nose.*

35

Eden stood inside her walk-in closet and pondered her options. The Zen Den's dress was decidedly casual, yet, as director of the facility, Eden chose to maintain a somewhat professional appearance. Yesterday she'd worn a light blue, cotton pantsuit paired with low heels. Today she vacillated between a tan, wide-legged pantsuit and a silk wrap dress. She decided on the latter, wore her hair down and lightly turned under, and opted for open-toed sandals instead of pumps. She sprayed on a light, floral cologne, grabbed her brief-case and laptop, and was out the door. Her official hours were nine to five, but old habits died hard. When working on the Hill, Eden routinely arrived a half hour or more early for work. She pulled into the parking space leased by the Zen Den at 8:35.

A shiny black Prius pulled up right beside her SUV. Alex emerged from the vehicle, looking more like a *GQ* model than an MD. Instead of what Eden assumed were trademark black jeans, today he wore a casual black suit, the accompanying stark white shirt open at the collar, revealing olive skin deeply tanned by the sun. The dark aviator sunglasses and five-o'clock shadow on his chin gave him a roguish air. *He doesn't come close to Jansen,* Eden mused as he walked to open her car door. *But he does look good.*

"Thank you and good morning," Eden said, easing out of her car.

"An early bird, I see," Alex answered. "Just like me."

"This isn't something you should get used to, necessarily. But it's nice to feel on top of things while getting my feet wet."

I'd like to get on top of you . . . and get wet. "You look nice today, Eden. I like your hair down."

"Yes, well, don't get used to this either, Dr. K. The ponytail/bun thing is more my style."

"Please, call me Alex." He unlocked the main door and then held it while Eden entered. "Are you a coffee or tea person?"

"Neither this morning. I had a protein smoothie before leaving home. But when I need a lift, I normally reach for green or chai tea."

"I love Starbucks's soy chai lattes."

"Me, too! And what about the new soy strawberry frappes?"

The two conversed easily until they reached the kitchen. Alex stepped inside, and Eden continued to her office. A few moments later, Alex knocked on her door. They spent the next half hour finishing up the fifteen-minute conversation from the previous night and sharing marketing strategies that would appeal to both mainstream and avante-garde audiences. Later Eden wouldn't remember how the fact that Alex was divorced, with a seventy-five-year-old mother whom he visited regularly in his native Greece, came up. When Ariel arrived, talk of favorite eateries led to the three of them deciding to dine at RFD. At the end of the day, when Alex suggested a glass of wine at Chaya, it seemed a logical conclusion to the end of a productive day.

There was the old saying "Time flies when you're having fun" and such was the case with Eden. She only became aware that it was seven-thirty PM, almost three hours past quitting time, when, amid a peal of laughter, she answered her phone. "Hello?"

"Well, it sounds like somebody is having a good time."

Oh, shoot. "Jansen, where are you?"

"Where I said I'd be about now. In front of your house." Pause. "Where are you?"

"On my way. Just leaving work. See you in ten minutes."

36

As she headed toward Santa Monica, Eden saw the thundercloud brewing beyond the mountains. It bore Jansen's face. She'd assumed he would phone her when he was on his way over. But when it came to men, experience should have taught her what happened when one assumed. Things ended badly.

I'm not going to participate in his attitude, she silently affirmed. *Just do you, Eden. Peace and love. Just do you.* She saw Jansen's truck as soon as she pulled up to her condo, waved, and continued to the parking lot. She exited her car, came around to the front to let him in, and greeted him with a hug. "Sorry I'm late, baby. Time got away from me."

Jansen hugged her and then stepped away, doing a slow perusal from head to toe. "You look nice," he said, his eyes narrowed, mind churning. "Real nice."

"Thank you." Eden's answer was as light as her step as she turned and walked toward the stairs.

"Smell good, too," Jansen observed, along with the

sway of Eden's booty-licious as she mounted the stairs in front of him.

Eden turned and gave him a killer smile. "All for you, baby."

They reached her condo and went inside. Eden sat down her computer and briefcase and then turned to face Jansen. "You look good, too," she whispered before raising up on her tiptoes and planting a juicy kiss on his succulent lips. When she would have ended it, he wrapped his arms around her and deepened the exchange. His fingers became lost in her hair, his free hand searching for bare flesh but instead coming in contact with soft silk. He eased his tongue out of her mouth, placed whispery kisses along her cheek and jawline, and then reached for her hand and walked them to the couch. "So . . . tell me about this job, love."

Eden removed her shoes, plopped on the couch, and placed her feet underneath her. Her eyes sparkled with unabashed excitement as she leaned into Jansen's embrace. "Jansen, I think I'm going to *love* this job."

"That's good."

Eden shared the basics of what her job entailed, as well as some of the characters who made up the Zen Den. "Instead of calling us staff, they refer to us as 'community members,'" Eden said, using air quotes for emphasis. "Only my second day there, and it already feels like family. I can see myself growing with this company, baby. I submitted a very rough outline of my plans for the center to Alex, and he is just as excited as I am."

Jansen had been idly rubbing Eden's arm, but at

the mention of another man, his movement stopped. "Who's Alex?"

Don't go there with him, Eden. Remember, peace and love. "Alex Kostopoulos, my boss, and the center's resident physician."

"Uh-huh. Is he the reason you dressed so sexy for your nine-to-five, and why you forgot there was another man waiting for you to come home?"

Eden sat straight and put distance between them. "Jansen, don't do this. Dr. K is my boss—"

"Oh, so now he's Dr. K, when a second ago he was Alex. Y'all on a first-name basis already?"

"I am not going down this road with you." Eden stood and walked out of the living room and into her bedroom.

"Why?" Jansen asked, following. "Is it because you've started down the road with somebody else?"

"Can you hear yourself?" In spite of her resolve to stay calm and peaceful, she felt her heartbeat increasing, her voice rising. "Obviously not, because if you could, you'd realize how stupid you sound."

Jansen's volume rose as well. "Oh, so one day in the presence of the good doctor, and the policeman is stupid. Is that how it goes down?"

In seconds, calm and peaceful had a fight with pissed off, and lost. "Are you kidding me? Did you really say what I just heard?" Eden headed for the closet. "You're a piece of work, Jansen McKnight," she continued from inside it, peeling off her dress and taking off her jewelry. "If all you came over here to do was piss me off, mission accomplished. I don't need—no, I won't *stand* for this drama in my life." She marched out of her closet clad in panties and bra. "I don't know if this possessiveness is an alpha male or Scorpio or McKnight attribute, but it isn't cute. When I'm with someone, it's one at a time. I'm in a work environment where there are men. I interact with them, go to lunch with them, and, yes, share a glass of wine with them after work. I really like this job and plan to keep it. So if you have a problem with anything I just said, let's end this now and go our separate ways. I don't have the time or patience for your bullshit, Jansen McKnight." Eden ended her tirade winded, fists clenched, chest heaving.

Jansen had endured this verbal assault with legs spread, arms crossed. Now he moved toward her with the stealth of a panther. "Oh, no?" he asked, his voice a deadly whisper. His eyes had darkened to an eerie black, and were it possible for his shoulders to become broader, chest to become wider, and legs to become longer . . . they had done so. Eden took a step back as he continued his approach, but he stayed her with a sure, strong hand. "So you don't have time for my bullshit, huh? Well, do you have time for this?"

With a singular movement, Jansen both closed the two feet between them and wrapped her in his arms. His mouth came down on hers: hard, heavy, demanding, relentless. Eden's impulse was to fight him, and she briefly tried to wriggle out of his arms. But then instinct took over—noted the hardness of his muscled chest, the sinewy strength of his toned biceps, the hardening shaft announcing its intent. Jansen's hands lowered, sculpted themselves to her cheeks, and pressed her firmly against him. Her nipples pebbled with excitement, the familiar tingling spreading from her core to the apex at her thighs.

"Jansen." The whispered name held urgency and understanding.

"Baby," he answered, his hands roaming over as much flesh as they could reach. He slipped fingers inside her lacy thong, found her treasure, rubbed her to wetness. "This is mine, girl. Anybody out there trying to get at it . . ." Jansen dropped to his knees and pressed his face into the furnace of her desire. His tongue was rough and strong, the fabric between it and its goal causing a delicious friction.

"Mmmm," Eden breathed but could say no more.

Still on his knees, Jansen backed her up, pinned her against the wall. He spread her legs and reclaimed the territory his mouth had known just seconds before. Eden's thighs trembled; she grabbed on to Jansen's shoulders for support. He placed a strong hand under her thigh and lifted her leg. She felt vulnerable, totally exposed, and excited beyond belief. Jansen nipped and kissed the insides of her thighs before moving aside the lace with his tongue. Eden emitted a shout when his soft, wet oral instrument made contact with her budding flower. Remnants of Kory's song ran through Eden's mind as she succumbed to the mind-numbing pleasure of Jansen's magical tongue on her pulsating paradise. He licked, sucked, kissed, tugged. She went crazy, stroke by stroke. Just as she felt the rumblings of a cataclysmic climax, Jansen stopped. Eden's legs buckled, and she slid to the floor.

Jansen reached into his shorts pocket and then hurriedly shed both them and the white tee he wore, sans underwear. His sword stood at attention, ready for battle. He handed the condom to Eden. "Put it on," he quietly commanded.

Eden complied. In a moment of sheer wantonness, she ripped the thin rubber from its plastic encasement and edged it up his shaft with her mouth. Jansen grabbed the back of her head, moaning her name over and again. The moment she'd shielded him completely, he dropped down, covered her, and took her right there on the bedroom floor. It was raw and nasty and sexy and beautiful—Jansen and Eden dancing the dance to the song they knew best, the tune they grooved to most perfectly. For twenty, thirty minutes, they remained lost in its melody. But every song has an ending, and theirs was no different. Eden cried out her release. Jansen growled his agreement. They lay sweaty and spent atop the Persian rug that covered the area around Eden's bed, the silence punctuated only by their breathing.

Eden prepared to rise, but Jansen stopped her. "I couldn't wait to be here, feel you in my arms."

"I'm uncomfortable, Jansen," Eden answered. *And it has nothing to do with our being on the floor.*

"Oh, I'm sorry, baby." Jansen hurriedly rose, bringing Eden with him. Again he reached to place his arms around her.

"Baby, let me use the bathroom. I'll be right back."

Eden hurried into the room and closed the door. She ran cold water, splashed her face, and looked in the mirror. A troubled expression looked back at her. As always, Jansen had loved her ferociously and tenderly at the same time. She'd experienced multiple orgasms, screaming, so intense was the pleasure. *Then what is wrong, Eden?* She gazed at her reflection. *Why don't you feel good now?*

As Eden soaped her towel and washed herself, the answers came. And then one final question. *What are you going to do about it?*

37

"Jansen, we need to talk." Eden had walked out of the bathroom, gone straight to the closet, and donned her favorite fluffy cotton robe before she spoke. Now she stood at the foot of the bed, looking down on the perfection that lounged across her bed in black boxers.

"Come here, baby," Jansen whispered.

"I prefer the living room." Eden walked out without waiting for an answer. She went into the kitchen, put on water for tea, and tried to calm her suddenly jittery nerves. She knew where this reaction was coming from and was determined to push past the fear. She took a breath, squared her shoulders, and walked into the living room, or lion's den, depending on one's point of view.

Jansen eyed her as she walked in. He sat stone-faced, arms crossed, his black T-shirt and jeans adding to his dark countenance. Eden opted for the chair instead of the couch where he sat. She sat down, looked at him, looked at the floral arrangement on her side table. For a while, neither spoke.

"What's wrong with you?" Jansen finally asked.

"I . . . need to share some things with you. How I'm feeling."

"About what?"

"Jansen, please don't get defensive. As simple as sharing one's thoughts may seem, this isn't easy for me. But if we're going to be together, I've got to do it."

"If? What's this about, Eden?" Jansen's eyes narrowed. "Does it have anything to do with this Alex dude you mentioned earlier?"

"Why would you think that? What I'm sharing involves only the people in this room."

"Oh, really? Well, excuse me if I draw a line between your hanging out with this boss you just met and our suddenly having problems." Jansen's body was taut, his look intense.

The discomfort that Eden had felt in the bathroom returned. *I can't do this.* "Jansen, I . . ." A whistling tea kettle interrupted her. "Would you like a cup of tea?"

Jansen shook his head. "No, I'm cool." His demeanor suggested he was anything but.

Eden went into the kitchen and used her nightly ritual to try to relax. She placed the loose-leaf tea into the infuser, sat the mesh holder into the ceramic teapot that was a gift from her mother, and poured in the water. After slicing a lemon and pouring a liberal amount of honey into a mug, she placed it and the teapot on a tray and walked back into the living room.

You could cut the tension with a knife. Eden ignored it, continued her deep breathing and her ritual. She placed two lemon slices in the mug. As she swirled the infuser, a citrusy lavender aroma reached her nostrils.

She inhaled deeply, poured the tea into her mug, and took a tentative sip. Jansen watched her every moment. Silent. Waiting.

Eden took another sip before placing the mug on the table beside her. "Remember how you and Michael used to protect me from the bullies? How I'd ask the teacher if I could leave class early, rather than risk meeting someone who'd threatened to fight me after school? I never liked confrontation, Jansen, ran from it as much as I could." She looked at him as she took another sip of tea. His face was still stony, but he'd uncrossed his arms.

"While married, I did the same thing, though not at first. When we first got married, Gregg and I discussed things, gave our points of view, and came to a mutual agreement—even if that was an agreement to disagree. But like I told you before, Gregg changed. Or maybe he became more of who he really was, who knows? But the bottom line is, he stopped caring about how I felt or what I had to say. Voicing my opinion became the sure precursor for an argument, or worse. One of the things I've learned on this spiritual journey back to myself is that I have to live in my truth, no matter what. I have to share my feelings with those who matter to me." Eden stopped, met Jansen's gaze.

Jansen broke the stare, stood, and walked to the window. He stood there only seconds, but to Eden, it felt as if an hour went by. When he turned around, both his demeanor and voice were subdued. "So who am I reminding you of right now? Your monster husband, or the school bully?"

"What you're reminding me of is how important it

is to communicate calmly, rationally, the way we're doing right now. You're nothing like my ex-husband, Jansen, and you've either bullied or pestered me half my life, so that's nothing new." Eden offered a soft smile. Jansen caught it and shared one of his own.

"You're possessive by nature, and a part of me likes that. It makes me feel needed, protected even. But I can also see where it could cause problems. I haven't been on the job a week, and already you're questioning me about my boss. Your accusatory tone both earlier and moments ago doesn't make me feel good. If every interaction I have with another male is questioned, trust is not at the foundation of our love."

"So you love me."

Pause. One second, two. "Yes, Jansen. I do."

"Come here." He reached for Eden's hand, and this time she took it. He led them back over to the couch. He sat down, and she sat down close to him, facing him. Jansen continued to hold her hand as he looked at her. Then he looked away.

"What is it, baby? What are you thinking?"

Pause. Three seconds, four. "I'm not one for much talking. With me, action speaks louder than words."

"Brooding, deliberate, not one for showing your emotions. . . ."

Jansen raised a brow in Eden's direction.

"Traits of a Scorpio."

"Baby, you'd have to read more than a zodiac sign to figure me out."

"No doubt. But you do have many of its characteristics, especially the good ones."

Jansen's skepticism remained, but now interest accompanied it. "What are those?"

"Loyal, intelligent, passionate to the *extreme!*"

Jansen performed a sideways once-over and drawled, "I take it that's not a problem."

Eden punched him playfully. "You take correctly." A moment of companionable silence passed between them. Eden breathed slow, her heartbeat steady. She felt her hand in Jansen's and imagined many evenings like this.

"You're right about me being loyal," Jansen finally said. "Which is probably why I'm possessive, if that's what you want to call it. Maybe I'm old-fashioned, too, because when I'm with a woman, she belongs to me— nobody else. And I'm hers." Jansen looked fully at Eden. "That's just how it is."

Many comments warred for dominance in Eden's mind: the fact that women were people, not possessions. That she was almost twenty years past legally grown, and her father's name wasn't Jansen. That loyalty had obviously gone on vacation when he'd cheated on his ex-wife. But she chose to choose her battles in order to win the war. She loved Jansen and wanted to be with him. She believed in her heart that possessive, demanding proclivities aside . . . he was a good man. Staying focused on the goal of this conversation, mutual understanding, she asked, "What about trust?"

"What about it?"

"Do you trust me, Jansen?"

Pause. Five seconds, ten, twenty . . .

"Well, do you?"

"Men aren't so different from women, you know. We don't want to get hurt either."

"I remember a conversation where you told me you'd always keep it one hundred with me. . . ."

"I believe the exact phrase is one hun-ned."

"However it's said, it meant you'll be truthful with me. And I'll do the same. I've never been one to date around or play the field, Jansen. I'm not interested in starting now."

"Good." Jansen reached for her. "Now can we stop talking and let our bodies conversate?"

Eden didn't resist when he placed his arm around her, tilted her chin, and engaged them in a deep, languid kiss. When he moved aside her terry-cloth robe and gently tweaked her nipple, she welcomed the move. Jansen was like a drug her body needed on a regular basis. She'd always enjoyed intercourse, but with Jansen, she couldn't get enough. So when he undid the belt and placed his hand between her legs, she opened to welcome him. She skimmed the band on his shorts, reached her hand inside, and found hard, throbbing flesh. *Mine,* she thought with mild surprise. And then she thought of something else—the other topic she'd planned to discuss with him. But when he eased off the couch and down on his knees, pulling her forward while spreading her wide and then dipping his head to her nether lips, Eden's mind zeroed in on one thing: pleasure. There would be time later for further discussion. Right now Jansen's tongue was talking to her, and she was thoroughly enjoying the conversation.

38

The rest of the week passed smoothly. Eden planned to personally try all the preventative and healing methods offered at the center so that in addition to her administrative acclimation, she'd experience Reiki, hypnotherapy, and the best massage she'd ever had. After a month off, Eden felt good being back at work and easily settled into her workday routine. She also remembered how much she looked forward to Fridays, no matter where she was employed. Even though her Capitol Hill job regularly called for working on weekends, Saturday and Sunday were still her favorite days of the week.

Alex tapped on Eden's open door. "Big plans for the weekend?" he asked before stepping inside.

"Spending time with family, friends. You?"

Alex shrugged. "The usual, I guess. Shoot a couple rounds, get some sun." All week Alex had pondered how best to ask the question that most interested him. Finally he could take it no longer and decided to ask outright. "Are you married, Eden?"

All week, Eden had anticipated the question and didn't hesitate in her answer. He'd acted professionally, but Eden wanted Alex and everyone else to make no mistake about her status. "I'm in a committed relationship."

Alex nodded. "Lucky guy. What does he do?"

This time, there was a slight pause. "He's a police officer."

Alex didn't try to hide his surprise. He walked over to Eden's desk and sat down in one of the two chairs that faced her. "A cop? As in crime-chasing, gun-toting officer of the law?"

Eden nodded.

"Forgive my saying so, but that is probably the last profession I'd guess for your partner."

"I understand." Eden further established her boundary by adding, "Jansen is a special man. I'm the lucky one."

"I look forward to meeting him," Alex smoothly replied. She'd said committed relationship, not marriage. In Alex's mind, that simply meant she was with the best one until the better one came along. On one hand, Alex knew he was playing with fire, that he'd be better off focusing on someone other than a "committed coworker." On the other hand, there was very little that this only son from a well-to-do Greek family desired and didn't get. He'd wanted to become a doctor. It had happened. He'd wanted to practice in the States. It had happened. And now he wanted Eden Anderson. As far as Alex was concerned, it was only a matter of time.

* * *

Rivulets of hot, sudsy water poured over Eden's shoulders and down her back. Knowing the consequences but being unable to resist, she'd stuck her head under the nozzle and allowed the pulsating stream to massage her scalp and neck. She thought the master bath one of the best rooms in Jansen's house. Comparatively, Jansen undoubtedly had the better, more comfortable home. Eden thought if only he'd get rid of his mini arsenal, it would be a perfect abode. His gun collection was the reason she'd missed luxuriating in this steel and marble paradise. She'd been here only once since the weapons discovery, had used whatever excuse necessary to get him to come to her place. She knew she'd have to have the conversation one day. But not now. Not now when things were magical, when her declaration of love had brought out an even more attentive, more passionate officer who was a gentleman.

"Come on, woman!" Jansen commanded from just outside the shower stall. "We need to leave in less than an hour."

"Almost done." Eden rinsed the conditioner from her hair, turned off the water, and stepped out of the shower. She wrapped the nearest towel around her wet hair. Before she could take two steps to retrieve one for her body, she was in Jansen's arms. "Jansen, we've got to hurry, remember?"

"Baby, when I see you like this, all clean and wet, I forget about everything else."

Eden shook her head as she wiggled free from his embrace. She hadn't known many men, and of the ones she had, she'd never met anyone who compared to

Jansen McKnight. He'd come over to her place every night that week, and still he'd ravished her as soon as she'd stepped in the door. Something about being in his arms stoked her flames of desire to heights heretofore unknown. There'd been no resistance as he'd undressed her in the living room before placing her on the dining room table and treating her as his meal. They'd ended up in the kitchen, where things had happened with a counter, a footstool, and a jar of chocolate syrup that then led to the shower, hair washing and, if she'd had time, a nap.

Ninety minutes later, Jansen and Eden strolled into the Greek, an intimate outdoor amphitheater nestled in the tree-covered hills of Griffith Park. For them, the night was perfect, dressed as they were in lightweight sweaters, jackets, and jeans. Jansen enfolded Eden's hand in his as they navigated the almost six thousand patrons waiting to groove to the sounds of Maxwell, Anthony Hamilton, Jill Scott, and Erykah Badu.

"Baby, do you want us to get our seats and then come back for the food basket?" They'd ordered "The Superstar," which consisted of breads, cheeses, a Greek salad, for Jansen a peppercorn top sirloin steak, and for Eden a bottle of cabernet sauvignon. "Those sandals look sexy as hell, but I don't want you to be uncomfortable"

"Oooo, you are so sweet to ask, but no, these shoes are comfortable, I don't mind standing."

Jansen shook his head. "Women."

Eden laughed. "Men." She leaned over and kissed him on the cheek. He put an arm around her, pulled her close, and kissed her for real.

"Jansen!" A voice from much too close to either Jansen or Eden came between their lips.

Jansen pulled back and looked around, the scowl evident even in subdued lighting.

An attractive woman dressed in a skintight animal-print mini, heels two inches higher than Eden's and a weave long enough to have helped an Indian woman pay off her house, stepped up to Jansen. Grabbing his arm, she exclaimed, "I thought that was you!" She wedged herself in front of Eden and proceeded to engage Jansen in an intimate hug.

Or tried to. Jansen immediately stepped back, pulled her arms from around his neck, and reached for Eden. He anchored her to his side, his expression as stern as it was civil. "Tami," he said with a restraint that Eden couldn't help but admire. "This is my heart, Eden Anderson."

Jansen's "heart" soared with a lot of admiration and a little pride. If this was what it felt like to be possessed, Eden was ready to rethink her position. She couldn't help but compare him to Gregg, her ex-husband. In the same situation, Gregg would have acted as if Eden weren't there, would have flirted shamelessly with the other woman and may even not have been above walking off to have Eden fend for herself. *When I'm with a woman, she belongs to me . . . and I'm hers. That's just how it is.* It felt good not to have to guess where one stood with her man. Eden leaned into Jansen's protective, supportive embrace and extended her hand. "Nice to meet you. Tami, correct?"

Tami looked at Eden as if she wore doo-doo on her face instead of a smile. Woman-to-woman telepathy told Eden everything she needed to know, including the fact that this woman should have gotten an Oscar for the grin she tried to maintain through her limp-as-a-noodle handshake. "Nice to meet you, Esther."

"Eden," Jansen corrected. "As in, the beautiful garden."

"Oh, how quaint," Tami responded. She turned to Jansen, and her smile became authentic. She tossed her lengthy mane, licked what Eden had to admit were perfect lips set in flawless skin, and in a voice as sexy as Marilyn Monroe and Pam Grier combined asked for a private moment of Jansen's time.

"I don't think so," he responded without hesitation. "Anything you want to say to me, you can say in front of her. There are no secrets between us."

"Fine," Tami spat, her cool facade slipping just a notch. "I see that your attention is temporarily diverted, but I just wanted you to know that all your things are still at my house waiting . . . and so am I."

Jansen pulled Eden even closer to him. Another step, and she would have been standing on his feet instead of beside them! He turned to face her. "Eden, I dated Tami before you arrived. Unlike the committed relationship that we share, Tami and I had a nonexclusive relationship for about three months, during which time I visited her at her house because I rarely let women come to mine. I may have left some clothes there, probably some DVDs, toiletries, or whatever." He looked from Eden to Tami and continued. "There is nothing I left at your house that I want, Tami. Nothing."

Tami's skin reddened under the assault, but she regained her cool. "Hmph. Baby, I was there. I know what we have, and I know there is no other woman on this planet who can make you feel the way I do."

"You're right," Jansen countered. Eden's heart sank. To think that someone else had enjoyed the pleasures to which she was now addicted brought almost tangible pain. Jansen continued. "But there's someone who makes me feel like I've never felt before, feel things in ways I never thought I could. And you're looking at her." Eden's heart soared.

They retrieved their basket, found their seats, uncorked the wine, and toasted the evening. Neither mentioned Tami. It was as if the nasty exchange had never occurred. Jill sang about love in E-flat, Erykah viewed life from a window seat, and Maxwell cried a fistful of tears. And something happened with Jansen and Eden. Their love deepened, expanded, took off on pretty wings. They enjoyed the concert immensely, but the music their bodies later played was what they loved the most.

39

"Look, Mike. I'm not trying to say Kobe ain't a bad baller, I'm just saying LeBron is more of the total package, an all-around player!" Jansen argued passionately, hand gestures further emphasizing his point.

"Kobe is *full* of game," Michael countered. "He's going to go down as one of the greatest players of all time!"

"And LeBron isn't? If you believe that, I've got some oceanfront land in Mississippi to sell you."

Eden and Bridgett looked at each other, their unspoken message one of "this argument will never end unless we end it." Eden knew her brother, and she knew Jansen was just as stubborn as Michael. Bridgett probably knew Michael even better than Eden. They let the men ramble for another moment or so, discussing how this Cheesecake Factory in Marina del Rey was their favorite and how the insanely divine weather and ocean views made southern California worth its earthquakes, traffic, and high-priced real estate.

Finally Bridgett had had enough and stepped in to change the verbal tide. "Speaking of land in Mississippi . . ." she began. "Oh, hell, there's no way I can use that for a segue. But I do want to change the subject."

For a moment, no one spoke. Eden looked at Bridgett. Michael looked at Eden. Jansen looked at Michael. Bridgett crossed her arms and smiled.

"The floor is obviously yours," Jansen said sarcastically, rocking back in his chair. "Are you going to tell us or what?"

"Yes, big brother," Eden added, looking from Michael to Bridgett and back. "What's the news?"

Michael shrugged. "A little change in lifestyle. Nothing too serious."

Bridgett swatted him. "Well, some things are going to happen sooner rather than later," she countered. "Life keeps moving—it's up to us to keep up with it."

Jansen sat up as the waitress brought their orders. When she left, he continued. "Okay, did I miss some part of this conversation, Bridgett, or did you start in the middle?"

Bridgett laughed. "I may have started in the middle. I just knew I had to start somewhere, or we'd be in a basketball Twilight Zone for the rest of the afternoon."

"So what's up, Mike?" Jansen repeated. "You have something to tell us, or what?"

Eden stared aghast at the couple and for the first time noticed the twinkle in both their eyes. *OMG, Big Brother has been hooked. He's head over heels in love with Bridgett Chambers!*

After a beat, in which Michael and Bridgett swapped goo-goo-eyed expressions, Jansen and Eden took sips from their drinks, and even the seagulls waited for an explanation, Eden quietly exploded. "Well, out with it already. What the heck is going on?"

"Well," Bridgett said coyly, "I can show you better than I can tell you." She held out her left hand and proudly showed off the diamond ring sparkling from her third finger.

Eden gasped. "Michael! You're getting married?"

Jansen clapped his hands together. "Big Mike! You finally stepped up to the plate. Congratulations, man."

Eden grasped Bridgett's hand for a closer examination of the ring. "You done good, bro," she announced. "Congratulations. I'm really happy for you guys."

Jansen motioned to their waitress. "This calls for a toast. Lunch is on me, as well as the celebratory bottle of bubbly!" After the waitress came over and stated the options, Jansen asked, "Bridgett, Mike will drink anything. So would you like the Veuve Clicquot or the Moët?"

"Actually," Bridgett said, her demeanor once again uncharacteristically shy. "I think I'll have cranberry juice or sparkling water."

"What? You've just announced some of the biggest news of your life, and you're going to go Ocean Spray on us?" Jansen shook his head decisively. "I don't think so."

Eden placed a hand on Jansen's arm. She looked from Bridgett to her brother and then back again. "Wait a minute. Is there a second part to this announcement?"

A subtle pride emanated from Michael as he answered. "I'll put it to you this way, weed: Mama's about to get that grandbaby she's been yakking about."

The conversation flowed from bachelor/bachelorette parties to possible wedding locations and baby names. The four stayed at the restaurant for almost two hours, leaving only because a phone call reminded Michael he was due in London soon, and he and Bridgett hadn't started to pack.

As they drove back to Gardena, Jansen was quiet, his mood subdued. Eden now knew this was part of his personality trait, but when he reached over for her hand, still silent, this conversational Libra could stand the mystery not one minute longer.

"What is it, baby? What are you thinking?"

"Why are you always asking me that?"

"Because it's the only way I'll know, and half the time even the direct approach yields no result."

Jansen smiled, gave her hand a squeeze, and kept driving.

Eden looked at him a moment and then out the window. How was it that she had fallen in love with a man who preferred quiet contemplation when she could talk a blue streak to the moon and back! They continued the journey, almost twenty minutes, in silence.

When they reached Jansen's home, he turned off the engine and looked at her. "So you want to know what's on my mind?"

He was looking at her with such intensity that suddenly Eden wasn't sure whether she wanted to know. Curiosity won out. "Yes, Jansen, I want to know."

"I'm thinking we should cancel our plans for the movies and spend the rest of the night trying to make a baby."

40

The brooder had rendered the talker speechless. Eden opened her mouth, but for the life of her not a word would come out.

Jansen fixed her with a smoldering look that made her shudder, walked to her side of the car, and helped her out.

Still, from Eden, no words.

They walked to the front door. Jansen unlocked it, let them in, closed the door behind them, and walked into the living room. Eden followed. Quiet. For the first time she understood the phrase "the cat's got her tongue." Except, in this case, instead of a cat, it was a baby-making idea that had her mute.

Eden sat on the couch while Jansen walked into his office. She could hear him fumbling around and clicking computer keys as he checked e-mail messages. He began to whistle Maxwell's "Pretty Wings." And words still continued to elude Eden's mind, much less her speech.

After five minutes or so, Jansen returned to the

couch. "What are you thinking, baby?" he mimicked, taking Eden into his arms, laying a sheet of paper he'd brought out with him to the side.

She smiled, heart pounding with a sudden rush of love for this passionate, sensitive alpha male. "Why are you asking me that?" she whispered, parroting his earlier comment.

"Because . . . that's the only way I'll know." His tone was playful, yet Eden beheld the sincerity in his eyes, his need for an answer and more.

"Well . . . I can tell you that while I'm open to the idea of babies, I'm not ready to make one tonight. But I am very interested in practicing our techniques so that if we do decide to cocreate a human being, we'll get it right."

"I took an AIDS test," he murmured into her hair.

Eden pulled back. "What? Why?"

Jansen reached for the paper that announced his negative results. "Because I want to love you with nothing between us. I want to feel all of you and want you to feel all of me."

Eden couldn't help but be amazed that just when she thought she knew the man beside her, he flipped the script to a new, wonderful page.

"Have you been tested since your last partner?" Jansen asked.

Eden nodded. "Last year during my annual gynecological exam."

"Eden, as long as we're together, I'll be faithful to you. Do you trust me?"

Eden nodded against his chest. "Yes, but we still have to practice safe sex, Jansen. I'm not on the pill."

Jansen placed soft kisses against her temple. "I'll be careful."

"I think that's what my daddy told my mama the night I was conceived."

"Ha!" Jansen's tone turned serious. "Would having my baby be so bad?"

"I want children." Eden pondered the question for several seconds. Her heartbeat increased as she continued. "But only if I'm married to their father."

Once again, the brooder brooded. They stayed that way, cuddling, silent, for a long time.

Finally, Jansen pulled away and stood. "Come on, little garden," he said, reaching out his hand to her. "Let's go practice."

41

Monday morning came, and Eden was still floating on the cloud she and Jansen had created. They'd spent the rest of Saturday night and all day Sunday talking . . . and practicing. They'd discussed Tami, Jansen's ex-wife Yolanda, and even Chandra Brockman. Eden opened up more about Gregg—the first time he hit her, and what happened when she left. It was while driving home at 6:30 the next morning that Eden happened upon a revelation: this was the first time she'd truly been in love. The other times, including those spent married to Gregg, had only been warm-ups to this moment. Until she'd experienced Jansen's deep, all-consuming love, Eden was unaware that there were sheltered parts of her heart that had never seen the light of day, that she'd never felt comfortable enough to open up and allow others entry. But she had on Saturday night. And all day Sunday. She thought that as long as she was with Jansen, which she hoped was forever, she'd remain open, to allow their love unlimited access.

She'd been stuck on "Pretty Wings" since the concert and hummed the tune as she entered the building.

"Well, looks like somebody had a good weekend." Alex was standing by the coffeepot when Eden entered the kitchen.

"I did," Eden replied. "How was yours?"

"Great. The weather was gorgeous—took a few friends out on the boat."

"Sounds like fun."

"What I love most about LA is living on the beach." Eden reached for her perfectly doctored tea and was almost to the door before Alex stopped her. "Eden, did you check your e-mails this weekend?"

"Negative, doctor. I didn't even turn on my computer."

Alex chuckled. "Good for you. I sent a note on Saturday about a lunch meeting today. You'll be meeting the coordinator of next month's mini health fair."

"What time?"

"Twelve-thirty. You can ride with me if you want."

"Thanks, but I have to run an errand. I'll meet you there."

"No worries." Alex told Eden where they were meeting, and Eden headed to her office.

The morning passed quickly, and at half past noon, Eden pulled up to the restaurant where she, Alex, and the coordinator were meeting. She quickly checked her makeup, grabbed her briefcase, and headed inside.

Once inside the restaurant, Eden spotted Alex right away. He'd garnered a corner booth and immediately waved her over.

"You know all the cool veggie spots," Eden said once she'd sat down.

"It's the company I keep," Alex replied. "Christina, the coordinator for the health fair, is also vegetarian. This was her choice."

A waiter came over to take their orders. Alex explained that they were waiting for a third person. Just then an attractive brunette walked to their table. "Sorry I'm late," she said as Alex stood and she kissed first one cheek and then the other. She turned to Eden. "Hello, I'm Christina. I've heard wonderful things about you."

"They're all true," Eden said, laughing. She held out her hand. Christina shook it but also leaned over and offered Eden the same two-cheek greeting.

"I'm famished," Christina said. She immediately picked up a menu. The three shared small talk until the waitress came over and took their orders.

"I'm very excited about this fair," Eden said to Christina. "How did you get involved?"

"I met Alex several years ago, when my sister was a patient. We became friends, and when he accepted the position at the center, I knew I wanted to help spread the word not only about the facility but about the idea of living holistically. By inviting the community in to experience free samples, if you will, of what we offer, we not only educate attendees about how to live healthy but hopefully gain new clients as well."

"Christina is being modest," Alex said. "Before retiring, she was one of London's preeminent cardiologists."

Eden's eyes widened. "You're a doctor?"

"Yes, though I no longer practice. I used to spend seventy, eighty hours a week on the job. After my dad died, and my sister almost did, I realized life is too short not to spend it doing what one wanted. I still consult and try to educate the public with events like this one."

The three discussed the health fair during most of the meal before it veered more toward the lives of those at the table. Christina asked Eden about life in Washington, and Eden learned about Christina's career in London.

"I haven't traveled through Europe much," Eden said after Christina had commented on England's lush countryside. "But London is one of my favorite cities."

"Have you visited Greece?" Christina asked.

"No, but because that is my boss's birthplace, maybe I should schedule a visit."

"You absolutely should visit my country," Alex said. "I'll be your personal tour guide."

"You should take him up on that, Eden. I've had that experience and, trust me, it's amazing." Christina winked at Alex before leaning over to kiss him, this time on the mouth.

Oh, so it's like that? Eden remembered her conversation with Ariel about how naturally flirty was the doctor and how rumor had him being quite the ladies' man.

"He's revered in his country, especially in Parieus. There he is a superstar."

"I'd say it's a smart group of people who recognize the importance of doctors."

"Ha! His skill with a scalpel is only part of the allure. In addition to being extremely handsome, I'm sure you know that Dr. Alex Kostopoulos is a very smart man."

"I think intellect follows anyone with an MD behind their name."

"Yes, but not many see those initials before they turn twenty-five."

"What?"

"Oh, come now, Christina."

"Look who's being modest now." Christina's voice took on a sultry tone. "Alex has a one-forty IQ, was one of the youngest to ever graduate Stanford University, and donates a third of his salary to relief efforts throughout Europe. He has a very big heart . . . among other things."

Eden and Christina laughed heartily at Alex's obvious embarrassment. She liked this feisty woman, obviously brainy but equally down-to-earth. It also relaxed her knowing that Alex's amorous attention was elsewhere. *Maybe Ariel is right. Maybe I have read too much into Alex's statements.* He was a big flirt and, for now, involved with at least one person of which Eden was aware.

"It was such a pleasure to meet you," Eden said once the lunch was over. "I look forward to getting the materials you promised to send."

"My pleasure as well," Christina responded. "You have excellent energy. I'd love to spend time with you socially. Alex, perhaps we should invite Eden over next weekend to hang out with us on the boat."

"Sounds like a great idea," Alex responded.

Shortly afterward, Eden left and returned to the office. She was feeling better than she'd felt in years, maybe ever. She was so glad to know that the little hitch in the giddyup that she'd perceived—Alex's interest— was simply a product of her overblown imagination. Ariel had been right. Instead of worrying about her boss's intentions, Eden simply needed to focus on what she wanted instead of what she didn't want. She worked the rest of the afternoon and then headed down the hall for her visit with Dakkar, the master masseuse. As she walked the short distance down the hall, she counted her blessings: the job of her dreams, a man she adored, and a brother about to become a husband and father in short order. Life was grand, couldn't be any better . . . could it?

42

"Baby, I'm tired. Why can't you come to me?"

"I was there all weekend. Why can't you come to Santa Monica?"

"True that, you did spend the weekend. But seriously, Eden, since you've moved I've logged the most mileage."

It was true. And Jansen didn't know the reason. Other than their first auspicious meeting, and the conversation at Michael's house, they'd not talked about guns in general or Eden's abhorrence to them in particular. Thankfully, his fleshly weapon had kept her mind off the steel ones, but still, the visit had not come without continual mental adjustments on her part. She'd skirted the issue, but just like she'd had to come to grips with other unpleasant occurrences in her life, having to deal with this one was just a matter of time.

"Who do you think works harder? Me or you?" Jansen had put in a ten-hour day. It had not been pleasant, and he wanted, no, needed Eden to help take his mind off the day's events.

"Jansen, your job is harder. But mine is also challenging. Work is work."

"What, you don't want to see me?"

"You know that isn't true."

"Then come over." Although Jansen would never admit it, or perhaps even acknowledge it, this was now just as much about her capitulating to his demands as it was about the travel.

Eden sighed. *I might as well deal with this last little stickler so I can go on and enjoy this man.* "Okay, Jansen. But I'm not spending the night. I'm only going to stay a couple hours."

Forty-five minutes later, Eden knocked on Jansen's front door. He answered almost immediately, pulling her into his arms and, as per usual, kissing her as if he'd not seen her just yesterday.

"How was your day?" Eden asked when she came up for air.

"Better now." Jansen reached for her hand, pulling her toward his office.

Immediately, a vision of the large handgun resting in the top desk drawer came to Eden's mind. "Wait, let's hang out in the living room."

"In a minute. But first I want to show you what I have for you."

Once again he moved toward his office, but Eden resisted. "I don't want to go in there."

Jansen scowled. "Why not?" Then, shrugging, he continued. "Fine, wait here." He walked into his office and returned with a small gift bag.

"What's this?"

"Just a little something to keep me on your mind."

Eden removed the tissue from the top of the bag and then reached inside. Her response was deadpan. "Pepper spray? Really, Jansen, we might have to work on your romance skills."

"Baby, protecting the one you love is about as romantic as you can get. I checked out the area around where you work and found that crime is very much a part of the landscape. I'll feel a lot better with your having that on your key chain. I also want to show you a couple defensive moves, as your carrying a gun is probably not an option."

"Not at all."

"So that's my compromise. Look, don't even think about it as for protection, if that will make you feel better. Think of it as just another girlie thing you have in your purse."

Eden's look was sarcastic even as she had to admit that the jeweled case the spray came in was quite attractive.

"Thanks, Jansen, but . . . I don't know how comfortable I'd feel carrying this around. It's almost as if in consciously protecting oneself, you're subconsciously saying there will be a need to in the future."

"That's a bunch of BS, baby, seriously. Do you lock your doors at night? Well, do you?"

"Of course."

"And does that mean a burglar is waiting in the bushes, or is that just good common sense?"

Eden stared at Jansen for a long moment. He didn't blink. "Okay, point taken." She put the spray back into the gift bag and placed it near her purse.

"Why don't you go ahead and put it on your key chain."

"I'll do it later."

"Humor me and do it now. Please."

Eden huffed and puffed before pulling her keys from her purse.

"Here, baby, I'll do it." Jansen easily attached the spray to Eden's chain, placed the chain back into her purse, and pulled her into his arms. "You know I'm only looking out for your best interests, right? That I don't know what I'd do if anything ever happened to you?"

"Nothing is going to happen to me, Jansen."

"I know, baby. As long as you're with me, which I hope is for a very long time, I'll make sure of it."

They retired to the master suite where Jansen relayed an abbreviated version of the day's events. They'd arrested Terrell Ford, the man who'd assaulted Mayleen "Sassy" Smith, but Jansen didn't feel they had evidence sufficient enough to hold him long.

"It's one of the things that frustrates me about the system," Jansen concluded. "There are innocent men behind bars and guilty ones walking free. I've met dozens of Terrells—master manipulators, skillful liars."

"He denied breaking into that neighbor's house?"

"Of course he did. Denied ever having committed a crime in his life, even though we have the rap sheet to prove otherwise."

"Turn over. Let me give you a massage." When he complied, Eden straddled the small of Jansen's back and began to work on his tense neck and shoulders. "Even Superman couldn't save the whole world, Jansen.

We have to feel good knowing we've done the best we can. That's all that's required of us."

They fell silent then, Eden kneading, sending subliminal love rays to Jansen's body, Jansen moaning his appreciation. Shortly thereafter, she was the one moaning while Jansen massaged her body from the inside out.

Later, back in the living room, Jansen was making his argument for her delayed departure. "Baby, it's late. You can spend the night, leave here when I do, around six, and have plenty of time to get to work."

"No, I won't."

"Yes, you will. You said your hours are nine to five."

"On paper. But I'm normally there from eighty-thirty to six."

"Why? Who are you trying to impress?"

"Myself. I plan to be fully up to speed on everything concerning the center within six months. Then I plan to plug into the national network and work my way into the upper eschelons of the holistic community's movers and shakers. I love this job, Jansen, helping people live better lives." When he continued pouting, she added, "I love you, too."

Ten minutes later, Eden was in her car headed home. She let out a yawn and, to keep herself awake, turned the satellite radio to a station playing upbeat tunes. Jansen had that way about him—he sexed her with such an intensity that afterward she could fall asleep straight away. *It would have been nice to spend the night,* she mused. And then, *I wonder if he'd be willing to get rid of all except his service revolver, and even place it in the garage for the night.* Eden switched lanes, turned up the volume, and bobbed her head to

a song about airplanes and making wishes. Even for
the fairies Ariel adored, Eden felt her desire would be
a tall order. Jansen, ridding his home of weapons at her
request? Eden yawned again, glad that she was less
than fifteen minutes from home. "I doubt it."

43

"Why don't you just tell him already?" Ariel suggested in the ethereal, singsong voice that was her style. After a busy couple days, she and Eden were finally sharing girl time during a lunch break.

"Because I don't want to argue," Eden replied. "Jansen loves his guns, and if I suggest he get rid of them, he'll say he can't because, one, weaponry is a part of his job, and, two—well, two is that they are a part of him."

Ariel eyed her friend, green eyes boring into brown ones. "Then if that's true," she said softly, "you'll have to learn to love that part of him, too."

"That's easy for you to say; you don't have to see one strapped to your man's hip."

"No, but I'm no stranger to guns. I actually have fond memories of them." Amid Eden's dubious expression, Ariel hurried on. "Back in Nebraska my grandfather was a huge hunter and farmer. My brother and I spent summers on his and my grandma's one-hundred-acre spread. He taught me how to shoot, and for fun we'd knock cans off fence posts or blast pop bottles. I can handle anything from a .38 to a rifle, and I have the county-fair blue ribbons to prove it!

"Because of our different experiences, guns don't hold the energy for me that they do for you. Sometimes," Ariel continued in a manner wise beyond her years, "the universe places us in situations to help us grow, help us love from a totally giving, totally selfless place. There's a reason you love Jansen so fiercely, why your lives are so inextricably linked."

"So I can accept violence?"

"So you can accept a person's choices and point of view. Tell me this—besides the obvious reason of what they generally represent, why do you dislike guns so much?"

"Besides the obvious, I have an especially strong dislike of guns used by the police." Eden told Ariel the story about her ex-colleague, Renee Newton, and how her brother had been gunned down by law enforcement.

"I'm so sorry about your friend's brother," Ariel responded. "It makes it totally understandable for you to feel as you do. But have you ever considered trying to change your position on Jansen's chosen profession instead of trying to make him change who he is?"

Eden reared back and almost went sistah-girl. But she kept her neck from rolling and her hands off her hip as she responded. "Why in the devil would I do that?"

"Because inanimate objects—anything, really— only has the power we give them. Yes, guns are weapons that do great harm. But that is only because of the choices made by the person who owns them. In and of themselves they are simply masses of energy held together to form a unit used for destruction. The truth of the matter, Eden, is that that mass of steel is harmless. It has no power. Those weapons don't have to make you feel the way you do about them. You could simply change the way you feel and look at Jansen's guns the way you look at him—with unconditional love. Love overcomes hatred and fear. And in the end, love always wins."

Eden sat back, folded her arms, and tried not to look at Ariel as if she'd grown a second head. "I will *never* love guns."

"Well," Ariel said with a shrug after she'd finished the last of her garden burger, "I guess you're ready to get back into the dating game. Because Jansen is a police officer, officers carry guns, and you're unable or unwilling to reconcile yourself to that fact. Because of that thought vibration, you're sending a message to the universe that you don't want to be with him. And sooner or later, whether you tell him or Spirit does, Jansen is going to get the memo."

For the first time since their meeting, Eden had not left Ariel's presence in a better mood. In fact, when she returned to the office, she felt a headache coming on. She thought about attending the next yoga session but then remembered the to-do list on her desk, the one she wanted completed by the end of the week. Eden hastened her stride to her office, determined to bury all thoughts of Jansen's guns and why she should love them under a mountain of work.

"Oh, excuse me, Om." Eden had rounded the corner and almost knocked their diminutive shaman over.

"No worries, dear one." Om started to walk away but then noticed Eden's countenance. "You are troubled."

"Just preoccupied," Eden quickly responded.

"It is more." He stood there, his eyes fastened intently on Eden, and waited for her response.

"I'm fine, really."

"There is nothing more satisfying than to give to one who is always giving to others. Would you like to come into my office for an energy healing?"

Eden had yet to experience what others in the office had raved about. Ever since he'd shocked her with his handshake, Eden had been leery about succumbing to his energetic influence. Still, his was one of the center's offerings she had not tried. At the thought of not being plagued by the icky feeling her conversation with Ariel had caused, she found herself nodding and following Om into his space.

She couldn't keep the smile off her face as she entered. *Office* was the last word she'd use to describe this eclectic space. For starters, there was a patient, or "client," table where a desk would have been. The walls were painted a soothing blue, the lighting was subdued, candles burned, and the subtle smell of citrus filled the room, and the table between them was filled with crystals and healing stones. Completing the decor were various statues of spiritual masters and a large original picture of the sun.

"Please take off your shoes and lie over there," Om said quietly. He walked over to a table, picked up a few stones and a couple vials, then walked over and placed them on the table near Eden. She followed Om's instructions and lay on her back.

"Is there a specific issue involving energy you wish to dissipate, any pain or illness?"

Eden took a deep breath and decided to be honest. "My boyfriend is a police officer, and I have a problem with the guns he keeps at his house. I need to change the way I feel about them and about his choice for career."

Om nodded. "Have you personally had a negative experience involving guns?"

"No, but I've been close to those who have."

"I see."

"I don't like guns, and I feel that if people didn't own them, no one would die from being shot."

"I will work to release the negative energy caused by the memory of your friend's unfortunate incident and open your heart chakra to the art of allowing your boyfriend the right to live his own authentic life. Is this in line with your desire?"

Eden nodded and fought the tears percolating near the tips of her eyes.

"Believe that all is well, Eden, because it truly is. Please close your eyes and take three deep breaths for me—in through your nose, out through your month. That's it, good. And another." Eden complied. "Excellent. And one more, this time holding for eight counts and releasing for eight." Eden heard Om rubbing his hands together. "I am going to place a little peace and calming oil at your temples and forehead."

Om's touch was featherlight. He lightly massaged her forehead and temple, and Eden began to relax.

"I'm now going to harness the healing energy and direct it toward your body," Om almost whispered.

"I will not touch you, but you may feel itchiness or goose bumps. Don't be afraid. Everything is divine energy, and that is what you're feeling."

Om moved soundlessly, but Eden correctly guessed he was near her head when a wave of heat began at the top of her skull and coursed downward, like lava, inside her veins. She relaxed more and more, continued to breathe evenly, at one point almost falling asleep. When the twenty-five-minute session was over, Eden left Om's office both energized and serene. She walked toward the front in search of Ariel to tell her she'd been right about two things. One, Om was amazing, and, two, she needed to tell Jansen how she felt about his guns and find a way to make her peace with them.

44

Jansen sat at the traffic light and watched a woman cross the street with her three children. One was in a stroller, while a second one, a little girl who appeared to be around four years old, helped her mother push it. The son, who Jansen guessed to be around six, ran in front of them, dashed back to tickle the baby in the stroller, and then turned and once again raced toward the curb on the other side.

I wonder what my children will look like? Ever since learning of Michael's pregnancy, Jansen had pondered his legacy more and more, and with whom he'd create it. Eden seemed the perfect choice. Like him, she wanted children. She was smart and would make a great mother. And he was madly in love with her. *But only if I'm married to their father.* Eden's comment from their conversation on the matter had stayed with him since she'd made it. Maybe that was why he'd been researching wedding rings online for the past couple days. Because, for Jansen, that minor detail could definitely be handled.

The beep of his cell phone interrupted his thoughts. He immediately recognized the Chicago number. "Nicki! I thought about you and Cameron just this morning. How's life in Chi-town?"

Her audible sigh was the first clue that all was not well. "Cameron got picked up last night, Jansen."

Jansen's jaw clenched. "Why?"

"He was hanging out with a group of friends when a fight broke out. Some of the kids involved are gang members, and when the cops found that out, they took in everybody."

"Is he still in detention?"

"No, I called Terry. He went with me and helped get him out without me having to pay any money."

"Terry's a good man," Jansen answered, remembering that one of Chicago's premier defense attorney's was also Nicki's cousin. "What did they charge him with?"

"Unlawful gathering, disturbing the peace, and possession."

Jansen was so thrown by the last charge he almost hit the car in front of him. "Possession of what?"

"Weed."

"You have got to be kidding."

"I wish I were." Nicki sighed again. "At least it was that and not crack. Then we'd really be in trouble. As it is, Terry thinks because this is a first offense, he can get the charges dropped."

"Cameron and I talked about this all the time. He promised me he'd stay away from drugs."

"Cameron has changed a lot since you saw him, what, a year and a half ago? He isn't that cute, precocious little boy anymore. He's turned into an angry young man—been that way since he visited his father in Denver."

"The one he hadn't seen in ages?"

"Yeah, Daniel's wife guilt-tripped him into calling Cameron and paying for his visit down there. Guess she seemed it only fair that because he was taking care of her sons that he should try to make peace with his own."

"I take it the trip didn't go as planned."

"Cameron definitely did not come back with warm fuzzies, if that's what you mean. He resents the fact that her boys get to grow up with his dad—couldn't stand the way Daniel doted on the daughter they had together. It didn't seem fair to him, and it isn't. Of course I told him life isn't always fair, but what twelve-year-old wants to hear that? That's when he started changing, after that visit, and I think that's when he started smoking. Terry does what he can, but he's got kids of his own, plus he and Cameron have just never been close. Not like the two of you were. He looked up to you as a true father figure. In fact, one time he told me he wished you were his dad."

Jansen's gut clenched. "I feel bad, Nicki. I should have kept in better touch with him."

"Yes, you should have," Nicki said without rancor. "But everybody's got their lives to lead. He was sick when he came home from visiting his cousins in Kansas City and found out he'd missed your visit."

"How can I help? What do you want me to do?"

"I don't know what you can do from LA. Cameron needs a firm, guiding hand through these teen years—

a male hand. Maybe just calling and talking to him on a regular basis will help. Maybe he'd think twice about his actions with you back in his life." They were silent a moment, thinking how quickly time had passed. It seemed only yesterday that Jansen was taking Cameron to the mall and playing video games. That bright-eyed, energetic kid had been full of promise. Jansen didn't even recognize the boy Nicki described. "I don't want my child to end up a statistic," Nicki continued, her voice near a whisper. "It's rough for a boy here in the streets of Chicago. I don't know how to keep him safe."

They talked a few more moments, and Jansen made sure to get Cameron's cell-phone number before they ended the call. Even after hanging up, the conversation stayed with him—while he picked up his dry cleaning, went through a fast-food drive-through for dinner, and even after he'd arrived home and eaten the meal. Jansen couldn't help but compare what Nicki had said about Cameron's anger to the anger he'd felt when his father had died. But for his uncle, Jansen could have gone down the same ugly path. The path Terrell Ford had chosen, and so many others like them. By the end of the evening, a plan began formulating in his mind. He reached for his phone and dialed Kathryn's number.

"Mama, I need your advice on something."

"Well, good evening to you too, son." Kathryn chuckled. "What's on your mind that's more important than a greeting?"

"I'm thinking about having a friend's son come stay with me for a while, a boy I used to mentor in Chicago. He's growing up and needs a man to teach him how to be one."

There was a pause before Kathryn asked, "Where's his father?"

"In Denver raising another family."

"Did his mother ask you to do this, and, if so, does she have a more personal stake in the matter?"

"Nicki was my neighbor in Chicago, and became a good friend. We were never more than that. I'm not attracted to her in that way, and she knows that isn't going to change. Her son, Cameron, is a smart, funny kid with a bright future ahead of him. I want to stop him from messing it up."

Kathryn asked a few more questions about Nicki and her son and then said, "It takes a village to raise a child, Jansen. And it takes a real man to step in and help somebody else's seed. So I say take it slow the way you've planned and remember that I'm here to help. Oh, and one more thing."

"Yes, Mother?"

"While you're out there taking care of other's kids, will you please think about having some of your own?"

45

"I don't know, Jansen. Taking care of a child is a huge responsibility, especially a teenager." Eden and Jansen sat in his living room where he'd shared his heart about having Cameron come to Los Angeles. "Not to mention the fact that there are drugs and violence here, too. If the boy wants to get into trouble, he'll find it no matter where he lives."

"That's just it, Eden. I don't think Cameron is in trouble because he went looking for it. I think he's just trying to belong somewhere, and he's looking up to the men who are paying him the most attention. This is a good kid, reminds me a lot of myself when I was growing up. I think I can make a difference in this child's life. In fact, after the earlier conversation he and I had on the phone, I'm sure of it."

Eden took in Jansen's serious, thoughtful countenance, and her heart swelled. How many did she know who would step up to the plate and make the future of another man's child his responsibility? Not many. As much as she loved Michael, and as good a man as she thought he was, she couldn't see him doing it. And any child would want to run the other way if her ex, Gregg, offered his services.

"I think you're wise to start with the Christmas vacation, see how that goes."

Jansen nodded. "I'd already planned to ask for some time off around that time." Jansen had planned to surprise Eden with a New Year's Eve getaway in Las Vegas, but he decided she didn't need to know that. He felt within himself an urgency to help Cameron. If he didn't, and something happened to the boy, he'd never forgive himself.

"You'll also want to start planning for the possibility of him spending the summer. Who's going to watch him while you're working? How will he socialize? Things like that."

"I know some good kids through the basketball program, and a few guys on the force have boys his age."

"What about Alberto? He probably knows some as well."

"Yes, he does. His older sister has a son around Cameron's age. So he'll do all right. As for my working, Cameron has been a latchkey kid since he was six, seven years old. He's very responsible. I won't expect anything less while he's a guest in my home. Plus, Mama said she'd help out. She doesn't have the energy to keep up with him—heck, she could barely keep up with us—but she'll be a good influence around him . . . as will you."

"Me? I don't know about that."

"I do. All that positivity and good vibrations? You'll be great. Plus, it will be good practice."

"For what?"

"For when our son gets his age."

Eden lay back on the couch and put her feet in Jansen's lap. He immediately began to massage her feet. "Jansen, I have to ask you something."

"What's that?"

"What about the guns you have all around the house?"

"What do you mean 'all around'? Wait." Jansen dropped her foot and crossed his arms. "Have you been snooping?"

"Not purposely," Eden replied. "Well, a little," she added.

"Uh-huh."

"It started that day I stayed here and used your computer. I was looking for cleaning solution to wipe the screen when I saw the gun in the top drawer. Then I noticed the gun cabinet and became curious as to just how many weapons you have around the house. I didn't dig deep, mind you, just opened a drawer here and there. I couldn't believe how many were in the house. Actually, it freaked me out."

Jansen picked up her foot again, thoughtfully massaging up to her calf and back. "Is that why you don't like staying here anymore, always trying to get me to come to Santa Monica?"

Eden hesitated and then decided to be truthful. "Yes."

Jansen let out a deep breath.

"I'm working on it," Eden hurriedly continued, "this abhorrence I have for violence in general and weapons in particular." She shared Ariel's story about life on a

Nebraska farm and learning to shoot. Then she told him about her coworker's brother being killed and how it had affected her. Not wanting him to feel judged, Eden conveniently left out the fact that his killer had been a man in blue. "Have you always liked weapons? I don't remember you and Michael playing cops and robbers growing up."

"No, but we played the hell out of cowboys and Indians."

"Ha!"

"You don't remember our plastic six-shooters?"

"No, but now that you mention it, I remember the water guns."

"You should. We napped up your hair more than once with a spray-down."

"That you did. I still owe payback for those showers."

"Ha! Forgive me, baby." Jansen placed a kiss on the sole of her foot.

"Okay, I do. But forgiving ain't forgetting. . . ."

"Guns are to be respected," Jansen said after he'd finished massaging one foot and picked up the other. "I'll teach him about guns—how to load and unload them, how to make sure there's no bullet in the chamber. He'd probably love the shooting range. I'll decorate one of the paper dummies with all of Cameron's bad habits—have him kill 'em."

"Now there's a thought," Eden sarcastically muttered.

"And here's another one. You should come, too. If you'd handle firearms a little bit, you'd stop being so afraid of them."

"No, thank you. I'll let that be you and Cameron's male-bonding time."

Jansen gently pulled Eden down farther on the couch and then covered her with his body. "Speaking of bonding, can we do some of that right now?"

"We can, but it's that time of the month, and I'm cramping. Let's make this a cuddle night."

Jansen groaned. "Oh, God. Not the *C* word." He kissed her neck and then began nibbling her ear.

"I'm afraid so."

"Baby, you know I want it."

"Jansen, stop it!" Eden exclaimed even as she wrapped her arms around him.

"I read somewhere that making love is good for stopping cramps."

"All righty then. The next time *you're* cramping, we'll try it."

46

Eden made a beeline for the green tea as soon as she stepped into the office. *I have got to stop spending the night at Jansen's during the week.* Even though they hadn't done it, he'd kept her up half the night anyway. The more he'd talked about Cameron coming to visit, the more excited he'd gotten. She didn't even know the boy, yet looked forward to his visit.

She reached her office but, noticing that the light at the end of the hall, kept walking. "Good morning, Alex," she said, peeking her head in the doorway.

"Good morning!"

"What time did you get here?"

"About ten minutes ago."

Eden's eyes widened. "And your desk looks like that?" There were papers strewn from one side to the other, along with folders, magazines, and the LA *Times*.

"You're looking at organized chaos; it's a masterpiece."

"If you say so." Eden took a sip of tea. "What time are we going to see the dancer?"

"Two o'clock. I figured we could do lunch first and go from there."

"You said she's at Agape, correct?" Agape was a large spiritual center founded and directed by *The Secret*'s Michael Beckwith.

Alex nodded.

"Then I know the perfect spot for lunch. Ariel turned me on to it. It's in Redondo Beach."

"Perfect. Let's leave at, say, noon?"

"Sounds like a plan!"

Eden walked down to her office with pep in her step. Since meeting Christina, she felt more comfortable around Alex and had relaxed her guard. They hadn't come out and said so directly, but even Stevie Wonder could have seen that the two were lovers. And even though Ariel had told her he flirted with everybody, Eden still felt better knowing he was seeing someone. She liked Alex, understood why women went gaga over him. Heck, if she weren't dating Jansen, she probably would have been among them. Now she was happy to have him as a colleague—technically her boss. She pulled up her to-do list and began tackling projects, already anticipating good company, a great meal, a fabulous time at Agape, and whatever wonders the day would bring.

"Hey, where's the Prius?" Eden asked when Alex stopped in front of a sporty Mercedes.

"I wasn't in a Prius mood," Alex responded.

"I like the Prius because of its environmental benefits. But this is gorgeous!"

"Thank you." He pressed the unlock button, opened

Eden's door, and closed it once she was safely inside. Moments later they were on the road.

"Do you attend Agape?" Eden asked.

"Not regularly, but Christina does. She was there recently when Maash-t Amm Amen was a guest."

"The dancer?"

"Yes. She's the one who created this healing dance called *het heru*. I watched a DVD of her with Christina and knew she'd be the perfect finale for our fair. She's in demand all over the world. We're lucky to get her."

"I can't wait to meet her and see the dance."

Alex merged onto Sepulveda from Lincoln at sixty-five miles an hour. The car handled so smoothly it felt more like thirty-five. He saw a patrol car and tapped the brakes.

"Aside from Jansen, I'm usually not happy to see the police, but in this case—thank you!"

Alex laughed. "Sorry, bad habit. We drive much faster in Europe, and it's easy to speed in this car. You can't even tell you're going fast."

"I've heard about the autobahn, but I haven't had the pleasure—or pain, depending on how you look at it— of being on it."

"It's not so bad."

"I'm sure race-car drivers say that about the Indy 500."

"Ha!" They reached a light, and another patrol car sat on the side of the street, its lights flashing. A policeman exited the vehicle and walked ahead to the parked car in front of him, his hand on the butt of his gun.

Eden and Alex watched in silence. "You know," Alex said once the light turned green and they proceeded through it, "most European police don't carry guns. And percentagewise, our crime rate is lower. Isn't that interesting?"

"Very."

"I hate guns."

Eden looked at Alex. "Me, too!"

"I really do. I think all weapons should be outlawed, thrown into a heap, and burned."

The conversation turned yet again after that. Eden learned more about Alex's idyllic childhood, and she shared her growing up amid the urban sprawl. Later, Alex raved about the Green Temple, Eden's restaurant choice, and Eden fairly beamed as she watched the *het heru* healing dance. They met with the dancer, and after securing her for the health fair, headed back to the car.

"Would you mind if I make another stop?" Alex said. "It's a little out of the way, but he's a doctor friend of mine I'd like you to meet."

"Sure," Eden said, buckling up and tilting her seat back after she'd put on her shades. It was a stunningly beautiful California day, and she was in no mood to hurry back to the office. Alex turned on the radio and cruised up the Pacific Coast Highway.

"Would you prefer that I change the station?" he asked.

"No, I love classical music."

"Good."

Alex glanced at Eden once and, seeing that her eyes were closed, took another longer look, as long as he dared while driving. *You are a beautiful woman, Eden*

Anderson. You'll be the perfect partner, and we'll make a great team.

Eden and Alex spent the entire afternoon at his friend's oceanfront home in Rancho Palos Verdes. The doctor and his wife were delightful and ended up writing a six-figure check to the center's foundation. Even though she knew she had a mountain of work, and had completed only three items on her long to-do list, Eden felt fabulous—she'd thoroughly enjoyed her day. As she drove home she again realized what a great guy Alex was and thought that if she weren't dating Jansen, she'd definitely go out with the doc.

47

"Hey, baby." Eden adjusted her earpiece and eased into rush-hour traffic for the short drive home.

"Hey, little garden. I missed you today."

"Don't you miss me every day, every second that I'm not with you?"

"No doubt. I called the office on my lunch hour and on break. Then I tried your cell phone. Where were you?"

"Out with Alex." Eden thought of how that sounded and quickly added, "He and I had meetings all day." She told him about the dancer and the donor.

"Oh, okay. Cool." Jansen's tone was smooth as he battled his emotions. He was jealous by nature, but ever since his heart-to-heart with Eden, he'd vowed to try to keep the green dragon in check. Eden trusted Jansen. The least he could do was return the favor.

Cool? No outrage? No interrogation? There is a God! Eden thought. "So, baby, I thought I'd stay home tonight. I got a little behind in work, and with the health fair coming up, I want to stay on top of things. You have marked your calendar, right?"

"What day is it again?"

"Jansen! It's the first Saturday in October, and before you tell me you work on Saturdays remember that you already promised to be there. It's a big deal for me, baby. I want you to come into my working world, meet my colleagues, and see what we do."

"Okay, weed, guess there's no getting out of this woo-woo shindig."

Eden laughed at Jansen's use of her expression. "Absolutely not."

"So I'll let you slide tonight, but don't think I don't know when your girl leaves the building."

"My girl?"

"Your period, woman. It should be over by Sunday morning. Which means I'm going to tear it up on Sunday night."

Eden stifled a moan, her kitty flip-flopping with anticipation. "You are so bad, Jansen McKnight."

"But it feels so good, doesn't it, Eden Anderson?"

"That it does. I cannot tell a lie."

Eden arrived home and, after preparing a light dinner of soup and salad, plopped down on the couch with her laptop. Christina had sent her the final list of participants. Eden wanted to familiarize herself with all who would be attending and send an introductory greeting to those she'd not yet met. She decided to first check her e-mails and was surprised to see several from Facebook. Scrolling down quickly, she saw a message from her friend Renee and immediately clicked it open.

Hey, girl: Sorry I've been MIA—I haven't been on here for a minute. Been meaning to call you, especially since I had my number changed (stalker, long story, details at eleven). But you know how crazy the Hill can get, especially since my Congressman has decided to change his mind again and run for reelection. Now we're all scrambling. ::sigh:: Here's my number. Either you call me, or I'll call you, and we'll talk this weekend. Renee.

Eden typed a quick reply:

My number's the same. Looking forward to catching up.

She went through the other messages, responded to those from holistic organizations that pertained to work, prepared for bed, and called her mother.

"Hey, girl," Phyllis said when she answered the phone.

"Hey, Mom. I'm not going to talk long, just giving you a quick call before going to bed."

"Kinda early for that, isn't it? It's barely ten o'clock."

"Yes, but I'm tired. I didn't get a lot of sleep last night."

"Uh-huh, out with the doctor . . . or Jansen?"

"Mom!"

Phyllis laughed. "I'm just messing with you, Eden. How's work?"

"I love my job, Mom," Eden said. She told Phyllis about her day and about the health fair. "You should come and stay with me that weekend, Mom—attend the festivities. You haven't been to LA in a while, and you know Michael is headed back over to London.

You could split your time between him and me and come to the fair with Kathryn!"

"I might come visit, but I don't know about all this new-age medicine. That stuff sounds rather suspect to me."

"Don't knock it until you try it. At the very least you could get a nice massage from a very handsome masseuse and eat delicious food that's healthy for you."

"Well, you know that fine men and good food will get me every time. And I do need to come there and check out our newest family member."

Eden laughed. "You'll love Bridgett, Mom."

"I do already. I've talked to her on the phone several times. She seems like a sweet girl."

"She is."

"And I'll get to see Jansen, too."

"Uh, yeah."

This time it was Phyllis's chance to chuckle. "You know I've got Ma-dar."

"What's that?"

"That's a mama's radar. Sooner or later, I know everything. Oooo, baby, that's Larry at the door. I have to run."

Phyllis clicked off the phone, leaving Eden with her mouth open. There was only one reason a man visited a woman at ten o'clock at night. *My mother on the receiving end of a booty call?* "Say it isn't so!"

Eden blocked out the visual of her mother's potential intimacies with thoughts of Jansen. She tossed and turned once she got into bed, knowing she needed the rest but missing her man.

48

Sunday came, and Jansen and Eden found themselves once again in the company of the Gonzalezes. It was Alberto, Jr.'s, birthday, and the yard was packed with what Eden guessed was a hundred people, most of them related. The only thing more plentiful than food on the long picnic tables was the love that fairly teemed in the air. Eden sat in a circle of Delphia's sisters, aunts, and cousins, being grilled as if she were on trial. Her crime? Being single and childless at thirty-four.

"Girl, what are you waiting for?" Delphia's sister, Lucia, asked, her lyrical accent turning the question into a song.

Delphia's mother tsked and shook her head. "When I was your age, I was a grandmother already." She leaned forward in her chair and whispered in a conspiratorial tone. "You want your baby to have to come through a raisin or a dried-up prune? Better to birth it through a peach, girl, fuzzy and soft, with no wrinkles!"

"Or since you're dark," Delphia's cousin added, "maybe more like a plum!"

"It doesn't matter what fruit you choose," yet another cousin offered, "as long as it isn't spoiled!"

The women laughed so hard they wiped tears from their eyes, and Eden joined them. She could see why Jansen so enjoyed this family and why he considered Alberto such a close friend.

Alberto's seventy-five-year-old great-grandmother, who didn't look a day over fifty-five, waved the women silent. "If I had that *hombre guapo* in *mi casa,* I'd never come out, and give him *muchos bebes!* Looking at his son makes a man feel *muy bueno. Mirada!*"

The women turned and saw Alberto prancing around with Alberto, Jr., riding on his neck. His daughter, Luciana, tugged his pant leg, begging her turn. Then she eyed Jansen, who carried another child on his shoulders, the boys dueling with plastic swords and having the times of their lives. Eden watched, took it all in, and remembered Jansen's conversation about keeping Cameron and having children of his own. She thought about Bridgett's pregnancy. Twenty-seven-year-old Bridgett was about to give Phyllis her first grandbaby while her thirty-plus daughter carved out yet another career. *These women are right,* Eden mused. *I'm not getting any younger. Maybe it's time to give Jansen what he and I both want . . . whether we're married or not.*

"Come here, you," Jansen growled as soon as he and Eden later stepped inside his house. "Ever since I first admired you in this sexy pink dress, I've wanted to take it off."

"Be my guest," Eden purred after Jansen pulled his tongue from her throat. "I want to take a shower."

Jansen squeezed her cheeks, patted her behind, and then directed her toward the stairs. Once inside the master bath, he made quick work of getting them naked and then turned on the spigots. "Instead of a shower, how about a bubble bath?"

"Sounds good."

Jansen plugged the tub and poured in a liberal amount of a sandalwood-fragranced bubble bath. "It'll take a few minutes for the tub to fill up," he murmured against her chest before taking a nipple into his mouth.

"I—it's okay," Eden stammered, her stomach tightening and kitty meowing its fervent request to play with the snake.

Jansen reached for a condom lying on the counter. "I want to make good use of this time . . . now . . . while we're waiting."

He tore open the package and took out the condom. Eden stayed his hand, looked deeply into his eyes, and said the words that were music to any man's ears. "I don't want anything between us," she whispered, her breath hot and wet against his ear. "I want to feel you, all of you, inside me. Can you give it to me, baby? The way I want it? The way we both want it?"

As her answer, Jansen lifted Eden up against the wall, secured her there with his arms, and guided his hot, pulsating shaft inside her with one long, sure thrust. He growled. She moaned, wrapping her legs around his waist. He pulled out to the tip and plunged to the base, over and again. It was hard to tell which heat clouded the wall-length mirror—the running water or the lovers' desire. Eden's toes curled with the intensity of her pleasure. Jansen pulled away from the wall and used his pillarlike arms to bounce Eden up and down on his shaft: harder, deeper, more. *More!*

"Jansen," Eden panted, tears of pleasure once again forming in her eyes. "You feel so good. This feels so good."

"Oh, so you like this bad boy, huh? You like me being nasty, giving it to you raw."

"Yes . . . yes!"

"Mmmm, take it in, baby. I want to give it to you. All. Of. This." Strong pumps punctuated each word he ground out. He lowered her so that one foot touched the floor as he held the other leg under the knee, giving him even greater access to Eden's lair. He gyrated his hips, whispering her pet name: little garden. A few more seconds, and they both cried out as Jansen filled Eden with love.

The next morning, Eden was awakened by a bright shaft of sunlight seeping through the partially closed blinds. She blinked several times, trying to come out from under a deep sleep. She squinted at the clock: 8:45. "Oh, no," she groaned, not even having the strength to be mad that she'd overslept. Nothing could make her feel bad about what had transpired last night. She'd simply have to make up the time. After checking her calendar to make sure her morning was free of appointments, and sending e-mails to Alex and Ariel telling them she'd be in that afternoon, she nestled back into her lover's arms and returned to dreamland.

49

September went by in a blur, and this, the week of the health fair, was insanely busy. Eden averaged ten hour days, working alongside Alex and Christina, making sure everything went off without a hitch. As was his manner when he went more than a day without sex, Jansen was testy. *And to make matters worse,* Eden thought as she wearily eyed his number on her caller ID, *I'm going to have to tell him no again.*

"Hey, baby."

"Dang, girl. You're still at work? You practically live at that place."

"Just this week. I'm taking a few days off after the health fair and will make it up to you then. Promise."

"Uh-huh. And how do you plan to do that with your mother in town? And my mother hanging with her."

Eden lowered her voice to its sultry quality. "I'm sure you'll find a way."

"Girl, don't play with me. You know how I get when I'm backed up. I haven't seen you all week!"

"Uh, excuse me, but did you just say backed up in

reference to time without sex?" Eden giggled but suppressed it when Jansen didn't join in.

"Oh, so my torture is funny to you?"

"No, baby, I'd just never heard that term used quite that way, that's all. Look, I'm late for a meeting. I'll call you later after I see how much I get done. Maybe you can come over tonight."

"Call me!"

"I will. Love you."

"I love you, too."

Eden's smile widened as she got off the phone. *Backed up? Really?* She shook her head and laughed out loud.

"I'm glad someone is in a happy mood," Alex said, coming into her office. "I'm about to pull my hair out."

"Why, what's going on?"

"There's not enough hours in the day for all the people who want to meet with me. And our celebrity list is growing. Will and Jada Smith just confirmed their appearance at the event.

"I know, Christina told me. Isn't it fabulous?"

"We need to make sure the VIP area is flawless. . . ."

"It will be, Alex. Don't worry. Christina has hired one of LA's top decorators to handle that room. We're going to transform the yoga/pilates room into their private oasis and move those activities outside."

"I know I shouldn't worry but . . ."

"Sounds like it's time for a yoga session yourself, or an appointment with Dakkar."

"I agree with you. But Dakkar is out with one of his regular clients."

"Well . . . you need to see him as soon as he gets back."

"I think you're right."

"Ah, right there, man," Jansen said when Dakkar pressed his thumb and forefinger across the back of his neck.

"This is what happens when you go weeks without me, dog," Dakkar calmly replied. "Someone in your line of work, or any type of work with heavy stress, needs to be worked on regularly. I've told you this."

"A lot going on, man, but you're right. I can tell the difference when I'm running or working out. The hot tub is no replacement for this deep-tissue action." Dakkar worked on Jansen in silence a while before Jansen asked, "How's business?"

"Great! I've secured a steady gig in Santa Monica, which is giving me access to a whole new group of clients, celebrities, and whatnot."

"Oh, yeah?"

"Yeah, a place called the Zen Den."

"I know about that place. That's where—"

"There's this fine sistah who works there," Dakkar interrupted. "But I think she might like a lot of milk in her coffee. She's always hanging out with this Greek doctor who works at the center. I'm pretty sure he's digging her, too."

Once again Jansen fought the green dragon. *Don't jump to conclusions,* he told himself. *There could be more than one sistah working at this place.*

"Yeah, buddy, Eden Anderson is the kind of woman

you'd take home to your mama. Know what I mean? Whoa, dog, relax. I just handled this area, and you're tightening up again."

Jansen took slow, deep breaths and tried to rein in his emotions. There was no reason to suspect Eden of anything. She'd told him about all the time she spent with Alex, knew they'd been in daily meetings regarding the fair. She'd all but threatened him to attend the fair. *Surely she wouldn't do that if she was going behind my back with this dude.* Or would she?

50

Hundreds of visitors lined the streets in and around the Zen Den. In a move nothing short of a miracle, Christina had pulled city strings and had the block on which the center sat closed off to traffic. A harpist played on the stage erected in the center of the street, directly in front of the center. Street vendors lined the block, and booths of healthy food abounded. The mood was festive, joyful, and yet surrounded by an aura of peace.

Inside the Zen Den, Eden mingled with the guests, not knowing whether she was coming or going at any given moment. Phyllis had arrived the day before, and in anticipation of her arrival and their oncoming lack of privacy, Jansen had kept her up half the night before that. Still, excitement overrode Eden's weariness. She observed the goings-on even as she participated, thankful yet again that she actually got paid to do this job!

A little after two, she looked up to see a small contingency enter the building. Phyllis entered chatting with Bridgett, while Michael, Jansen, and Kathryn brought up the rear. Eden clapped her hands together and made a beeline for her family.

"I'm so glad you're here!" she exclaimed, giving her mother a quick kiss on the cheek before reaching for Jansen. "Especially you," she whispered with a bit longer kiss on the mouth. She knew her mother was watching, but she knew, too, that Jansen would be scrupulously observing her behavior. In the past few days he'd asked several questions about Alex. Eden wanted to make sure Jansen understood his importance in her life. She couldn't wait to introduce him to her boss as the man she loved.

Eden greeted the other family members before leading them on a personal tour of the facility. Phyllis and Kathryn held a skeptical view, while Bridgett seemed thoroughly interested in the center's offerings. Jansen and Michael conversed among themselves as Eden led them back from her offices through the main lobby to the backyard where, finally, Phyllis and Kathryn were impressed.

"Wow, baby, this yard is something special," Phyllis enthused, looking over the meticulously manicured landscape and taking in the fountains, flowers, and ponds. "I would love to watch the sunset in an atmosphere like this!"

"And look at the large koi," Kathryn added. "You think one of these would work in my backyard, son?"

"Sure, until Uncle Jeff came over. Then they'd end up either fried or blackened, served with grits!"

"I know that's right!" Kathryn agreed amid the laughter.

"Oh, Mom, Miss Kathryn, there's the masseuse I told you about. Come on, it's time for your appointments."

When the two older women turned and looked where Eden had pointed, their eyes sparkled, and large grins spread across both their faces.

"Surely you don't mean to tell me that tall, dark, strapping young fella there is getting ready to put his hands on me," Phyllis whispered as her eyes hungrily drank him in.

"Mom!" Eden was more than a little embarrassed to see the unabashed desire that underlaid the words. Of course she knew her mother was grown, and did what grown people did, but Eden hadn't been around to see it. Her parents had still been married when she'd left for college; their separation and divorce had happened when she'd been gone for five years. Larry Bates was the first man she'd heard her mother mention. *But she's only fifty-eight and still healthy and vibrant. She still needs to . . .* "Dakkar!" Eden called out to her colleague to staunch her thoughts. When it came to parents and children, there was such a thing as too much information.

Kathryn hadn't said a word but looked uncharacteristically demure as she stood by Eden's side to meet the trainer. For these two older women, Dakkar—with his stocky build, chocolate skin, sparkling white teeth, and trademark locs—was like a cool drink of water in a desert land. Dimples winked at them when he smiled, bowed slightly, and kissed each hand in greeting. "It's my pleasure to meet you," he told first Phyllis and then

Kathryn. "I trust I can provide you with an enjoyable experience."

"You're providing me with one already," Phyllis murmured and then raised her hand to her mouth when she realized that had been spoken out loud. "What I meant to say was my daughter, Eden, has already sang your praises."

Good save, Mom, Eden thought, swallowing her laughter. "Dakkar, this is my brother, Michael, and my friend Jansen."

"What a small world," he said after he'd given Michael a brother's handshake. "Eden, Jansen has been one of my clients for the last three years."

Eden turned to Jansen, dumbfounded. "You get massages? From Dakkar? I never knew that."

Jansen shrugged, squiggling his eyebrows playfully. "There are a lot of things about me you don't know."

Eden approached Jansen teasingly, fully aware that her mother wasn't missing a step, could probably count the hairs in Eden's brow, so closely was she checking out the scene. "What other woo-woo activities are you involved in that I don't know about? Have you been secretly taking yoga classes or practicing tai chi?"

Jansen snorted. "All right, don't push it."

"Eden, I have to hand it to you. I've been trying to get this guy on a healthier path for years. Guess I didn't have the right amount of curves," Dakkar finished with a wink. A look passed between him and Jansen, both thinking of the conversation about Eden shared during Jansen's massage just days ago.

Eden missed the silent exchange. Her focus was on

Alex, who was conversing with a group on the other side of the room. She wanted to catch him before he got away again. "Well, you have a chance to redeem yourself with Miss Kathryn," she said once her attention returned to Dakkar. "She's going with you while I take Mom and Bridgett to the next tai-chi session." After Dakkar had led a still smiling Kathryn away, Eden turned to her brother. "Jansen's coming with me, Michael. Would you like to do tai chi with Mom or check out some of the other festivities?"

"I think I'll grab a smoothie and go check out the music. I might get some ideas to incorporate into our album."

"Okay, cool. Let's all meet back up in an hour."

Michael headed for the door while Eden, Jansen, Bridgett, and Phyllis walked toward the opposite hallway. Alex finished the conversation with the group he'd been talking to and walked toward her.

"Alex, I'd like you to meet my family. This is my mom, Phyllis. Mom, this is Doctor Kostopoulos."

"It's a pleasure meeting you, ma'am," Alex said, reaching out to shake Phyllis's hand. He continued to hold Phyllis's hand between both of his as he continued, "I can see where Eden gets her loveliness."

Phyllis's eyes glistened as brightly for Alex as they had for Dakkar. "Oh, I don't know about that," she said, obviously enamored by gleaming white teeth and feral green eyes. "It's a pleasure to meet you, doctor."

Eden introduced Alex to Bridgett and Michael before turning to Jansen. "This is my friend, Jansen McKnight. Jansen, Alex."

The two men sized each other up as they conducted

a staid handshake. "Nice to meet you," Alex said in a perfunctory tone.

"Likewise," Jansen answered, equally unenthusiastically.

Alex turned back to Phyllis. "You've raised an extraordinary woman, Phyllis." In comrade fashion, he put his arm around Eden's shoulders. "The center runs brighter, tighter because of her stellar administrative and management abilities."

Phyllis's response was interrupted by Jansen, who stepped around her and up to within five inches of Alex's face. His voice was low, barely above a whisper. "If you want to keep using that arm, doc, I suggest you get it out from around my woman."

Alex released Eden and turned to Jansen with a look of surprise. "Oh, I'm sorry, Jansen. I wasn't aware Eden was property."

Jansen's jaw clenched, but he said nothing further. Stormy green eyes met molten chocolate ones. Jansen imagined performing a karate chop to Alex's solar plexus, while Alex dreamed of injecting Jansen with something that would make him sleep for a very long time. Phyllis and Bridgett watched the standoff with extreme interest, wondering if there was going to be a beat-down between the meditation room and the statue Eden had explained was the angel of peace.

The tense moment seemed to last an eternity, but only seconds had passed before Ariel's whimsical voice filled the air as she rushed up to the group. "Eden! Oh, my gosh, is this your whole family?" Ariel looked between those standing in the semicircle. "I'm so glad to meet you all, so glad you came out." Without waiting for introductions, Ariel turned to Phyllis. "You've got to be her mother. Not only do you have the same facial features, but your aura is just as bright and sunny as your daughter's." Ariel closed her eyes, took a deep breath, and lowered her voice to a conspiratorial whisper. "Your very essence is *amazing.*"

Eden laughed at Phyllis's barely veiled expression of confusion but didn't feel now was the time to tell her mother that Ariel was an aura-seeing fairy channeler who believed that in another life she'd been married to Galileo. Alex excused himself from the group, and Eden introduced Ariel to everyone. After Ariel said her good-byes and Eden had pointed her mom and Bridgett in the direction of the tai-chi room, she turned to Jansen. "Okay, lover, what would you like to see next?"

"The exit," Jansen said, unsmiling.

Eden grabbed Jansen's hand and led him to her office. After closing the door, she turned to him. "I'm sorry about that," she said.

"I don't like him."

"Alex is just a big flirt, Jansen. He's—"

"Don't make excuses for his disrespectful behavior. A man putting his hand on another man's woman, in front of him, is an invitation to trouble." Eden put what she hoped was a calming hand on Jansen's forearm. He brushed it off and walked to the other side of the room. "That man has no idea who he's messing with."

Eden walked over to Jansen. "Baby, Alex knows how I feel about you and why I come to work skipping with a smile on my face. He was just trying to get under your skin—that testosterone-chromosome thing that thrives on competition. I'll talk to him about it—"

"I don't want you to say a damn thing to him about me. Let me handle my business, baby."

"That's exactly what I don't want to happen. Alex is my colleague, Jansen, nothing more. I don't know what possessed him to act like he did, but it won't happen again. It is my desire to be a part of this center for a long time, which means you and Alex are going to have to find a way to coexist." Eden took a deep breath and noticed the stern expression that still graced Jansen's face. She hugged him from behind and laid her head on his strong, wide back. "Please, baby. Let it go . . . okay?"

Jansen turned and hugged her. "Okay, baby." He kissed her forehead. "For you, I'll chill out."

They walked out of Eden's office and back to the main lobby area. Jansen looked out and saw Michael sitting by the stage. After he kissed her cheek and went to join him, Eden made a beeline for the kitchen, where out of the corner of her eye she'd seen Alex heading. It was time to give someone a piece of her mind!

51

Eden walked up to Alex and Christina, who were chatting amicably while sharing chips from the same paper bowl. "Excuse me, Alex, a word, if I may?" They'd barely made it back to his office before she closed to the door and angrily reeled around. "What in heaven's name do you think you're doing?"

Alex remained calm, his demeanor unruffled. "Call me touchy-feely, but I didn't see any harm in embracing a colleague. It wasn't like I kissed you or patted your rear." *And I want to do both, believe me.* "I don't think a man who was secure in himself and his relationship would have had a problem with it."

"Alex, I don't want to argue about this, and I don't want there to be problems with you and the man I love. It's true that you and I have grown closer during these weeks that we've worked shoulder to shoulder on this event. And while I feel comfortable with your innocent physical displays, Jansen is not. So because we will continue to have these types of functions and other social occasions that may involve you and Jansen being in the same vicinity, I'd like to know you'll both be adult enough to . . . get along."

"But, Eden, you know me. I'm expressive, and often my hands are a part of that. I'll place my hand on your arm, squeeze your hand, or tweak your cheek—it's nothing! What kind of jerk—" Eden cleared her throat. "All right," he continued, his hands raised in surrender. "I'm sorry for touching you in front of your boyfriend. In the future I'll keep a respectable distance and my hands to myself."

Eden let out a breath of relief. "Thank you."

The next two hours went by without a hitch. Phyllis and Kathryn had had their massages, and after initially balking, were now sitting in a beginner yoga class. Michael was talking with the percussionist of the band who'd just played, and Bridgett had gone in search of her favorite thing these days . . . food. Eden was talking with Ariel when she felt a pair of large, strong hands grip her shoulder.

"Hey, you," she said, giving him a wink and an air kiss. "We were just talking about you."

"All good, I hope."

"What else is there?" Ariel asked, her green eyes sparkling as she looked from Jansen to Eden and back again.

"Ariel said that even without a uniform she would have guessed you to be law enforcement or some type of security. She also said she thought she could best you at the target range."

Jansen's eyes widened. "What? A woo-woo shooting expert?"

Ariel laughed and told him about her country roots.

"I can knock off a cola can from fifty feet," she boasted. "Blindfolded," she added with a lyrical laugh.

"Ha! Sounds like I'd have my work cut out for me," Jansen said. "Maybe you can join Eden and me when she goes for her shooting lessons."

"Oh, no. I'll leave the fun with fire power up to you guys."

Jansen asked Ariel what types of guns she'd used, and they continued chatting about kick, recoil, and other firearm verbiage of which Eden wasn't privy. *Sounds Greek to me.* She looked to her side and saw Alex approaching with Christina. *Well, speak of the devil. . . .*

Jansen saw Alex seconds after Eden, and the smile he wore disappeared.

"Jansen," Alex began as soon as he reached the trio. "I need to apologize for my earlier actions. While I did not intend to upset you, your reaction proved otherwise." Jansen cut his eyes from Alex to Eden. "We'll undoubtedly be seeing each other in the future. I don't want there to be any hard feelings or bad blood between us. So I wanted to apologize, and I also wanted you to introduce you to my friend, Christina Montague."

Jansen hesitated only briefly before extending his hand. "It's all good."

52

Eden, Phyllis, Bridgett, and one of Jansen's sister-in-laws joined Kathryn in the large, airy kitchen of her Long Beach home. The men, which included Michael, Jansen, and Jansen's brothers, gathered in the dining room around a mean, competitive domino game. Their trash talking filtered in and out of the women's conversation, which bounced between food, movies, yesterday's health fair, and now . . . men.

"Girl, I hope you don't think your dating Jansen came as a surprise," Phyllis said, pulling the potato and vegetable casserole she'd assembled out of the oven. "You can't keep anything from your mother."

"Obviously," Eden replied. When the evening before had come and gone without Phyllis saying anything about what she'd seen at the center, Eden knew her mother hadn't been surprised. She'd believed it to be mother's intuition. Now she knew it was just Michael's big mouth. "That boy gets on my nerves!"

Kathryn and Phyllis shared a look between them. Neither felt it necessary to tell Eden that Jansen had been the first one to spill the beans, having shared the news about his and Eden's first date. Kathryn had promptly called Phyllis, overjoyed that what she'd wanted for years was finally happening—that her son would wake up and see that Eden was one of the good ones. Michael's tattletale phone call had come about a week later.

"What difference does it make?" Bridgett asked, eating almost as much of the salad as what went into the bowl. "I'll tell anything moving or breathing that Michael is my man. In fact, I'm thinking about taking out a wedding announcement in *USA Today*." When three pairs of wide eyes turned in her direction, she added, "Just kidding."

"Well, just for the record," Kathryn said as she basted a rump roast in its own seasoned juices, "I couldn't be happier. I could do worse for a daughter-in-law."

"Ha! That sounded like a backhanded compliment, Miss Kathryn."

"Wasn't meant to be, child. I've known you since you were knee-high to a grasshopper; that you're one of my best friend's daughters is a bonus. Let that boy step out of line one time, and we'll be on him so fast it will make his head spin. He'd better treat you right, act like he's got some brought-upsy."

Eden thought back to the night before and how Jansen had treated her. He'd been "up" all right, almost half the night, and that he'd been anything but gentlemanly was why Eden's body seemed to tingle still. She'd been so pleased that Alex's health-fair antics hadn't been mentioned, that Jansen had indeed put the incident behind him. Or maybe that was what had fueled him, and why Jansen had sexed her to within an inch of her life—branding her time and again, thrust after thrust.

In the dining room, bones were being slammed, smacked, and spun on the table.

"Take this, my *brothah*," Jansen's younger brother howled as he put down the double six and got thirty points. "You know the boss man rules. All y'all getting ready to sing Donald Byrd. *Fallin' like dominoes*—ha!"

"Man, shut up," Jansen replied, placing a double five on the board and increasing his lead over his sibling. "Your butt has the fewest points of anyone sitting here."

When the men around the table laughed, Michael chimed in. "Don't let 'em get you down, son. Because they're getting ready to be right where you are." Michael played his last bone, a double trey that locked the board and clinched the game. "Lost!"

Groans and curses dotted the trash talk as the men pushed all the dominoes into the bone pile and started a new game. As Jansen reached for his bones, he glanced up and caught Eden and his mother sharing a laugh. His heart clenched and filled his body with love for her. *She belongs here,* he thought, remembering how his mother had often babysat her when she was six, seven years old. How he and she would work puzzles together before it became uncool for him to hang out with someone's kid sister. Back in the day, he hadn't wanted her anywhere around. Now he never wanted her to leave.

Bridgett joined them, and now both Michael and Jansen seemed more preoccupied with what was going on in the kitchen than the domino game. Michael watched as Eden put a hand on Bridgett's stomach. *Yeah, that's my seed growing in there,* he mused as his chest swelled with pride. *I'm getting ready to be a father.* He couldn't wait.

Jansen followed Eden into her condo, using his foot to kick the door closed while his hands balanced containers of sock-it-to-me cake. Eden had run ahead of him to use the restroom, a testament to all of Kathryn's spicy, nonalcoholic sangria tea she'd drank that afternoon.

"That feels better," she said, joining Jansen in her bedroom. He'd already pulled off his shoes, jeans, and shirt and now lazily gazed into the dresser mirror, eying his five-o'clock shadow. Eden stripped off her tan jeans, jeweled T-shirt, and bra and donned a cotton baby-doll lounging dress that hit midthigh. She slipped into a pair of fuzzy yellow house shoes, pulled her hair back into a ponytail, and headed for the kitchen. "You want to start the movie while I warm up the cake?"

Jansen swatted her behind as she passed him. "Sounds like a plan."

Moments later they sat cuddled up on Eden's chenille divan, eating divinely moist cake with warm glaze. In between bites they shared kisses and laughed at the antics of Paul Mooney and others in the Robert

Townsend classic, *Hollywood Shuffle*. In the month they'd seriously dated, watching these urban classics was just one of many things Eden and Jansen had discovered they both enjoyed. The one-thousand-piece puzzle they'd recently purchased—and that now lay spread out on a card table in one of Jansen's guest rooms—was another. They both were suckers for sweets and loved dogs, nature, and the Lakers. They also relished making love. Jansen had always been insatiable; for Eden, nightly loving had been an acquired taste.

"Mmmm, look at that," Jansen purred, gently brushing a glaze-tipped fork across Eden's barely covered nipple. "I've gotten glaze on my baby." He continued to lightly graze the fork over her peak until it hardened into a dark chocolate pebble.

"You sure have," Eden eked out through a suddenly constricted windpipe and awakening nana.

"Well, I can't have that," he whispered, smoothly setting the saucer on the coffee table in front of them. "Let me . . . clean that up."

Jansen dipped his head inside her wide bodice, his tongue immediately finding its goal. He flicked the nipple back and forth with his tongue, swirled it around the areola and then sucking her full into his hot, wet mouth. Eden gasped with the impact of his mouth on her breast. Jansen kissed his way up her neck, eased the dress off her shoulders, and gave attention there before licking the side of her face, nibbling her earlobe, and placing wet kisses along her temple.

Then he reached for the fork, swirled it into the glaze. Now Eden knew why he'd requested she pour extra on his slice. She held her breath and watched the gooey substance come toward her, watched in awe as Jansen lowered the fork to the other nipple and repeated the process. Eden squirmed and moaned, reaching for Jansen's T-shirt, wanting to feel his flesh.

Jansen's laugh was throaty, knowing. "Patience, little garden. I like to take my time with dessert." He eased the dress over Eden's head, directed her to lie back, and then slowly rid her of the beige bikini panties she wore. His pupils blackened with desire, and for a moment he simply stared at her. Eden grew more heated under his intense perusal, her mouth watering in anticipation of things to come. Jansen dipped the fork in the glaze over and again and, like an artist, began to paint Eden's body with the sweet treat—her breasts, stomach, inner thighs . . . and elsewhere. Then his tongue gave special attention to everywhere the fork had been.

Finally it was Eden's turn. Jansen stood and removed his shirt and boxers. His arousal sprang up like a python—stood at attention like a private greeting brass. He stood beside the divan, waited, and watched to see what Eden would do. She was unsure at first, but then, smiling, she rose to her knees, ran her fingers through the glaze, and rubbed them up and down his engorged shaft. Soon, as Jansen had so expertly demonstrated, her tongue followed the frosted trail as she licked, sucked, nibbled, and squeezed.

"Mmmm," Jansen growled. "Damn," he barely whispered, followed by a hissing sound as Eden took in as much as she could. He reached for her hair, released it from its holder, and then began to massage her head as she massaged . . . his head. Jansen's legs began to shake, and Eden, emboldened with the power she wielded, turned toward the wall, grabbed the back of the couch, and commanded, "Now, Jansen. I want to feel you inside me. Hard. Deep. Show me what you're working with."

Her commanding tone turned Jansen all the way on. He spread her wide and plunged inside her with one long thrust—hard and deep as she had ordered. He spent the rest of the night showing her what he was working with—and then some.

53

After taking two days off to spend time with her mother, Eden returned to work. She was barely in the door when an unexpectedly early Ariel pounced.

"He's gorgeous! Eden! You didn't tell me you were dating a god!"

Eden laughed. "Okay, Ariel, I admit he's handsome, but that's a bit much."

"Eden, he's—"

"Amazing," they both said together and then laughed.

"Well, he is!" Ariel walked to the kitchen with Eden.

"Speaking of amazing, where was Travis? I just now realized he wasn't there, that I have yet to meet this artiste who has captured your heart."

"He's in a forest near Seattle attending a rainbow gathering/sun dance." When Eden cast Ariel a questioning look, she continued. "It's a communal meeting that involves meditation, visualization, and focus on peace, love, harmony, freedom, and community, among other things. But back to your guy—wow, what a bod.

No wonder you're willing to forego your reservations and handle his gun."

"Ariel!"

The sound of Ariel's tinkling laughter trailed behind her as she returned to her desk. Eden finished fixing her tea, shaking her head and smiling at Ariel's bawdy comment. Ariel was like the little sister Eden had never had. She was a bit flighty, and a tad extreme, but Eden knew the freckle-faced redhead had a heart of gold and emitted love like sunbeams wherever she went.

Eden entered her office and immediately began tackling a massive to-do list. She began with her e-mails, responding to the hordes she'd received from satisfied attendees of the weekend's health fair. She crafted a thank-you letter and had it sent out to all the practitioners, chefs, artists, and others who'd participated, and sent a special package to the City of Venice for their stellar cooperation throughout the day. The package included gift certificates for all of the Zen Den's offerings to be given to the employees at the mayor's discretion. Next she went through her regular mail, sorting from "important" to "file," from "pending" to "trash." Before she knew it, it was noon, and Alex was knocking at her door.

"I was beginning to think you might not come back." His smile was easy and his stride confident as he entered her office and sat down in a chair facing her desk.

"Wild bears couldn't keep me away from this place, Alex. You know that." Eden continued working, scanning over various memos and other items in her inbox.

"That I do. The health fair was a rousing success,

thanks in large part to your participation and organizational skills."

"You're too kind, doctor. Christina had everything under control by the time I came on board. I simply helped execute."

"And you did so brilliantly."

"Thank you."

"How's Jansen?"

Eden looked up from the paper she held and, seeing only sincerity in Alex's face, answered. "He's good."

"I really like your mom."

Eden smiled, remembering a point in the afternoon when she'd seen her mother conversing with the doctor, her flirty demeanor more fitted to someone sixteen instead of nearing sixty. Thankfully, her mother had waxed poetic about Alex only during their phone conversation, and not when Jansen had been anywhere around. "You impressed her, that's for sure. She thought you were the handsomest thing on the block— raved about your eye color and wanted to know if they were contacts."

"Ha! One look at my mother's eyes, and she'd have her answer." Alex stood. "How about some lunch? I called RFD and got the specials for the week—BBQ Bello and Buddha's Belly."

Eden groaned. "I am so there! Just give me about ten minutes to organize my desk, and then I'll meet you in the lobby."

Lunch was lovely. Alex was more laid-back than Eden had ever seen him, and she wondered how she'd missed his cutting sense of humor. As they tasted each other's dishes—the chilled, marinated portobello with mango, avocado, and other vegetables topped with spicy ranch dressing, and the Thai-inspired noodle dish that made up Buddha's Belly—Alex plied Eden with stories of his antics as a seventeen-year-old college student, and passing the medical board at an unprecedented twenty-seven years old.

"You could say I was driven," Alex concluded as the waiter brought over helpings of gluten-free chocolate cake and apple-fig crisp. "But after fifteen years I began to get bored, wanted to expand my concept of healing. That's when I went to India and trained for three years under a brilliant doctor and surgeon named Thadmi Kaur. I also spent time in China, Tibet, and Africa."

"Africa?" Eden's surprise was evident.

Alex nodded. "Sat at the knee of village doctors and wise old women who'd never gone to school, much less college, but could cure anything that ailed you and dress a wound better than any I've seen. One of the more fascinating concepts I heard was the use of okra to bring about less painful childbirth."

"Okra?" Eden's forkful of chocolate cake stopped in midair. "I'm all ears."

"They believe that ingesting large amounts of okra during pregnancy helps line the vaginal cavity with a slippery substance, aiding the child in its passage through the chamber. I watched a woman give birth, and I swear she simply squatted down, grunted, and out came a baby!"

"Ha!" Eden's guffaw caused other patrons to look

around and smile. Soon Alex joined in the merriment, and the more they laughed, the funnier the story seemed, until they were holding their stomachs and wiping their eyes.

Eden sat back from the table and placed her napkin in her plate. "Alex Kostopoulos, you are one of a kind."

"That I am, Eden Anderson . . . that I am." Alex picked up his water and winked at her over the glass.

I'm a lucky woman, Eden thought. *And so is Christina.*

The afternoon flew by, and soon Eden was on her way home. As soon as she reached the condo and changed clothes, she returned the missed call from Jansen.

"Hey, baby."

"Hey, weed. You coming over?"

"Jansen! We discussed this. I'm staying at my house, and you're staying there. I'm worn to a frazzle, you insatiable beast. And as much as I'll miss you, I'm looking forward to a hot soak in the tub, bed by nine, and at least eight hours of uninterrupted sleep."

"Sounds boring," Jansen replied, a pout evident in his voice.

Eden chuckled. "You'll live."

They chatted a moment longer, and then Eden retrieved her laptop and sat perched against her bed's headboard. She'd decided to check her personal e-mails while the tub slowly filled. There were a ton of Facebook messages. Many were from her holistic friends—suggestions to *like* this and invitations to that. She bypassed them for a more thorough inspection later and scanned her inbox for personal messages.

"Renee!" Eden exclaimed when she saw the name

Renee Newton in her inbox. She hurriedly clicked the e-mail and read the note that contained Renee's number and a request to call ASAP. Eden went to the bathroom, turned off the water, and retrieved her phone to dial her friend.

54

"Renee Newton!"

"Eden Anderson!"

Eden turned out the lamp next to her bed and crawled beneath the covers. She hadn't talked to Renee in months, and even though she'd reached her goal of lights out and in bed by nine, she knew that actually going to sleep might be a while. "How are you? DC? Life? Oh, my gosh, girl, we've got so much to talk about!"

Renee chuckled. "Eden, it is so good to hear your voice. Where do I begin?"

"Most people would say at the beginning, but, heck, I say plunge right into the middle and spread out from there!"

"Ha! That sounds like a plan. Wait, hold on, let me grab my hot chocolate." There was a rustling sound as Renee pulled her large mug closer to where she was huddled under a throw to ward off October's east-coast chill. "Okay, first off, are you sitting down?"

"Lying down, to be exact. And just to show you how much you rate, I put my place off limits to my boyfriend so I could get to sleep early, and here I am talking to you."

"I'll make it worth your while, Eden. There was a pregnant pause before Renee added, "I'm engaged!"

Eden squealed, sitting straight up as she did so. "Shut up!"

"Is this news enough for you?"

"Stop it!"

"Hmph, it's a little too late for that, thank God. My June wedding will be in the Bahamas, so update your passport, and if you're slacking, start exercising. I want all my bridesmaids to look fabulous!"

"Oh. My. God, Renee! You could have told me anything but this." Renee Newton was that friend who put the *P* in *picky* and whose long list of "must haves" put the *P* in *perfect*. Among the absolute deal breakers were if a man did not have an MBA, made less than six figures, was under six feet tall, had a criminal record of any kind, rented instead of owned, or had a less than seven hundred credit rating. Her husband—she'd insisted many times—would have all these attributes plus a few more, just to surprise her. "I am so happy for you, girl. Okay, details, tell me everything!"

"For starters, his name is Lance Whorton; he's from New Orleans, Louisiana; and I met him when he was here on business."

"A Southern man, huh? I've heard they grow 'em good down there."

"You heard correctly!"

"So, what does he do?" *How much does he make? How many degrees and from what Ivy League school?*

For the first time since saying hello, there was a brief pause in the conversation. "He's, uh, into physical fitness."

"Sounds like a perfect fit for someone who likes to work out herself four to five times a week. So are you saying he owns a training center of some sort, maybe for professional athletes?"

"Not exactly."

No matter how grand, unless it was a Bally or 24 Hour Fitness chain, Eden couldn't imagine him making enough money to give Renee the type of life she demanded. "Okay, girl, I know a stall when I hear one. Break it down for me."

Renee sighed. "Okay, but I've already heard enough 'I told you so's,' so spare me."

"Okaaaaay," Eden answered, drawing out the word.

"He's a personal trainer."

"Girl! What's wrong with that? Some of those guys make tons of money. Remember that guy who trained Oprah and then went on to write books and all kinds of stuff? That's nothing to be ashamed of."

"Trust and believe, he's no Bob Greene. He didn't graduate from college, rents an apartment in a modest neighborhood, and lived at a Louisiana correctional facility for four years—from seventeen to twenty-one."

Eden was stunned into paralysis. She held the phone away from her head, stared at the picture of Renee she'd programmed into it, and wondered who this was on the line with her good friend's voice and manner but incredulous conversation!

"You're shocked. I know. It's not what I planned."

Eden finally recovered her voice. "That's putting it mildly." A moment of silence passed, and then, "How tall is he?"

Pause. "Six-foot four, two-twenty. Solid muscle, massive strength. Think LL Cool J with even more swagger. Yet the kindest, most thoughtful human being you'd ever want to meet."

At least you checked one item off your list, Eden thought. "Wow," she said.

"He was in DC accompanying a client on an extended stay. I met him at the gym."

"You've gone to that gym for years, seen tons of fine men. What was it about . . ."

"Lance."

"Yes, what was it about Lance that was different?"

"Everything. It's hard to explain, but there was this presence about him that went beyond physical, though that, too, was pretty awesome. But he was focused and methodical; he wasn't checking out every woman who walked by—just took care of business and left. The third time I saw him there, I went up and introduced myself."

Eden had forgotten Renee's rule about the man having to make the first move. "You stepped to him?"

Renee laughed. "I know. All I can say is God has a wicked sense of humor. Lance is almost everything I said I'd never settle for. But now that I'm in the situation, I realize it's all about perspective. In throwing out that crazy list of expectations, I've found a man who exceeds my wildest dreams of happiness, who makes me feel whole and complete, protected and loved."

Eden laid back down. "I know what you mean."

"He makes me . . . What—you do?"

"Yes."

"Uh-oh. Sounds like it's time for somebody else to spill some beans."

The smile came through in Eden's voice. "Well, for starters his name is Jansen McKnight. He's my brother's best friend who I've known most of my life. He moved back to LA almost four years ago after his divorce." Eden paused and waited for Renee's response. There was none. "Renee?"

"Uh, I'm here, Eden. What did you say his name was?"

"Jansen McKnight."

"And you say he moved back to California?"

"Yes."

"From where?"

"Chicago. Renee, why all of these questions?"

Pause. Major pause. Five seconds, ten, thirty . . .

"Renee, you're starting to worry me. What's going on?"

"Is he a police officer?" Renee's voice, which moments ago had been jubilant and animated, was now low and dull.

"Yes," Eden responded, her heart beating faster, Jansen was a consummate ladies man. Is it possible that he and Renee dated? That they . . .

Renee interrupted Eden's uncomfortable thoughts.

"Around thirty-eight, thirty-nine years old?"

"Yes. Renee, do you know Jansen?"

"I've never met him, but I know of him."

"How?"

"Jansen McKnight is the cop who killed my brother."

55

Five minutes had passed since Eden hung up the phone, and still she didn't move. She simply sat there, staring into space, replaying the last part of her good friend and former colleague's conversation in her head.

"Jansen McKnight is the cop who killed my brother."

"Are you sure?"

"I'd bet my engagement ring on it. There were five officers placed on administrative leave following . . . Steven's murder. Jansen McKnight was one of the names listed. I remember all their names."

"But if five men were suspended, how do you know Jansen was the . . . reason your brother died?"

"If five men fired five guns, does it matter which bullet pierced Steven's heart?"

Eden sat the phone on the bed and placed her head in her hands. Her mind reeled, unable to process what she'd been told. Scenes from her whirlwind romance with Jansen played in her mind like a slideshow: their first real kiss in Michael's guest bathroom, the subsequent first date and unforgettable night. Intimate dinners, unforgettable nights, walks by the beach, unforgettable mornings, watching old movies, reminiscing, and unforgettable afternoons.

Then a different set of scenes began to play: her place and seeing Jansen's gun before he deftly tried to hide it under his clothes. His place and the gun on his bedroom dresser, and in the office, and a drawer in the kitchen, and in the well-stocked cabinet. Michael's house and the weapon that was never far from him. And the most distressing scene of all—at Michael's. Big man. In deep shadow. With a gun pointed at her chest.

Eden shuddered as she swallowed a gasp. "Jansen," she whispered, her hands going to her mouth, tears forming at the tips of her eyes. "Oh, baby, what have you done?"

The cell phone rang. Eden looked at the caller ID. Jansen, just as she'd figured. Now the tears fell, one by one, a stream of sadness down her face, pooling into a glob of abject despair. She silently implored, *Why this? And why now?* Now, when everything seemed perfect, and she'd decided to "allow," per Ariel's suggestion, and coexist peacefully with Jansen, his weapons, and his career choice. Now, when Jansen had opened more fully to her world, often joining in her yoga sessions and eating less meat. Thoughts of the coming weekend entered the equation. One of the biggest hurdles yet was about to be jumped as Jansen had agreed to join Alex and Christina on his boat. Both of their families knew and approved of the union. "It was perfect!" Eden ground out between gritted teeth. "Almost too good to be true," she whispered. She threw one pillow against the wall, and then another, and then all of the half a dozen that dotted her bed. Too keyed up to sleep, she paced and cried, and not wanting to risk even seeing his name right now, turned off her cell phone.

Jansen laid back, idling rubbing his manhood while waiting for Eden to pick up the phone. When the call went to voice mail, Jansen looked at the clock: 9:48. He waited for the beep and then left a message. "Hey, sleeping beauty. I see you got your wish and are probably already in dreamland. Enjoy it, baby, because this weekend I'm going to make it up to you. Check this, I traded Saturdays with a guy who needs next Sunday off. So he's going to work my Saturday this week, and I'll work his Sunday. That means we can hang out a little later on Friday, you know, at this kumbaya meeting at your boy's house. Only for you, little garden, would I go through these changes. Any other time, that brothah would have become well acquainted with my fist . . . a few times. Guess you're making me a better man. I miss you, baby. I want you with me all the time. I love you more than anything. Call me."

56

"Eden, it's him. *Again.*" Ariel's voice was compassionate yet firm. "I don't know what's going on, but . . . don't you think you should take his call?"

"Still in a meeting, Ariel," Eden curtly replied into the phone intercom. "For the rest of the morning I do not wish to be disturbed by anyone."

Eden tried to refocus on the report in front of her but soon dropped it on the desk, stood, and walked to the window. This October morning was cool and overcast, with California's habitual "sunny and seventy" having gone the way of her idyllic romance. She'd done nothing but think about what Renee had said and knew no more of what to make of it this morning than last night. Sleep had not come easy. She'd managed just a couple hours, giving in to slumber amid a lone bird's dawn lullaby. The shrill of the alarm had awakened her, and for a few glorious seconds she was free of thought and memory—it was just another day. Then she'd stretched and remembered. After showering and dressing, she'd turned on her phone, noting missed calls from her mother and more from Jansen. She had also seen that there were messages. She hadn't yet the strength to listen to them.

Eden returned to her desk, determined to work. An inner-office instant message popped up on her computer. *Alex.* Ariel says you are not to be disturbed. Is everything okay?

Eden's hand hovered over the keyboard as she formulated an answer. Busy, focusing. What do you need?

It can wait. Lunch?

Just the thought of food caused Eden's stomach to flip-flop. Thanks, but no. I'll order in.

Somehow Eden managed to get through the morning, actually return a few phone calls, answer some e-mails, and respond to the report she'd been sent. When Christina phoned, Eden was glad Ariel had ignored her mandate and put the call through. She accepted the invitation for lunch, and for a little over an hour she was able to take her mind off the Jansen/murder madness. She and Christina discussed the health fair, its successes and failures, and began setting up the foundation for an even bigger one next year. The miso soup had been comforting and healing, and Christina's effervescent personality had been beneficial as well. When she walked back into the center and saw Ariel sitting at the front desk, she actually smiled. The upturn was short-lived.

"Jansen called."

"How many times?"

"I've lost count. But the last one was five minutes ago. He said if he didn't hear from you within the hour, he was coming down. It sounded like he meant it."

Ariel's eyes bore into Eden. They were full of questions and compassion. "It's not my business—"

"No, it isn't—"

"But." Ariel visibly swallowed. "A heavy heart is a sign that something needs to be gotten off one's chest." Her voice was low, gentle. "I'm here, Eden."

"Let me call Jansen," Eden replied. "And then maybe I'll talk about it."

Eden bypassed her office and walked to the end of the hall.

"She lives!" Alex said once she'd tapped on his office door. "Did you make a dent in it?"

"In what?"

"The workload."

"Oh, that. Actually, yes."

"And you held out for a better invitation, I see."

Eden smiled. "You spoke to Christina."

"I called her just as she was leaving the restaurant. She said you'd met her."

"Yes, decided I needed the break after all and some fresh air. Was there something you wanted to discuss?"

Alex peered at Eden, noted the slight puffiness around her eyes, the eyes that did not twinkle as they usually did when she smiled. He took in the slight redness around her nose and the tightness of her mouth that silently negated the asking of questions. "It can wait," he finally said, turning to retrieve a file behind him and then facing her once again. "Maybe we can discuss it over lunch tomorrow. By then I'll have better organized my thoughts."

"Sounds good."

Eden walked to her office and shut the door. Once

again her stomach was in knots. She dreaded making this phone call but feared Jansen coming to visit even more. Eden had no doubt that Ariel was right. Jansen had meant what he'd said about coming down. There was one thing for sure about him—he didn't make threats, but promises.

Please let me get voice mail. I'll just leave a message and . . .

"Baby, finally! I was about to put out an APB on you, girl." Jansen nodded at Alberto, signaling that he'd meet him by the patrol car. He had a couple minutes of break time left and walked to the side of the coffee shop. "That was a long meeting, lasted all morning. Is everything okay?"

Eden took a deep breath. "I wasn't in a meeting, Jansen. I was busy trying to gather my thoughts and make sense of some things."

Silence.

The brooder. Eden could imagine the slight furrowing of eyebrows, could see his eyes narrowing and the slight puckering of those talented lips. She closed her eyes against his image.

"What's the matter, Eden?" Jansen said at last.

"Something I can't get into over the phone. Would you like to meet, say, around six in Culver City? That's halfway between you and me. There's a restaurant on Sepulveda at—"

"Whoa, baby, what the hell is this meeting-halfway nonsense? We've never met halfway a day in our lives. It's either your place or my place, and I don't mind driving."

"Jansen, please. I'll explain everything when I see you and . . . you'll understand."

"Fine, Eden, but I'm telling you now. This doesn't feel good."

"No, it doesn't." Eden gave Jansen the name of the restaurant. "I'll see you there."

It was the only workday Eden could remember in which she wanted time to slow down. By the time she reached her car, her nerves were frayed and, once again, her stomach roiled. When she got to the restaurant, she pulled into the parking lot, walked in, and immediately saw Jansen at the bar nursing a beer. He looked as gorgeous as she'd ever seen him—his buffed chest filling out a stark white muscle shirt that was tucked into black jeans, emphasizing a narrow waist and thick thighs. Her step faltered, but with resignation she pressed on. His eyes bore into hers as she approached him. He did not smile.

"Hey," she whispered, leaning forward to kiss him lightly on the mouth.

"Hey."

"Let's get a booth."

"Do you want something to drink?"

"No, I'm good." She walked to the last booth, the one farthest from either the door or other patrons, facing away from the room so she couldn't be seen.

She'd hoped Jansen would sit down on the other side, but instead he slid in beside her, took her in his arms, and seared her with a mouthwatering kiss. "That's better," he said when he finally released her. "I don't know what that little peck up front was about."

You can do this, Eden. You've got to do this! She

scooted away from him and leaned her back against the wall. "I talked to a friend of mine last night. Renee Newton?" She wondered if the name would ring a bell.

Jansen shrugged. "And?"

"She knows you."

"Renee Newton?" Jansen scowled, took a swig of beer, and then shook his head. "The name is not familiar. Where does she know me from?"

"Chicago."

"Chicago? Renee Newton . . ." Jansen's voice trailed off as he pondered the name, rubbing his chin thoughtfully. "Baby, I'm drawing a blank. Where did she say we met in Chicago?"

"Actually, it's more like she knows *of* you. It's her brother with whom you . . . had the encounter."

"Oh, okay. What's his name?"

"Steven. Steven Newton."

Jansen raised the bottle to his lips but just before it reached them, realization dawned. He slowly lowered the bottle to the table and turned his body toward Eden. His feelings were in his eyes: fear, judgment, regret. "What did she tell you?"

Eden looked at Jansen a long moment—willed away the tears that threatened to fall. "Is it true?" she asked, her voice barely above a whisper.

"What exactly are you asking me, Eden?"

Her lips began to tremble with the effort it took for her to remain calm. "Did you kill her brother?"

Jansen let out an audible sigh, rested his forearms on the table, and hung his head.

"Well . . . did you?"

"It's not cut-and-dry, Eden—"

"Isn't it?" Eden pushed the question through clenched teeth. "It's either yes or no."

"There's more to it than that."

"Jansen, I've got to know. Did you do it?" A single tear ran down her face, the only part of her body that moved.

"My gun was fired along with others, yes."

Eden felt a gush of air leave her lungs. She became light-headed and for a moment couldn't breathe.

"It was a no-win situation, Eden, and the only way out. Other lives were at stake and—"

"Whose lives? Yours? The other officers?" Anger slowly built at the core of Eden's being and spread outward. "Was his life any less valuable because he wasn't in uniform?"

"Eden, you don't know all the facts."

"And I don't want to know them! Here's what I do know. Steven was someone's son, brother, two children's father. I don't care what he did, Jansen. He didn't deserve to die."

"So that's your verdict, huh? I'm guilty without even a chance for rebuttal? You obviously listened to your friend's side of the story. But you don't want to listen to mine?"

"No, because nothing you say can justify taking a life or can bring his back. Now please move. I've got to get out of here."

57

"Greetings from the Zen Den! This is Ariel. How may I help you?"

"Good morning, Ariel."

"My word, Eden. What happened to your voice?"

Crying part of the night; screaming the other. "Rough night. I won't be in to work today."

"Is Jansen with you?"

Pause. One tear, two. "No."

"Would you like me to come over?"

Eden's voice quivered. "I can't ask you to leave the center."

"Melanie can cover for me. Her first class isn't until ten-thirty."

"Ariel, it's okay."

"It absolutely is. Everything is in divine order. Now what's your address?"

Twenty minutes later, Eden sat with a steaming mug of lavender-infused tea sprinkled with what Ariel referred to as "peace powder." White candles burned, as did a fragrant oil from a brass statue Ariel claimed was the Hindu deity of love. Aside from a long, nurturing hug and whispers of "all is well" and "love is all there is," there had barely been five words spoken between them. Ariel had waltzed into Eden's home as if she lived there, went to the kitchen, fixed the tea, and now sat quietly at the edge of Eden's bed. Eden rested against the headboard, her arms on her knees, amazed that against all odds she actually felt better. Not a lot— only a notch or so above horrific—but at this point she'd take any improvement she could get.

Another ten minutes went by without conversation. Ariel sat still, almost statuelike. Eden eyed her love-centered friend: legs crossed, eyes closed, hands resting comfortably in her lap, a slight impish smile on her face. *Meditating, no doubt. Or talking to her fairies.* Eden almost smiled. But not quite.

"Would you like more tea?" Ariel asked without otherwise moving or opening her eyes.

"I'm fine, thanks."

"When did you last eat?"

"Yesterday, but I'm not hungry."

Ariel nodded. "Okay."

Five more minutes went by. Eden repositioned the pillows and half sat, half lay against the headboard. Ariel uncrossed her legs and stretched.

Eden breathed in through her nose and out through her mouth, once, twice, and again. "I . . . I want to talk about it. But I can't seem to push the words past my lips."

Ariel waited, silent.

"It's about Jansen."

Now Ariel turned to face Eden directly. She placed

her elbows on her knees and balanced her chin on steepled fingers. "I'm listening."

"He killed someone." There, the horrible truth had been spoken aloud, yet again. Eden almost expected the ground to begin shaking beneath them. Her world had surely wobbled off its axis when met with this news.

Ariel didn't flinch or move. She slowly closed her eyes, inhaled, opened her eyes, exhaled.

"It was my friend's brother, or, rather, a colleague I knew in DC." Eden recounted the very brief account of the incident Renee had shared—namely that there had been a standoff, and after almost ten hours, her brother had been shot multiple times and died of his injuries.

"I'm so sorry," Ariel said, her voice barely above a whisper. "For everyone involved: your friend, her brother, you, Jansen, the other police . . . everyone."

A chirping bird, the one Eden thought lived near her windowsill, caught her eye. When she looked out the window, she noticed the gardener pruning the neighbor's bushes, a cat stealthily crossing from one yard to the next, a bicyclist coming down the alley. Amazing how, mere feet away, life went on normally when she knew hers would never be the same again.

"What did Jansen say?"

Eden sighed. "What could he say, Ariel? He took someone's life!"

Ariel remained calm, her voice even softer than before. "Yes, but why? What was the circumstance, the chain of events that caused this tragedy?"

Eden shrugged. *If five men fired five guns, does it matter which bullet pierced Steven's heart?* Renee's words caused her to shiver even as they reaffirmed her position that no excuse would ever change the facts of what happened. Jansen had shot his gun, and somebody had died. Eden looked at Ariel, and the tears she thought were finished began anew as she echoed Renee's question. "Does it matter, Ariel? Does it matter what happened when the end resulted in a life being taken?"

Ariel quietly arose from the bed, retrieved Eden's mug, and left the room. Eden could hear her humming in the kitchen, hear drawers being opened and closed, along with noisy paper bags. She returned less than ten minutes later bearing a tray with two steamy mugs, a plate of raw veggies, and a creamy faux-cheese sauce. She placed Eden's mug on her nightstand, and the veggie tray in the middle of the bed. Then she returned to her spot in the center, facing Eden. She picked up a carrot stick and munched it thoughtfully.

"My grandpa served in the war, the Korean War," she began, her voice as melodic as if she were discussing flowers in winter. "He was only seventeen when he signed up, said he'd been greener than a hornet at the time and that nobody that young should go to war.

"He was barely out of basic training when the army got called over. The training gave the men bravado and a steely resignation to do their job."

"Is that what you're going to tell me? That Jansen was just doing his job?"

"I can't speak for Jansen, Eden. He should be the one to do that. I'm talking about Pa." Ariel took several sips of tea, ran a stalk of celery through the sauce, and quietly munched it. "My grandpa's unit was ordered to take over this territory that was strategic to their victory. The fighting was intense; he said that after a while one simply became numb to anything but the training needed to keep their comrades alive and stay alive themselves.

"One day Pa said he came face-to-face with the enemy, a young boy who looked about his same age or younger. He said they stood there, guns drawn, for what seemed an eternity. Pa had faced deer, rabbits, squirrels, coon, had even downed pigs and cows for curing. But never a human being, and never anything that could shoot back."

Ariel became silent again, sipping tea, munching on veggie sticks. After another long moment, Eden reached for a snap pea and munched it mindlessly. "What happened?"

"Pa said it was the strangest thing, but . . . the boy smiled at him. Really smiled. Pa froze. He looked that boy in the eye, with his olive skin and black hair, and just couldn't do it, couldn't pull the trigger. He thought maybe they'd both just turn around and walk away, meet up with their units, and if they had too, shoot each other when, as my Pa said, 'he couldn't see the white of his eye.' Just when Pa was about to lower his gun, two shots rang out. See, the boy had smiled because he'd seen one of his friends coming toward them, preparing to shoot my grandpa in the back. Fortunately, two American soldiers had also seen the Koreans. One trained his gun on the boy in front of Pa, and the other one took out the guy who would have been Pa's assassin."

Ariel had been looking out the window. Her eyes were glassy as she fixed them on Eden. "If it hadn't been for those two soldiers, my grandpa would have died, and I wouldn't be here."

The two women sipped their tea in silence. Ariel drew figure eights on Eden's silk, pale pink comforter. Eden stared out the window, looking for an answer to the dilemma she faced, other than the obvious one that would separate her from Jansen forever.

Ariel looked at her watch, stood, and reached for the tray. She took it to the kitchen, and Eden heard water running. After a couple minutes, Ariel returned. "I have to run, dear one," she said, coming over to give Eden a hug. "There are three sides to every story, Eden. And even that which we view as truth is—"

"—only an illusion," they whispered together.

Ariel reached for her purse and headed for the door.

"Ariel?"

She turned. "Yes, Eden?"

"Thanks."

"*Namaste.*" Ariel clasped her hands, did a slight bow, and left.

58

Eden lay down after Ariel left, but sleep eluded her. What she did realize, however, in those moments of stillness, was that she did feel better. The pain, actual ache, that had seized her heart upon leaving Jansen at the restaurant was abating. And she realized something else. Jansen hadn't called.

"Probably for the best," she murmured as she climbed out of bed and pulled off her pajamas. She ran the water as hot as she could stand it, poured in a generous amount of a lavender-vanilla mix, and turned on the jets. When the tub was filled she climbed in and thankfully sank into the searing liquid. She allowed the powerful jets to sooth the knots that were in her neck and shoulders. When images of Jansen kneading those very same muscles assailed her, she shook them away. Other images arose and weren't as easily dismissed. Her muscles involuntarily clinched. Even if she told her mind she didn't miss him, her body knew otherwise.

After a long soak, Eden washed her hair, did forty-five minutes of yoga, and then decided to organize the three hundred or so books that constituted her library. Anything to keep herself busy and her thoughts diverted. After setting up her iPod and scrolling to the first track of Jennifer Lindsay's debut CD, *Songs in the Dark*, she pulled all the books from their shelves and divided them by topic. Beginning with her politically oriented books, her largest collection, she began stacking the titles in alphabetical order. By the time the last track of the album began to play, she'd successfully organized the political section from *A* to *Z,* and instead of simply placing the books back on the shelf side by side, she became creative, laying some on their backs, other side by side, and, after scrounging her house, placing various items between the books for a more interesting visual. She was standing back, admiring her partially done handiwork, when the phone rang.

Immediately, she thought of Jansen but allowed a small smile when she looked at the caller ID. "Hey, Mom."

"Are you busy, baby? I can call you later on, if that's the case."

Eden quickly pondered what to tell her mother, deciding that less was better. "I've got a couple minutes," she said as cheerfully as possible. "What's up?"

"Kathryn said Jansen showed up on her doorstep last night looking like somebody shot his dog and killed his cat. When she asked him what was wrong, he said y'all had broken up but wouldn't elaborate. You two were like peas in a pod when I left just two days ago. What happened, Eden?"

So much for my plans to keep Mom out of this. "It's a long story, Mom, but I really can't get into it right now."

"Well, before you tell me you're getting ready to go into a meeting, you should know I called the job and talked to Ariel. She said you weren't feeling well. When I asked her if it was your heart that was sick that child closed up tighter than an oil-slick bottle with a childproof cap. I was impressed, especially after how, when we met, she talked nonstop. That's a friend right there."

Eden genuinely smiled for the first time in two and half days. "That she is."

"Is it another woman?"

"Mom, please."

"Okay, baby, I know it's none of my business."

No, it isn't.

"Is it his job?"

"Mom!"

"Okay, okay, but you should know Kathryn is beside herself; says she's never seen Jansen look this miserable, even after his daddy died. So whatever happened, I hope y'all can work it out. Because I watched you, Eden, you and Jansen. Saw how you acted when you didn't know anyone was looking. I know a fit when I see one, daughter—you know, the hand-in-glove kind, the white-on-rice kind?"

Eden wanted to rush off the phone. She was tired of crying, and listening to her mother threatened to open the floodgates again.

"Y'all are it, baby."

"Mom, I gotta go."

"Okay, Eden. I'm going to back out of your business. But don't be sitting over there with pride and stubbornness for company. Call me if you decide to talk about what's bothering you. And more importantly . . . call Jansen. Kathryn said he hasn't heard from you."

"Okay, Mom. I love you. Bye." Eden hurried off the phone, switched her iPod to the Black Eyed Peas, and dove back into her book project. She was determined not to give her mother's word one second's thought. When the phone rang again less than ten minutes later, she almost didn't even look at the ID. When she did, she answered. "Hey, Alex. I was going to call you a little later."

"I'm not calling about work. I'm calling about you. Are you okay?"

No! Eden wanted to scream as loud as humanly possible. *No, I am not okay!* "I've been better," she truthfully answered. "But don't worry, I'll be back to work on Monday."

"Oh, so I won't be seeing you and Jansen later tonight?"

"No."

Hmmm. Trouble in paradise? "Want to talk about it?"

Eden went off. "Why does everybody want me to talk about it? I don't feel like talking, okay?"

There was a long moment of silence. Alex cleared his throat.

"I'm sorry, Alex. I shouldn't have snapped at you."

"It's obvious you've got something on your mind, Eden." Alex paused again as though he wanted to say something further but decided against it. "I'll talk to you later."

Eden finished her library project, which had led to her organizing her drawers and closets as well, around six PM, and after finally feeling hunger pangs ordered

from a Thai restaurant near her house. She'd watched
about thirty minutes of *What's Love Got to Do with It*
when her buzzer sounded. Assuming it was her food,
she buzzed him in.

Instead of a delivery man, a uniformed driver stood
at her door.

"Uh, I think you have the wrong house."

"Ms. Anderson? Eden?"

Eden frowned. "Yes?"

"My name is Sullivan, and I was sent here by Dr.
Kostopoulos. He is requesting the pleasure of your
company at his Malibu estate. Dr. Christina Montague
will be there as well."

Eden stood speechless. "It is a casual affair," the driver
continued. "The doctor recommends jeans, T-shirt, a
light jacket to ward off the night chill. I'm at your
disposal, so you will be free to return home whenever
you wish."

Eden's door buzzer sounded again. "Hold on a
moment." She buzzed in the Thai delivery guy and
paid him when he arrived. "I just ordered dinner," she
explained to the driver as she watched the delivery guy
head back to the elevator.

"Dr. Kostopoulos employs an excellent chef, madam.
I am sure he will be able to replicate the dish you've ordered or prepare anything that you'd like. Additionally,
you are welcome to bring that with you, and we can
heat it up once we arrive."

For two days straight, Eden had been able to think
of nothing but Jansen McKnight and the terrible news
she'd learned about him. Suddenly it felt as if the walls
were closing in on her, and an evening spent at the

ocean's edge became an increasingly attractive idea. "You said I can come home at any time, correct?"

The driver nodded. "That is correct, madam."

"It will take me a few minutes to change clothes."

"I'll be down in the car, madam. Take your time."

Soon Eden was nestled in the back of a large black town car as they drove toward the Pacific Coast Highway. *What am I doing?* The driver turned onto the coast, and the ocean, in all its magnificence, came into view. *You may not know what you're doing, Eden Anderson, but you're about to find out.*

59

Eden thought she'd never laugh again, but here she was, with Alex, feeling true joy. The best thing she could have done for herself the last week was accept his invitation to Malibu. The atmosphere had been just the balm she'd needed. His elegantly appointed house sat about thirty feet from the ocean's edge. A large deck had provided the perfect place to watch the sunset, outfitted with a full outdoor kitchen, comfy deck furniture, and an oversize hot tub. It was from there that the chef had prepared a delectable meal of grilled vegetables, mushroom risotto, and a rice-based croquette that resembled crab cake. This delicious fare had been accompanied by a limited-edition Greek white wine from one of Alex's longtime family friends who owned one of the country's largest vineyards. Christina had called to cancel, citing a last-minute emergency. At first, Eden had thought it planned, but after speaking with Christina personally, knew otherwise. Alex had been a perfect gentleman, and when she'd said that friendship was all she could offer him, he'd said it was enough. He'd taken her out on the boat to the middle of the ocean, where they'd enjoyed a glorious sunset. Alex's world was so vibrant and interesting she'd actually had moments where Jansen wasn't on her mind. They were rare, but they'd happened. And for that she was grateful.

"I said you'd love it," Alex said, referring to the comedy benefit they were now attending in Palm Springs.

"You were right. This is just what I needed, Alex. I really appreciate your inviting me."

He hugged her good-naturedly—placed a kiss on her cheek. "You're welcome." Alex was ecstatic to be sitting there with Eden. He was sure that whatever had happened last week had involved the big, bad cop. He'd probed once, gently, and been promptly shut down. Eden had said the topic of Jansen was strictly off-limits. Alex hadn't asked again. *Slow and steady wins the race,* he thought as the next comedian took the stage, and he lightly rubbed Eden's shoulder.

Jansen's bad mood was perpetual, and Alberto worried. He'd never seen his partner this down or this quiet. He watched Jansen walk to the vehicle and could have sworn the brother had lost weight. The reason for his concern wasn't totally selfless—a partner whose mind was elsewhere could get them both in a world of trouble.

"Good news?" Alberto asked when Jansen got into the car.

Jansen snorted. Alberto backed the car out of the

station parking lot and headed toward La Brea. "They got Terrell Ford again," Jansen said.

"Oh, yeah? That fool never learns."

"Boys like him never do. He's looking at time now though." When Alberto threw him a questioning look, Jansen continued. "He used a weapon this time—first-degree burglary, felonious assault, drug possession."

Alberto shook his head. "You think he's part of the gang robbing in Baldwin Hills?"

"We'll soon find out. Some dudes will sing like canaries when they're looking at twenty-to-life."

"He's not going to get that much."

"He might. They're going to sentence him not only for these crimes but for the others he did and didn't get caught."

They continued in silence. Jansen grimaced and rubbed his eyes, remembering yesterday's conversation with Dakkar.

"Have you seen her?" Jansen asked, his face turned to the side as Dakkar kneaded the knots from everywhere.

"Look, man, I don't want to get into it."

"I'm not asking you to—I'm just asking have you seen her? Is she at work?"

"Yes, she was gone only the one day and came back on Monday."

"I bet she's hanging out with that punk-ass Alex. He couldn't wait for a chance to make his move. Am I right?"

Dakkar sighed, kneaded.

Jansen sat up abruptly. "Look, man. How long have I known you?"

Dakkar looked Jansen in the eye. "A long time."

"Then help a brothah out. Tell me what you know."

Dakkar turned to the jar that contained a mixture of shea butter, aloe, and herbs. He briskly rubbed his hands together. "I know they work together, brothah, that's all."

"She's in his office?"

Dakkar nodded.

"And he's in hers?"

Again, Dakkar nodded. "But that doesn't necessarily mean anything, man. Now come on, lie down and relax. You're going to tighten up the area I just smoothed out, and your rate is going to double for the extra work I'm doing."

"I just need to talk to her, dog," Jansen said after lying down. "That's it, just talk. She won't take my calls, and I'm better off not coming to the job. I'd take one look at that Greek asshole, and somebody would get hurt. I just want to talk to her, see her. . . ." Jansen whispered before falling asleep.

"Damn, man, where you at?"

"I'm sorry, Al, did you say something?"

"Only for the past five minutes." They arrived at the place of their latest investigation, a warehouse that had been relieved of over a quarter million dollars' worth of machinery. "Look, Jansen, she's gonna come back. Women be trippin', dog, it's what they do! My old lady trips on the regular—even when she ain't pregnant, I can find myself on the couch for no reason. Just give her space and let it pass."

"It's not that easy, especially when she won't even hear my side of the story. That shit's messed up."

"You still haven't told her?"

"Didn't you hear what I just said?"

Alberto tapped the steering wheel. He'd never been good at the emotional, heart-tug kind of situations. Most of the time he diffused such moments with humor. Now was one of those times. "Hell, if she won't take your calls, send her ass a letter. Do an Oleta Adams on her ass and go trailway-railway—planes, trains, and automobiles."

Alberto succeeded in getting Jansen to smile. "I think you've mixed Oleta with a little Billy Crystal."

"Whatever gets you out of the *P* funk. Come on, brothah. Duty calls."

60

Eden walked into her place, exhausted. Yet she was glad she'd insisted that Sullivan, the driver, bring her home. Alex had wanted her to stay in Palm Springs. After declining her own room in the four-bedroom penthouse suite, he'd offered her her own, smaller suite on another floor. But Eden didn't want to send any mixed signals or raise expectations—even though she hadn't failed to notice how much she and Alex had in common, and how potentially easy it would be to blend their lives. Yet while her body had been with Alex, Jansen had never been far from her mind. It had been only a week but felt like years since she'd seen, smelled, touched his addictive body. He'd weighed on her heavily all the way home. She'd almost called him. *Maybe on Sunday. . . .*

She entered her home and immediately prepared for bed. Planning on sleeping in the next day, Saturday, she decided to quickly check her e-mails and see if Renee had responded to her e-mail. They hadn't talked since the night she'd learned of Jansen's involvement in Steven's death. The silence had been awkward. Even though she knew they'd probably neared the end of their friendship, such as it was, Eden had written to try to clear the air, assure her there were no hard feelings.

She skimmed her inbox and read a message from Chandra announcing a trip to LA. *It will be good to see her,* Eden thought even though they'd talked only one other time after the first reconnection. She hadn't seen Chandra since high school. *I'm glad I didn't tell her about me and . . .*

Jansen! Eden's eyes widened when she saw an e-mail from *Blue Knight.* His face came to her immediately as the only one who could sport that moniker. She hesitated only seconds before clicking on the link. With the first sentence, her heartbeat quickened.

> Eden: There were children involved. Steven Newton fired into a playground crowded with kids. If we hadn't taken him out, some of them would have died. That's what happened. And while it wasn't an easy choice, and something I'll live with for the rest of my life, if given the same set of circumstances, I'd do it again. That's the short version. If you want to talk, call me. J.

Eden read the brief e-mail over and again. She tried to understand what hadn't been written—how Jansen was doing, how he felt about her now. It hadn't escaped her notice that there were no terms of endearment, no declarations of love. She wasn't "little garden," or "weed," but Eden. "Well, what did you expect?" she asked out loud. "You're the one who left without looking back." She read the horrid details yet again. *Could this be true? Could Renee's brother have instigated the event that brought on his demise?* The thought to call and ask her was quickly dispelled. How could she justify talking about it with Renee again until she'd at least talked once to Jansen?

Eden looked at the clock. It was almost two AM. She turned off the computer, deciding to follow her initial plan and call him on Sunday. *No, I'll go see him. That's it. I'll go to Gardena on his day off.*

61

"Sorry to wake you," Alex said upon hearing the sleepiness in Eden's voice.

"Alex? Do you know what day it is?"

Alex laughed. "Saturday, I know. And you know I wouldn't call unless it was an emergency. But I just got a call from a friend of mine, a member of the French parliament, with major connections here to people with deep pockets, people who are interested in the holistic lifestyle and will donate to our cause. He's going to be here for only one day. Can you meet us at the center? We'll do a walk-through and then take him to brunch."

"This sounds fabulous, Alex, but why do I have to be there?"

"Because he appreciates beauty," Alex said without apology. "Once he meets you, the money is as good as in the bank."

An hour and a half later, Eden strolled into the Zen Den. She didn't come in most Saturdays and forgot how bustling it was—by far their busiest day. She was surprised not to see Ariel and then remembered that today was Travis's birthday. Eden smiled. *I wouldn't be surprised if she didn't show up on Monday, due to matters of the heart.*

Eden met up with Alex and his dignitary, and after an extensive tour of the grounds, stood near the lobby while their guest used the facilities.

"I owe you big time," Alex said, beaming. "Francois was extremely impressed with you. But don't worry, I told him you were unavailable."

"Thank you."

"Hey, what are you doing tonight?"

"No plans, why?"

"There's supposed to be a huge meteor shower tonight, clearly visible here on the west coast. I was told of a place just outside the city where we could see it clearly."

"Alex . . ."

"My intentions are entirely honorable," Alex continued. "Have you ever witnessed such a shower?"

"Can't say that I have."

"They are pure magic."

Eden thought for a moment. "Now that you mention it, I did see that e-mail. Didn't read it though, but Ariel had mentioned it as well."

"Then you'll come? Tonight? Around ten o'clock?"

When Eden nodded, Alex gave her the details. The dignitary walked up just as he finished. "All set?" Alex asked, looking from the Frenchman to Eden. "Let's go."

Dakkar closed his eyes, and let out the breath he'd been holding. Like many in the center, he believed that nothing happened by coincidence, and there was a reason he'd been standing where he was—just inside the large storage room. Which was how he was able to overhear the entire conversation that had taken place between Alex and Eden. He reached for his phone without thinking twice. "Jansen, Dakkar. I've got news."

The day passed quickly, and by the time nine o'clock rolled around, Eden was actually excited to witness the shower with Alex. After brunch with him and Francois, she'd come home and Googled *meteor showers*. If what happened was anything like what had been described, they were in for a treat. She'd dressed casually in a brushed cotton warm-up and tennis shoes. Her hair was pulled back into a ponytail, and except for mascara and gloss, she was makeup free. She reached for her nuts, water, and jacket, made sure she had her cell phone, and headed out the door.

Jansen hit speed dial on his cell phone and dialed the station. "Sheila, Jansen. Did you get the information I asked for?"

"Is coffee black?" she asked with just the right amount of sexy in her voice. This attractive, plus-sized veteran had been after Jansen since he'd arrived. But it was harmless flirting. Sheila was married with children and no plans to leave her husband any time soon. "Who is this doctor, and why is he so important to you?"

"Never mind that, just give me the info."

Sheila sighed. "I do you a favor, and this is the

thanks I get? You'd better be glad you're a handsome
hunk, or you'd get *nada*. Do you have a pen?"

Alex cursed the faulty GPS that had directed he exit
onto Hawthorne from the 405. After turning right, he
realized how far he was from his destination and knew
he could have continued farther down the freeway. He
was already behind, having run into the bumper-to-
bumper traffic typical of a Saturday night in metropolitan LA. In hindsight, he should have used his driver.
But he'd wanted to flow independently tonight and for
the night to be with him and Eden alone.

"Come on!" he yelled to a slow-moving driver. He
downshifted, pressed the gas on his Mercedes, and
sped around them. Once he passed them, he didn't de-
crease his speed. The lights were in his favor, and he
flew through green after green. On his fourth attempt
he made it but saw a flash of bright white light behind
him. He'd heard about the cameras installed at certain
intersections, and how ridiculous were the fines. Alex
smiled and kept on moving. There was no price too
high when it came to Eden Anderson. She didn't know
it yet, but in her Alex felt he'd met the woman of his
dreams.

"Damnit!" Alex looked in the rearview mirror to
be sure he wasn't mistaken. He wasn't. He'd seen the
bright lights from the camera but hadn't seen the
police. Now bright red lights, accompanied by a short
siren, told him that once again he'd be delayed.

Jansen couldn't believe his luck. Or his timing. The
jet-black luxury auto pulled to the side. But Hawthorne

was busy. Over the outside intercom, he directed the driver to turn onto a side street. The driver complied. Jansen smiled. As soon as they'd turned and gone down a short distance, the Mercedes pulled over once again.

Alex jumped out of his car. "What's going on?"

"Get back into the vehicle," Jansen commanded in a tone that brooked no argument. Alex stopped short, turned on his heel, and stomped back to the car. Jansen waited until Alex had gotten back in his car. He pulled out his weapon, checked the bullets and safety, and then got out of the car.

He strolled up to the driver's-side window, which Alex had already opened.

"Here's what you need—license, registration, and insurance, right?" Alex handed the items out the window. He just wanted the jerk cop to write up the ticket so he could be on his way. When the officer didn't take the paperwork, Alex looked out the window. It was just before dark, yet the officer wore sunglasses. He couldn't make out his face, but something about him . . .

"Step out of the vehicle."

Now he knew. It was the same voice that had ordered an arm away from around a certain woman. Alex's blood boiled, but he figured now was not the time for confrontation. He had been speeding, Jansen was a cop, and he didn't want to go to jail. "Look, buddy, you tell me to get in, and now you're telling me to get back out. Just write the ticket."

Jansen leaned down to Alex's eye level. "Look, doc. We can do this easy, or we can do this hard. Now step out of the vehicle." Alex begrudgingly complied. "Now get into the backseat."

"What?"

"You heard me."

"I'll do no such thing!"

"Would you prefer the trunk?" Alex's green eyes turned almost black with indignation. Jansen smiled. "Look around you, doctor. This street is pretty isolated. It's Saturday night. People are out living it up." The smile disappeared. "Now, into the backseat. I won't tell you again."

Alex rose up to his full six feet. "You don't scare me, asshole. You'll pay for this."

"Yeah, well, not tonight." Once Alex was in the backseat, Jansen chained his legs and cuffed him to the door handle.

"What the hell are you doing? Do you have any idea how much trouble you're making for yourself? Do you know who I am?"

"I know who you think you are." Once Jansen had taken his cell phone and checked the car for anything that could help Alex escape, he straightened. "Just try to relax. I'll be back shortly." With that, he was gone.

Eden enjoyed the sounds of the water hitting the shore. Alex was right. Here, away from the city lights, the stars seemed brighter, closer. She'd arrived earlier than she thought, almost half an hour before their scheduled nine PM meet-up. The place seemed a bit isolated, but Eden wasn't afraid. This was a city filled with homes for the upper middle class, most of those residences hugging the shoreline. She looked over at the other lone car. *Another star-gazing couple,* she noted, a blond-haired man in the driver's seat, his companion's hair long and dark.

Eden eased down her windows a bit more, reclined in her seat, and closed her eyes. She'd intended to take a nap after returning from her time with Alex, but between overdue phone chats with her mother, Bridgett, Michael, and Delphia, along with wading through the e-mails she'd avoided all week, there just hadn't been time. *I'll just rest my eyes for a minute.*

And a minute was all the time she got. The next thing Eden knew, there was a knife to her throat.

Eden froze instinctively as she felt cold metal pressing against her skin. "What do you want?" she stammered. "I don't have any money on me." She looked up and noticed that the man who held the knife to her throat was the one she'd eyed in the other lone car in the small parking lot moments before. The person she'd thought was a woman was actually a long-haired man who demanded she unlock the doors and even now rummaged through her purse, scattering her items in every direction.

"She ain't got shit!" the long-haired man shouted. "Let's get out of here, man."

"Oh, no," Blondie drawled. "She may not have money, but I think we might be able to negotiate another form of payment." He slid the blade of the knife from her throat to her cheek, and across her lips. "You're a pretty thing, you know that?"

"Please," Eden whispered, hardly recognizing her own voice. "You don't want to do this. I'm expecting my friend any minute. Your friend is right. You need to leave." *Please hurry, Alex. Please!*

Long-Hair was becoming more nervous. "Come on, man. I signed on to rob a few folk, put some change in my pocket. But not . . . what you're thinking. I'm not down with this."

"Then move your ass!" Blondie shouted. "And if you breathe a word to anybody, I'll kill you."

Eden and Long-Hair's eyes met. She guessed him to be no more than nineteen years old, the man holding the knife a few years older. It looked as if the kid wanted to help her but didn't know how. "I'm sorry, ma'am," he said and took off.

"Well, now, little lady. It's just you and me. And I'm ready to party!"

Eden knew it might prove futile, but she tried reason. "You seem like a nice young man," she began.

"Shut up!" Blondie shouted, opening the door. Eden had already guessed him to be around five-foot-nine or -ten. But his was a stocky build, lots of upper muscle strength. Still, she wouldn't go down without a fight. She leaned back and began kicking, belatedly remembering the pepper spray on the key chain, and wishing she'd taken Jansen up on his offer to teach her self-defense moves.

Blondie found her fighting humorous. He easily grabbed her legs, using the knife to rip the top of her warm-up open in one quick move. Steel found flesh, and Eden felt a sharp pain near her navel. "Ow!"

Blondie's grin was lecherous. "You'd better stop struggling unless you want that pretty brown body tattooed with stab wounds." He grabbed Eden's arm and tried to pull her out of the car and into the backseat. Once her feet hit the pavement, however, she became a tigress—biting and hitting and screaming, all at once. And then she saw headlights turning into the parking lot. *Alex!* She tried to turn and run toward the car, but Blondie grabbed her and put the knife to her neck. "You make one move, and you die," he growled, beginning to slowly turn toward the vehicle that had so inconveniently interrupted his rendezvous.

"Police! Freeze, you asshole."

Jansen?

Blondie jerked around with Eden squarely in front of him. Jansen could see the glare of the headlights bouncing off the sharp metal at his garden's throat. He could take this guy out, no problem. Eden was several inches shorter than her captor. It would take one bullet, straight to the head. Jansen's finger tightened on the trigger; energy surged into his veins. He imagined tossing the gun to the side and taking this guy with his bare hands. Only years of military discipline kept him cool under pressure unlike he'd ever felt. But this situation was getting ready to end. And he was ending it now.

He pulled the trigger. Eden screamed. Blondie dropped to the ground. Eden ran into Jansen's arms. "Jansen, Jansen," she sobbed, holding on to him for dear life.

"Shhh, it's all right, little garden," he said, hugging her even as he eyed the wounded suspect. "Go sit in the car. I have to take care of this. Come on, baby, let go."

Eden buried her head in Jansen's shirt. "I don't want to see."

"You don't have to. It's only a shoulder wound, it'll heal. Now go get in the car. Don't turn around."

Within minutes, the local police were on the scene. They took the man into custody without incident. The responding officer walked over to Jansen. "She was lucky you were passing through, but . . . what were you doing so far out of your precinct area?"

"Off duty. On my way to see a friend."

The officer nodded. "I understand. One more question. How'd the suspect's nose get broken?"

Jansen looked the officer in the eye and spoke without hesitation. "I guess he fell down. This pavement is unforgiving."

62

One month later, and Eden's life looked totally different than it had before. She never would have guessed it, but as her mother often said, life was what happened while she was busy making plans.

Following her assault, Eden and Jansen talked about the Chicago shooting. Ariel had been right. There were three sides to every story and Eden was glad she'd finally decided to listen to Jansen's version of what happened. In her brief account, Renee had left out a couple of major details. Her brother battled a lifetime of mental illness. Steven Newton was assumingly off his meds the day he went on a rampage, killing his ex-girlfriend and her new lover. He arrived at the schoolyard seeking his third target—an eight-year old second grader, his ex-girlfriend's son. Steven held this little boy responsible for the relationship ending, and planned the ultimate revenge.

As for whose bullet actually killed him, no one could be sure. All of the officers fired from the same type of weapon, so all equally took responsibility for his death. Even now, all these years later, Jansen's regret was palpable. Not that he and his fellow officers protected a playground full of children, but that it took taking a life to do so. That night, following these reve- lations, the love-making had been soulful, exquisite, as Eden tried to ease Jansen's sadness with each touch, each kiss, each pelvic thrust. That night, their love got back on track.

The same could not be said for Eden's career at the Zen Den. She was no longer at the center. As much as she'd loved the establishment and had seen it in her future for years to come, too much had happened for her to stay there. After learning the details of how Jansen had been in the right place at the right time to affect her rescue, she'd scheduled a meeting with Alex for the first thing that following Monday. They talked for over two hours, during which time Eden phoned Jansen. He apologized to Alex, who after learning of Eden's near rape, was grateful that it was an armed police officer and not he who'd showed up on the scene. The two men reached an unlikely truce, and for that, Eden was grateful. Alex tried to convince Eden to stay at the center, she was an excellent fit for their es- tablishment, but Eden decided she wanted to work somewhere closer to home. Her new home in Gardena.

It was the one condition on which Jansen would not budge. He wanted to keep his little garden safe. The best way to do that—he'd adamantly explained after she yet again refused target practice at the shooting gallery—was under his roof. So Eden had placed her newly purchased condo back on the market, given a thirty-day notice to the Zen Den and, within that time, secured another job managing a metaphysical store. This five-year old establishment in Redondo Beach had just recently expanded to allow the addition of various spiritual modalities to offer their customers: chakra readings, hypnotherapy, mini-massages, and energy healing. The lower pay was offset by Eden's joy at finding another opportunity to immerse herself in what she truly loved—her mission and her man.

Eden's eyes shone with love as Jansen reentered the room. He carried a bottle of bubbly and a tray filled with fruit, veggies, soft brie cheese, and warm French bread. He sat the tray down in the middle of his king-size bed and then popped the cork.

"What are we celebrating?" Eden asked coyly. "Or are you already thinking about the two weeks until Cameron will be here, when I won't have you all to myself?" She honestly didn't think anything could top the festivities of the past month, when Jansen had sexed her every single day, sometimes twice—not only taking her to the moon and the stars but to other planets she hadn't known existed.

Jansen poured them each a glass and handed one to her. "Baby, every moment with you is a celebration, and Cameron will be at the other end of the hall. But I do have some news."

Eden sat up. "I'm all ears."

Jansen's eyes scanned her scantily clad body. "No . . . you're not. I was approached with an interesting opportunity to maybe get off the streets and pursue a . . . higher calling."

Eden almost spilled her drink. "You're going to be a preacher?"

"Ha! Not hardly, baby," Jansen answered, tweaking her nipple through thin, lacy fabric.

"Oh, my God. I was about to say—"

"No, this is a new program they're starting with the city of Los Angeles. An outreach situation that would pair law enforcement with some of these hardheads, a mentoring, guidance-type program that goes deeper than the once-a-week or twice-a-month outing but actually guides these young bloods out of the hood, through college, and beyond."

"Sounds impressive. What's the program called?"

"PULL—Police United for Lasting Legacies." Jansen appeared cool, but, inside, his heart sought hard for his woman's approval.

It came quickly. "I love it," Eden said. She raised her glass. "To PULL, and to you. Actually, only to you. You're my hero, Jansen. I love you."

They toasted and drank.

"Wait a minute," Eden said, her eyes narrowing. "Does that mean I'm never again going to see you in that sexy blue uniform with that fancy belt filled with gadgets for every occasion?"

"Oh, I'll still wear the uniform," Jansen responded. "And I'll still get to use these." With movements quicker than that of a panther, Jansen had gripped Eden's arm and secured it to a wrought-iron art piece above his bed.

"Jansen! What are you doing?"

Jansen's smile was predatory. "You'll see." He

reached into the drawer of his nightstand and pulled out another set of cuffs.

"No!" Eden tried to sound indignant, but secretly she was getting turned on.

"Yes," Jansen drawled as he reached for her other hand and licked the fingers before securely fastening it to the other side. "This is my reward for winning the dare. You, handcuffed. Me, free to have my way with you."

"Okay, wait a minute. Stop. Back up. What are you talking about? You haven't won a thing!"

"Oh, haven't I? Have you not been properly seduced— and improperly, too, for that matter? And aren't you right now in my home, and my bed, where you belong?"

Eden sputtered in an attempt to find words even as she jerked against the cuffs. "Surely, you jest," she countered, shivering as Jansen brushed his fingers across her stomach before drifting farther down and parting her lips to lightly flick her flower. Eden swallowed a moan before breathlessly responding. "If anything . . . I seduced you!"

"Oh, yeah?" Jansen asked with a chuckle, lightly licking and then kissing her flower. He stood, as he slowly pulled off his tank top and released the knot on his drawstring pants. "We'll see about that."

Eden took one look at "Mr. Magic" and knew hers was an uphill battle of which she'd gladly lose. After an hour of foreplay and several orgasms, Eden wrapped her legs around Jansen's waist, content to let the brothah think he'd won. Who was she to argue, when he had her singing soprano, seeing stars, and loving her to within an inch of her life? This was the man of her dreams and the father of the child that even now grew inside her. Eden felt yet another oncoming climax, held Jansen tighter, and beamed with satisfaction. Losing a bet had never felt so good.

Want more?
Turn the page for Zuri Day's

What Love Tastes Like

Available now wherever books are sold

Turn the page for an excerpt from
What Love Tastes Like . . .

I

Could anybody possibly be that fine? That's what Tiffany Matthews asked herself as she fastened her seat belt, took a deep breath, and clutched a teddy bear that looked as frazzled as she felt. The bear had an excuse—it was twenty-three years old. And so did Tiffany—she was exhausted. Graduating from culinary school and preparing for a month-long overseas internship had taken its toll.

There was yet another draining aspect to consider: Tiffany was terrified of flying. So much so that even after taking the anxiety pill her best friend had given her, she brazenly endured the curious stares of fellow passengers as they watched the naturally attractive, obviously adult woman sit in the airport, enter the jetway, and then board a plane with a raggedy stuffed animal clasped to her chest.

Tiffany didn't care. During a childhood where her mother worked long hours and her grandmother loved but didn't entertain, Tuffy, the teddy bear, had been her constant and sometimes only friend. No matter what happened, Tuffy was there to lend a cushy ear, an eternal smile, and wide, button-eyed support. This stuffed animal was also the first present she remembered her father giving her, when she was five years old. Unfortunately, his gift stayed around longer than Daddy did, a fact that after years of not seeing him still brought Tiffany pain. They were estranged, and while Tiffany would never admit it, having her father's first gift close by always felt like having him near. Tuffy brought comfort—during her childhood of loneliness, her teenaged years of puppy love and superficial heartbreak, her college years of first love and true pain, and now, while pursuing a dream her parents felt was beneath her. As the plane began its ascent into the magnificently blue May sky, and Tiffany squeezed her eyes shut, praying the pill would stave off an attack, she knew she'd take any help she could get to make it through this flight, even that of a furry friend.

It wasn't until the plane leveled off and her heartbeat slowed that she thought of him again—the stranger in first class. Their eyes had met when she passed by him on the way to her seat in coach. Tiffany had assessed him in an instant: fine, classy, rich. *And probably married,* she concluded, as she finally loosened the death grip she had on Tuffy and laid him on the middle seat next to her. *Clearly out of my league.* . . . Still, she couldn't help but remember how her breath caught when she entered the plane and saw him sitting there, looking like a *GQ* ad, in the second row, aisle seat. His close-cropped black hair looked soft and touchable, his cushiony lips framed nicely by just the hint of a mustache. But it was his eyes that had caused Tiffany's breath to catch: the deepest brown she'd ever seen, especially set against flawless skin that not only looked the color of maple syrup, but she imagined tasted as sweet. This information was absorbed and processed in the seconds it took the man two people in front of her to put his carry-on in the overhead bin and step aside so the people behind him could continue. The stranger had glanced up at her. Their eyes had held for a moment. Had she imagined his giving her a quick once-over before he resumed reading his magazine?

Tiffany tilted back her seat and placed Tuffy on her lap. Perhaps it was the medication or the lack of sleep the prior night, but Tiffany welcomed what she hoped would be a long slumber that would take her over the Atlantic, all the way up to the landing in Rome. If she was lucky, she thought, she'd wake up with just enough time to pull her seat forward and place her tray table back in its upright and locked position. And if she was sleeping, she wouldn't be thinking about how much she hated flying, and she especially would not be thinking about Mr. First Class. She knew she was kidding herself to think she made any kind of impression as she passed by the sexy stranger. How could she, dressed in jeans, a Baby Phat T-shirt, and clutching a tattered teddy bear? *No need to sit here fantasizing. If I'm going to dream . . . might as well do it in my sleep!*

Dominique Rollins, or Nick as he was known to friends, put down the magazine and picked up his drink. After staring at the same page for over five minutes, he realized he wasn't reading it anyway. For some inexplicable reason, his mind kept wandering to the woman back in coach, the sexy siren who'd passed him clutching a teddy bear as if she were five instead of the twentysomething she looked. His guess was that she was afraid of flying and the toy was some type of childhood relic, like a security blanket. But to carry it openly, in public, holding it as if it were a lifeline? *Too bad, because that chick is fine as chilled wine in the summertime.* Nick appreciated the stranger's natural beauty, but he liked his women successful and secure. Not that he was looking for women on this trip, he reminded himself. He wanted a carefree few days without any complications. Nick knew all too well that when it came to the words "woman" and "complication," one rarely appeared without the other.

Her eyes . . . Nick tilted his seat back and sipped his Manhattan. That was what intrigued him about her. In them was a curious blend of trepidation and intelligence, of anxiety mixed with steely resolve. The combination brought out his chivalrous side. A part of him wanted to walk back to where she was, sit her on his lap, and tell her that everything was going to be all right. His rational side quickly shot down that idea. One, she was a stranger; two, she'd hardly appreciate being treated like a child, clutched teddy bear notwithstanding; and three, Nick wasn't in the market for a woman—friend or otherwise—he reminded himself for the second time in as many minutes. He was grateful for his work and the newest acquisition that had helped to take his mind off Angelica, the woman who'd dashed his dream of their getting married and having a family together . . . and broken his heart.

Nick signaled the flight attendant for another drink and reached for his iPod. He didn't want to think about Angelica on this trip. He wanted to enjoy this mini-vacation in Rome, one of his favorite cities, and dine at AnticaPesa, one of his favorite restaurants and the inspiration behind the upscale eatery in his newly acquired boutique hotel.

Thinking about the quaint, thirty-four-room property he and his partners had purchased in Malibu, California, and were transforming into a twenty-first-century masterpiece, brought a smile to Nick's face. Following the global economic collapse, the men had outwitted their corporate competition and had gotten an incredible deal on the 1930s Spanish-style building. The group, four successful men with diverse and various corporate and entrepreneurial backgrounds, all agreed that it was the good looks and sexy swagger of Nick and another partner, Bastion Price, that sealed the deal with the sixtysomething, hard-as-nails Realtor who'd handled negotiations. This trip was the calm before the storm of Le Sol's grand opening, less than one month away.

Nick pressed the button that reclined his seat to an almost fully horizontal position. He tried to relax. But every time his eyes closed, he saw the short-haired, chocolate brown, doe-eyed beauty who'd passed him hours before, with those hip-hugging jeans and bountiful breasts pressed up against a tight, pale yellow T-shirt. *You're flying to Rome for pasta, not pussy,* he mentally chastised himself. Even so, his appetite had been awakened, and the dish he wanted to taste wasn't from anybody's kitchen.

2

Tiffany took a deep breath and tried not to panic. Her purse had been here just a minute ago, in the basket of her luggage cart, right next to her laptop. She mentally retraced her footsteps in her mind, remembering specific moments when she knew she'd had the Coach bag her mother had given her for Christmas. She'd definitely had it as she exited the plane, had fiddled with the strap as she and the handsome stranger shared casual pleasantries when finding themselves separated only by a rope as they snaked through the customs line. She'd looked in her purse, prepared to boldly give the man her phone number, but his turn had come up before she could find paper and pen. She remembered carefully putting her passport back in her purse after they'd stamped it, her mother's words echoing in her head: *Treat that passport as if it's the key out of that country, because it is.*

"Yes, I had it then," she said to herself as she remembered her purse being the last thing she placed on the luggage cart, after loading on two heavy suitcases, a carry-on, her laptop, and Tuffy. Then she'd rolled out of the baggage claim area in search of ground transportation. That's when a young woman who looked American but spoke with an accent had approached her and asked for the best way to get to the tourist sites in the city center. When Tiffany said she didn't know, the woman had excitedly gone on about it being her first time in Rome and admitting how nervous she was to be there by herself. Tiffany could relate. She was nervous as well. She'd felt a kinship with the foreigner, and at the time had thought the woman's shifting eyes were due to nervousness. Now she knew it was due to something else. *That bitch was watching out for an accomplice.*

"She took my purse!" Tiffany yelled, before even realizing she was speaking out loud. Several pairs of eyes turned to stare at her, but she was too panicked to feel embarrassment. "Help, those people stole my purse!"

Belatedly, Tiffany decided to give chase, her heavily laden luggage cart careening wildly through Rome's Fiumicino Airport. She steered the clumsy vehicle as if she were back on the streets of LA, doing a drive-by.

"Excuse me," she said to a woman whom she accidentally bumped in the butt, almost knocking her over. "Coming through!" she yelled as an older gentleman decided to stop and tie his shoe. She managed to bring the cart to a halt just before she broadsided him, stopping so quickly that her carry-on toppled off the cart and Tuffy flew forward and hit the man in the head. "My bad," she said to the bewildered man, who began berating her in rapid-fire Italian. "No-a speakie, no-a speakie," she replied as she gathered up her bag and her bear and began again in the direction she thought the woman had gone.

Five minutes later, she gave up the chase. The woman was nowhere in sight and now Tiffany doubted she could even recognize her in a line-up. Was her hair dark blond or brown? Was she wearing a blue top . . . or was it purple? The woman was Tiffany's height, five foot three, but Tiffany didn't remember whether she wore jeans or slacks, or a skirt, for that matter. She'd had colosseums, not criminals, on her mind as they'd talked.

"Damn." Tiffany plopped down on her luggage and put her head in her hands. She could feel the beginnings of an anxiety attack coming on and tried to focus on breathing deeply. But the gravity of the situation began to grow in her mind. She was in a foreign country, alone, with no passport, no money, and no idea how she'd gone from triumph to tragedy so quickly. She'd been so proud of herself as she'd stepped off the plane, having made it through her first trans-Atlantic flight without throwing up or peeing on herself—both unfortunate events that had accompanied past panic attacks. Now she was precariously close to achieving a trifecta, because in addition to these two scene-stealers, she felt ready to throw a two-year-old tantrum and assure herself a place in one of Rome's asylums for the insane. Tiffany began to shake with the effort it took to hold herself together. Trying not to hyperventilate— on top of not vomiting, peeing, or sobbing like a fool— was taking its toll.

"Are you all right?"

Tiffany froze at the sound of the voice flowing down to her ears, smooth and sweet . . . like maple syrup.

Without opening her eyes or raising her head, she knew who it was. *Just great. I probably look like a blubbering idiot, and here comes Mr. First Class to see me in all my crazed glory.* Tiffany hadn't imagined the handsome stranger as her knight in shining armor, but she had imagined doing things to him at night—before she'd forced herself to stop fantasizing and fallen asleep.

He placed a firm hand on Tiffany's shoulder. "What is the problem here? Can I help?"

Tiffany wiped her eyes, prayed there was no snot coming out of her nose, and stood. She took another deep breath and forced herself to look into the eyes that had melted her meow-meow on the plane. "My purse was stolen." Her voice was soft, barely a whisper. But it was all she could do. The energy that fueled her initial outburst was spent; now if she opened her mouth much wider she'd break out into an ugly cry.

He angrily clenched and unclenched his jaw. "Come with me." His tone was decisive, as were his movements. He placed his single carry-on bag on top of her luggage, took Tiffany's much smaller hand into his large one, and began navigating them through the terminal. Tiffany walked beside him silently, feeling as if the events taking place were surreal. She'd been in Rome less than an hour and already her life was upside down. When they reached the elevator, he quietly reached for the teddy bear in the luggage cart basket and handed it to Tiffany.

"Here, your friend will make you feel a little better."

His gesture was almost her undoing, yet Tiffany took Tuffy and clutched him to her chest. "Thank you," she stuttered. She knew it must seem silly to other people, but once she clasped her dear furry friend, she began to calm down.

The elevator doors opened and the stranger guided the cart and Tiffany inside it. Tiffany snuck a glance at him, and then not being able to resist it, took another, longer look. "Where are we going?"

"To the administrative offices," he replied. "I know someone there who can get us to a higher-up in airport security. We'll be able to get this straightened out without all the hassle. You'll have to fill out a report with the airport, and another with the police if you want this crime reported, which I suggest that you do. I won't ask you what happened. You'll have to repeat the despicable details at least twice as it is." He gave Tiffany's hand a reassuring squeeze. "By the way, I'm Nick Rollins."

His personable manners in the midst of madness brought a smile to Tiffany's heart, if not her face. "Tiffany Matthews."

"Even though I truly wish the circumstances were different, Tiffany Matthews, it is a pleasure to formally meet you."

Just over an hour later, Nick was once again leading Tiffany, this time out of the administrative offices and down to ground transportation. As assuring as it was to have this six-foot-tall mass of obvious authority walking beside her, looking nice and smelling good, something about his take-charge manner made her uncomfortable. For the moment, she was too grateful to complain. If Nick hadn't been there, Tiffany felt she'd still be sitting on her luggage, crying and waiting for God knew who to do Lord knew what.

"Thanks for everything you did back there," Tiffany said as they once again neared the elevator.

"No worries," Nick said comfortably. "I'm just glad I was here to help you. Trans-Atlantic flying can be exhausting. To have your purse stolen after having just landed is plain bad luck."

"I knew better than to turn my back on my cart, even for a second. But that woman, excuse me, that *thief,* distracted me on purpose, showing me a brochure of some famous fountain . . ."

"Trevi, it's the Trevi Fountain."

"It's the *trouble* fountain in my book, because that's what finding out about it cost me—nothing but trouble."

"On the good side, nothing was taken that can't be replaced, and what's more, your trip is bound to get better from here!"

The next thing Tiffany knew she was in Nick's chauffeured town car, getting whisked to the American embassy for an emergency replacement passport. On the way, Nick provided his satellite phone so that she could make calls to replace her traveler's checks, cancel her credit cards, and turn off her cell phone— all the while thanking her mother for bugging her until Tiffany had promised to write all of her credit card, passport, and related telephone numbers on a separate piece of paper and place it in her carry-on luggage. While she placed all of these calls, Nick was a calming presence beside her, handling his own items of business on the car phone. When she ended her call, he was still on his, a business call of some sort, she deduced. She busied herself looking out the window, taking in this place that looked so different from the streets of

LA. They passed several stately looking buildings adorned with statues and accented with fountains.

As she gazed out her window, Tiffany thought back over the past couple hours. How Nick Rollins had swooped in to save a modern-day damsel in distress. She remembered the deference those in the airline office had paid him, how the manager of the airport had referred to him as "Mr. Rollins." How the police had appeared out of nowhere and taken her report right there in the airline office, precluding her from having to actually travel to the station to fill out the report. Nick was obviously well known in Rome, or at least well connected.

It took just under an hour for Tiffany to fill out the paperwork regarding her stolen passport and the application to have a new one expedited to her. Throughout the process, Nick continued to be a reassuring presence beside her. His chivalry continued once they left the embassy and got back in the car.

"Please accept my gift of a hotel room where I'm staying," he said.

Tiffany started, so engrossed in present complexities that she hadn't begun to think of future challenges—such as eating, sleeping and navigating a foreign city with no money. "Oh, I couldn't," she muttered, her mind whirling with plan-B possibilities, of which there were none.

"I insist," Nick countered easily. "It's in a very nice and convenient location, and has a great restaurant with shops nearby. It will be the perfect backdrop for your introduction to Rome, and will prevent you from having to scramble around for a room on credit."

There was humor in Nick's voice as he spoke this last sentence, but Tiffany failed to find anything funny. She seriously doubted that there was a hotel on the continent that would extend credit to a traveling guest.

"I can't accept that kind of generosity," Tiffany said again, this time with less conviction. When Nick remained quiet, gently stroking his wisp of a mustache, she continued, "Only if I can pay you back, every cent."

Nick smiled, and a blessed showing of even, white teeth sent her heart flip-flopping with a different kind of anxiety. She was quickly, quietly, falling in lust.

Who is this man who's rescued me? Tiffany pondered the question as she and Nick continued casual conversation. *And what is he expecting in exchange for his kindness?*

GREAT BOOKS, GREAT SAVINGS!

When You Visit Our Website:
www.kensingtonbooks.com
You Can Save Money Off The Retail Price
Of Any Book You Purchase!

- **All Your Favorite Kensington Authors**
- **New Releases & Timeless Classics**
- **Overnight Shipping Available**
- **eBooks Available For Many Titles**
- **All Major Credit Cards Accepted**

Visit Us Today To Start Saving!
www.kensingtonbooks.com

More of the Hottest
African-American Fiction from
Dafina Books

D